Christopher L. Bennett

AMONG THE WILD CYBERS

eBooks
Pennsville, NJ

PUBLISHED BY
eSpec Books LLC
Danielle McPhail, Publisher
PO Box 242,
Pennsville, New Jersey 08070
www.especbooks.com

ISBN: 978-1-942990-96-3
ISBN (ebook): 978-1-942990-95-6

Excerpt from *Only Superhuman* reprinted with the permission of the author and Tor Books.

Cover Design and Robot Image: Mike McPhail, McP Digital Graphics.
Interior Design: Danielle McPhail, Sidhe na Daire Multimedia
Cover Background © GrandeDuc, www.shutterstock.com
Copyeditor: Greg Schauer

For Stanley Schmidt, who got me started.

Contents

Among the Wild Cybers of Cybele

From the journals of Safira Kimenye,
14/13/004 Anno Cybeleae
(10 November 2250 Solsys Equivalent Date):

During today's foraging, the loggers were attacked by a fandancer. They must have intruded onto its territory; the vertebrates don't hunt by magnetic fields, so it couldn't have found them appetizing. This was a large species of fandancer, with sharp tusks and a bony club at the end of its tail. It inflicted some damage – mainly on Bunyan, ever the bold and reckless one. Galadriel called a retreat – I picked up the signal on my earphone – but the biped hounded us relentlessly. Perhaps its terror at the alienness of the loggers drove it to such violence.

So the loggers lured it onto a compass rose. With my more limited senses, I couldn't detect the sedentary arthropod; its chitin camouflage blended perfectly with the grass. I saw them luring the 'dancer toward a particular patch of ground, but I was startled when that patch snapped shut, leaving a bare starburst pattern in the grass and trapping the fandancer inside a nearly solid, spherical cage of segmented limbs.

As we left, I could still hear the 'dancer fighting to break free from the compass rose. I can't help hoping it succeeds. It was only defending its territory – maybe even defending young. And dying slowly of thirst is a nasty way to go. But as I keep reminding myself, it's not my place or anyone else's to referee nature's battles.

Well. I'll be glad when Marc gets here. His enthusiasm always lifted my spirits. And having his support in this difficult cause will make the work easier.

Safira looked just as Marc Dupuis remembered: a tall, elegant woman with regal Sub-Saharan features and a blinding smile. She engulfed him with a warm embrace the likes of which he'd only dreamt of as her graduate assistant. But such fantasies were a decade behind him now—well, four decades, counting the long sleep from Earth to Cybele. He wasn't here to moon over Safira Kimenye, but to do a crucial and very delicate job. He returned the embrace with merely professional courtesy.

"It is *so* good to see a human face again," Safira beamed, "especially a friendly one. I'm so glad you're here."

"Really?" Marc teased gently. "I've kept up with your journal entries on CybeleNet. It sounds like the loggers have made you part of the family. You sure I won't just get in the way?"

"Oh, they're charming companions, all right. But I miss a human voice, the warmth of a friendly touch." She clasped his hands a moment longer, then helped him gather up the supplies that had come with him. They both took great care; it usually took weeks or even months for Safira's diffuse support network to track down the peripatetic researcher, so these supplies would have to last them both. Before leaving the drop site, Safira deposited a data crystal containing her latest journal entries for later pickup. It was an awkward way to transmit data, but of course Safira had disabled her wristcom's transceiver circuits to keep the wrong people from tracking her down.

The trip to the loggers' camp was a convoluted twilight journey through a forest of purple-trimmed bamboo-ferns. On the way, the Kenyan woman and the Moroccan man caught up on the news since they'd last met eight long Cybeline months ago, shortly before Safira's expedition had begun. But glimpses of the forest denizens kept them distracted. Arthropods of countless shapes and sizes swarmed through the forest, their developed lungs and circulatory systems letting them greatly outgrow their Terrestrial analogues. Sparrowasps, scorpionflies and dragonmoths hummed through the air, revelling in a niche undiscovered by the native vertebrates. After all, the tailed vertebrates had only two limbs apiece, adequate for 78-percent gravity, and evolving wings would leave them without a leg to stand on.

Yet the vertebrates were not completely grounded. Some could rear up on strong tails and climb the bamboo-ferns with grasping feet; others could leap into the lateral fern stalks and brachiate with prehensile trunks and tails. One species employed the implausible technique of flipping upward and hanging from the stalks by its legs, making its way blithely upside-down.

Safira frowned at Marc's quiet absorption of this image, which evoked hilarity in most observers. "Are you all right?" she asked. "You were always so eager, so excited by new discoveries. You seem more...subdued now."

Marc remained silent for a moment. "Well...I suppose I've got some things on my mind. Like how you'll convince the loggers they can trust a human other than you. Although," he smirked, "it can't be much harder than what I went through to earn your helpers' trust. They're... understandably protective of your charges. Without your endorsement, I doubt—"

The older woman smiled. "Think nothing of it. And that goes for both issues. I had to win the loggers' trust the hard way—teaching them to accept me and avoid others like me at the same time. But there's a shortcut for you." She unpocketed a small device on a chain and draped it around his neck. "This transmits a copy of their recognition signals. Admittedly, I haven't tested it, but it should ease your acceptance greatly."

"I can see why you haven't mentioned this in your journals," Marc said thoughtfully. "You don't want the hunters getting hold of this."

"No, it's not what I'd particularly prefer to get around their necks." The uncharacteristic anger barely reached her voice, but it burned in her dark eyes. "Never mind," she smiled, shaking it off. "We're almost there!"

They shortly emerged into a clearing dominated by (and presumably resulting from) a large, strikingly regular stockade of bamboo-fern stalks. "That looks like it could keep out an army of arthropods," Marc observed.

"It does. Routinely. The pincer-hounds find the loggers' magnetic fields particularly appetizing. And it's stronger than it looks."

"Right. The coating they secrete." As they drew nearer, Marc could see the crystalline sheen on the stalks. "Remarkable."

"Especially when you consider that the loggers are descended from survey probes, not builders. Their construction skills evolved purely as a defense mechanism."

Suddenly, a disguised hatch in the ground tilted open, and the loggers began to emerge. "They know I'm back," Safira said. "But they're wary of you," she added as the low-slung hexapods pulled up short of the humans.

"Perhaps I should keep my distance for a while," Marc suggested. "There's a tent for me in with the supplies. I could sleep out here tonight."

Safira had gone up to the troop leader and was stroking its gleaming carapace soothingly. "Don't worry," she said, seeming to address both human and logger. "They're already letting you closer than they'd let anyone else."

"Still, I'd rather not press my luck," Marc shrugged. "After all, those cutting arms of theirs are diamond-tipped."

"Don't be silly. For all the evolution they've undergone, their First-Law programming's still in effect. They won't hurt you." She caressed the blocky creatures of crystal and polymer like beloved children.

Safira soon persuaded Marc he would be safer within the compound. It was already too cool for the arthropods to remain active, but some vertebrates hunted by night. So, with delicacy, Safira led Marc and the loggers through a halting introduction built around human approximations of the loggers' submission behaviors. Much of their communication was electromagnetic, but the emitter around Marc's neck took care of that. Besides, the loggers' neural nets adapted quickly to new data. So, far sooner than would have been possible with biological animals, Marc was granted clearance into the sanctum.

The entrance tunnel was cleaner than he'd expected, the loggers having coated it with their plasticrystal secretion for stability. The interior space was broken by a regular grid of sharpened, crystal-coated poles pointing skyward. Its only other distinct feature (aside from Safira's campsite) was a materials dump, presumably supplying the auxons' building projects as well as their self-replication. Along with bamboo-fern stalks, polegrass, and the like, Marc saw stones, animal remains, and some fragments of auxon bodies. He assumed these must be scavenged, since the loggers weren't predatory.

Following his gaze, Safira explained, "We were attacked by a heliraptor yesterday. Until then, the stockade hadn't been designed to keep out flying creatures. The 'raptors have scared off most of the airborne arthropods hereabouts, and they usually haven't preyed on their own relatives before. This one must've been either newly evolved or newly migrated to the area. It was certainly the biggest I've seen."

"It inflicted casualties?"

"Nothing fatal," Safira replied. "It used a laser weapon—a mutated altimeter beam, I'd guess. Several loggers were injured—especially brave old Bunyan, of course. But they fashioned some polegrass stalks into crude spears. They managed to snarl the 'raptor's left rotor when the spears got caught between the blade and cowling. It went into a spin, but reacted quickly, of course, and managed to adjust its airfoils and limp away. And I soon heard the squeals of a rhinostrich. Not as good a source of replication material as another auxon—but certainly an easier kill," she finished proudly.

Marc surveyed the logger troop. "They seem pretty well-repaired now."

"The females did their job well." The "females" were those members of the self-replicating (or auxonic) cyberspecies who actually possessed the replication and repair equipment. The majority were made without such equipment to save materials. Upon their deaths, the females digested their remains and downloaded their acquired data, learning from their experiences and mistakes, thus redesigning the next generation to be better adapted to their environment.

"Bunyan got a leg cut off," Safira went on, "but he resisted having it replaced. Maybe I'm anthropomorphizing, but I don't think he liked being cheated out of another battle scar."

"*Hm*," Marc pondered. "Would vanity evolve in a basically asexual species, without the need to attract mates?"

"I think evidence of toughness and courage demonstrates his importance to the group, so he gets allocated more resources. Also, it demonstrates that his design is successful, so it might be favored in reproductive selection."

Marc took a moment to absorb the intriguing idea, then studied the defensive palisades. "So these were erected after the attack?" Safira nodded. "You think they'll keep the heliraptors out?"

"The plasticrystal will resist their lasers, so they can't be cut down easily. But 'raptors can hover and maneuver quite well. They should be able to work around this barrier." She smiled. "And then the loggers will develop a more elaborate one. They can't anticipate, but they learn quickly from experience."

Marc found himself alongside the materials dump, contemplating what must be Bunyan's severed leg. "I keep wondering," he mused, "if the auxons might evolve to build themselves out of the same, near-indestructible materials they used to build our cities. I mean, they already have diamite claws and fullerene muscles; why not go the rest of the way?"

"Because they were designed to evolve," Safira said. "And that means they had to be vulnerable. Death is a tool of evolution," she continued philosophically. "It's what weeds out the failures to make room for the successes. If they were indestructible, there'd be no selection mechanism, and they wouldn't adapt." The probes' designers back in

Sol System couldn't have anticipated all the conditions of an alien world. So, because they were sending self-replicating probes anyway (a few seed units being more economical than an army of drones), they had given them the ability to evolve, using both random Darwinian mutation and the more Lamarckian ability to modify their offspring based on experience. It was hardly a new idea; cyberengineers had known for centuries that evolving hardware or software often produced more effective design solutions than a conscious creative process (one more nail in the creationists' coffin, though the creationists still denied it).

"We know that," Marc countered, "but the auxons don't. They don't see the bigger picture, they just try to perpetuate themselves. An indestructible species might be an evolutionary cul-de-sac, but it'd be an enduring one."

"But it takes more effort to bond the atoms for such materials. More time and energy to craft them. They built our cities from those materials because we programmed them to. But now they're ruled by pragmatism, not programming. They perpetuate their `genes' just fine without being indestructible. So there's no point in wasting the energy to make themselves stronger than they need to be. Any more than for us to have armor shells or five hearts."

She shook her head. "That's the flaw with the government's propaganda about how the auxons will destroy the whole biosphere. They're not that superior. They obey the same natural laws as any animal." She grimaced. "But no matter how much I stress that in my journals, Berdahl and his people cling to their paranoia, and their mad campaign to exterminate the whole kingdom of auxonic life!"

Marc fell silent; the anger in her bearing demanded a respectful distance. He found her intensity beautiful but forbidding, like a mother tiger's. As much as he admired the sight, he had to turn away to hide his concern. With such passion for her cause, it would hurt her all the more when she learned of his betrayal.

It was early autumn in this hemisphere, and the mornings were chilly. Gamma Leporis was hotter than Sol, but Cybele was its fifth world, receiving only three-fourths the illumination of Earth. The seventeen-hour nights didn't help either. Still, the only place to bathe was a frigid stream, and it had to be done in the morning before the arthropods warmed to the hunt.

The cold water helped distract Marc from Safira's graceful, bronze body. A decade past, he'd have craved the sight and more. But this was supposed to be a professional relationship—even aside from his hidden agenda.

He continued to tell himself he wasn't really betraying her—that he acted out of respect and concern for her. He wanted the same thing Governor Berdahl did: not only to save their adopted planet from ecological catastrophe, but to save their mutual friend Safira from the horrible mistake she was making. Now she was blinded by her scientific fascination, her closeness to the auxons; but in the long term her wisdom would prevail and she'd understand that they'd acted for the best. He knew, though, that she would resent him for quite a while once his deception became clear. It would only worsen matters if he assumed the role of lover as well as ally.

Marc therefore strove to take their mutual nudity in stride. So it came as a surprise when he realized she was studying his body with open interest. "What?" she smirked when she got around to noticing his questioning expression.

"You...never looked at me that way back on Earth," he answered guardedly.

"My dear, you were barely more than a child then."

"And now?"

She appraised his anatomy frankly. "Grown up nicely." She grinned. "Oh, don't be so surprised. I haven't had a man in nearly a Terran year."

A number of emotions roiled through Marc, none presenting a clear course of action. But then Safira's attention was drawn elsewhere. "Hear that stridulation?" she whispered. "The pincer-hounds are stirring. We'd better get to the stockade." She strode determinedly past him toward shore...but gave him a swat on the rump which clearly said, *Later*.

With the pack of pincer-hounds figuratively barking at the gate, there was nothing to do but wait inside the stockade and talk. Safira seemed happy to continue her bald flirtation, but the loud washboard growling from outside gave Marc a convenient (and truthful) excuse for not being in the mood. He knew he was in no danger, but the sound was like chalk on a blackboard, only in bass.

The loggers seemed relaxed, but alert. Guided by the alpha female, Galadriel, they made well-practiced (or instinctively programmed?)

rounds, checking the integrity of their defenses. Amidst it all, though, Marc saw behavior uncannily resembling ritual comfort and bonding. He tried to take it in stride; after all, the loggers had evolved along a social model, and such behaviors were functional within that model. It was simply a logical outgrowth of a stochastic selection process, he told himself, and no reason to feel sympathy for the cybernetic probes. Especially since he knew what was coming.

In fact, it came sooner than he'd expected. Safira and the loggers reacted to the airborne engine sound before he noticed it, launching into a flurry of movement. "Another heliraptor?" he ventured innocently.

"Hunter drones," Safira snarled. "Shit, how did they find us so soon?" She pulled two plasma rifles from a case. Marc's eyes widened at the restricted weapons—and widened further when she tossed him one. "Aim for the optics! Only part they can't shield fully from the EM pulse."

"I, I've never used a gun!"

"Life is learning. Figure it out!"

In moments, the hunter drones came into range and started firing plasma bolts of their own, each mini-fireball making a curt *whoosh* like a whirling torch on fast playback. The pincer-hounds' grating chorus fell into disarray as the arthropods fled.

The loggers used the defense tactics they'd developed against the heliraptor, hurling polegrass spears along with rocks and stalk fragments. But the hunter drones had enclosed VTOL jets rather than open rotors; and the remote-controlled, non-evolving weapon platforms lacked the inbuilt vulnerability of the auxons. The drones took the loggers' attack unfazed and blasted back with much deadlier efficacy.

Safira shrieked as the first logger died, the bark of her plasma rifle meshing with her cry in bellicose harmony. Her skill was disturbingly good, and she blasted several drones squarely "between the eyes," scrambling their power systems and felling them. Marc fired toward the drones, trying to appear helpful without actually helping. His novice aim served this purpose well, enabling him to shoot in earnest and even broadside a drone or two without making a kill.

But his attack did have an effect. One of the drones he'd grazed turned and closed on him. Before he realized what was happening, Safira bore him to the ground, her close-cropped hair made a halo by the actinic bolt passing just beyond it—the bolt which had been aimed at his own skull.

He gasped—at the unexpected attack, at the shock of impact with the ground, and at the pressure of Safira's firm, warm body against his. Their eyes met and locked, frozen by the moment.

The kiss was spontaneous, surprising, and deeply unwise under fire. Marc was even more surprised to realize he had initiated it. Safira returned it electrifyingly for two seconds, then rolled off and blasted the drone's brains out.

As Safira executed the remaining attackers with efficient, maternal fury, Marc lay on the ground trying to absorb the event. That drone's operator had tried to kill him! He'd known emotions were running high, but he'd never expected such unbridled hostility from his own side. He knew Governor Berdahl would severely punish that hunter...but it made things a lot less clear-cut to realize there were fanatics on both sides.

In the end, there were two logger fatalities, whom Safira eulogized as Legolas and Daphne. The loss of a female hit her hard, for they were the least expendable, but she grieved equally for them both. There was no ceremony on the loggers' part; the females simply consumed the corpses for material with which to repair the numerous injuries sustained in the attack.

Bunyan had lost a cutter arm this time, and had been blinded in his rear optics. His carapace was partially melted, and his awkward gait suggested neurological damage. It amazed Marc that the battered cyber still functioned. When Safira cuddled the cold, hard mechanism and spoke fondly of his "indomitable spirit," Marc found it hard to retain his skepticism.

But repairs would have to wait, since the hunters knew their location now. The stockade was evacuated with no sentiment and minimal preparation—primarily the swift construction of a litter for Safira and Marc, to prevent them from leaving a chemical spoor. Safira had taught them this, but they now did it on their own initiative. The litter rode atop the carapaces of several large females. Safira and Marc had to cling tightly; the ride was remarkably smooth, but that was largely cancelled by the swift pace of the journey over variable terrain.

Galadriel took the lead, with Bunyan on her back. As the troop's prime defender, he headed the repair list. Already she was secreting around him the conductive gel that carried her repair nanites, while fine manipulator arms attended to macrorepairs. Other males formed a defense perimeter, alert for attack, while a few straggled behind to erase their trail, even to the extent of performing nanorepairs on broken plants. (Safira hadn't taught them that; it was a naturally evolved defense.)

Although they used the forest's purple foliage for cover, Safira scanned the sky for more hunter drones, weapon at the ready. "I don't know what I'll do once the planetwide satellite network's in place," she sighed at one point. "But we must carry on," she then said, smiling and placing her hand supportively on his. "The cause is too important to abandon, no matter how impossible it may become."

Marc couldn't help but clasp her hand warmly in return. "I don't think it's in your nature to give up, Safira. The more impossible a cause, the harder you work to succeed. That's why there are black rhinos in Africa again."

She returned his gaze with gratitude and warmth. Their hands remained clasped, and soon their lips met. They still had to cling to the litter, so they couldn't do much more; but it was enough to kiss for hours. When the troop finally stopped for the night, Safira and Marc were stripping and devouring each other before the litter touched the ground.

It was just sex, Marc insisted to himself as they lay comfortably intertwined the next morning. Just the natural response of a woman who'd been alone too long and a man who owed her his life. It was a perfectly understandable indulgence, and no strings need attach. He knew he could credibly pull back to a professional remove without complicating things further.

He had to admit, he was having doubts about his cause following the attack and his time with the loggers. But second thoughts were moot; the betrayal had been complete the day they'd met. All he could do now was try to minimize her pain.

Perhaps he could raise doubts in her mind about the auxons she so cherished—remind her of the stakes involved in their existence. Best, though, to start on peripheral questions. "Have you ever wondered," he began, "whether the auxon probes that were sent to other worlds might've undergone the same kind of evolutionary process that these did? Whether other colonists might have to face these same problems?"

Safira maneuvered to meet his eyes, her body sliding quite distractingly across his. "I've thought about it," she said. "But I think there were a few unusual things about Cybele. Aside from the tectonic activity, there was the sheer bad luck of having magnetic-sensitive predators who found the auxons' fields appetizing. That increased the attrition rate, and increased the likelihood of non-dormant probes evolving." The probes had been designed to fall dormant once their programmed tasks had been completed—while allowing new replication to balance whatever attrition might occur, so enough probes would be available to survey habitation sites and build cities upon receiving the command from Solsys.

"But other worlds might have their own dangers," Marc countered. "If attrition were excessive, the probes there might also mutate into nondormant forms, the better to avoid danger."

"True."

"And then a situation like Cybele's might be inevitable," he continued. "Without a mission to direct them, the auxons' preset behaviors would only last until they clashed with pure survival—whereupon they'd be weeded out in favor of more successful mutations. Eventually they'd end up with the same kinds of survival-driven behaviors as living animals, filling all the natural ecological niches: herbivores, scavengers...predators. Coming into competition with the native forms," he finished significantly.

Safira didn't pick up on this, perhaps deliberately. "I don't know if they'd evolve predation without first being preyed upon. What are the odds that another world would have magnetic-sensitive predators?"

"Some animals might attack them out of fear or territoriality. They might occasionally kill an attacker, and eventually they'd figure out that animal corpses are rich in the carbon and other elements they need for replication and fuel. Or they might discover it while sampling corpses, evolve into scavengers and then hunters."

"You're right," Safira smiled. "Life always manages to fill whatever niches it can find, and follows many paths to do so." She pursed her lips thoughtfully, alluringly. "But would they have the time? If *Arachne* had gotten here seventy years ago as planned, it would've found most of the auxons still dormant and awaiting instructions. The few active mutants would've been recycled and never gotten the chance to evolve further." The original colony ship *Arachne* had mysteriously vanished en route to Gamma Leporis. The vessel's presumed destruction had never been explained, but it hadn't kept the larger, more advanced *Anansi* expedition from making a second, successful try. "Maybe if the planet were farther away, with a longer interval before the colonists arrived....But ten parsecs is pushing the limits of practical colonizing range. There weren't many probes sent farther out than here."

Marc had to concede her point; in fact, he welcomed it. He wouldn't wish Cybele's crises on another planet. Beyond that, though, he found himself simply enjoying the moment. Here were a nude man and woman, wrapped in each other's limbs, casually discussing science and philosophy. It wasn't much like his grad-student fantasies of Safira, but it felt very right to the more mature Marc—an easy, comfortable union of erotic and intellectual rapports. Not a transient passion that would serve its purpose and burn out... more like the basis for a lasting, meaningful relationship.

Inarguably, he had to nip this in the bud. He'd served his purpose; he should leave now, before the other shoe fell on Safira.

But as he gazed into her dark, brilliant eyes, leaving seemed impossible.

Marc had convinced himself there were quite valid reasons to stay with Safira until the endgame. First, there was the concern that another hunter-drone operator might lose control. Marc felt it best to stay for her protection (conveniently forgetting who'd protected whom before). Also, he still hoped he could convince her to see his side, to surrender voluntarily and spare him her betrayed wrath.

On top of that, he was simply fascinated by the wildlife of Cybele, and their journey through the violet-hued wilds provided ample opportunity for observation. Safira focused more on the auxon species, but Marc was fascinated by the native fauna, the rich variations on the themes of arthropod and vertebrate. While only the arthropods flew, many grew vast and sedentary, such as the crabtrees, whose segmented limbs were camouflaged as bamboo-ferns, trapping prey in chitinous "fronds" and digesting them in Venus's-flytrap style.

The vertebrates had their differences too, as dramatized in a battle between a fandancer and an eleroo, champions of two distinct taxonomic orders. The stiff-tailed, scaly eleroo grabbed and struck with twin prehensile proboscises, leaping spryly about its foe, sometimes spinning to use its heavy tail as a truncheon. The downy-furred fandancer lashed forward with its more flexible tail, its fans of extended ribs pivoting back to keep the biped in balance. At times it would switch tactics, balancing with its rearthrust tail while swiping its ribfans forward to slash with sharpened tips. The pointed arguments of its ribs and tusks finally won out over the blunter attacks of the eleroo's trunks and tail, the scaled megalopod falling victim to blood loss. The 'dancer's bright fans fluttered in triumph (and warning to scavengers) as it tore into its kill.

The greatest discovery, for Safira and Marc alike, was also courtesy of the fandancer genus. The humans were among a grove of honeycomb stalks when they observed a small troupe of 'dancers with unusually large ribfans. The troupe seemed interested in the scorpionflies that rested in the fern-tufts—vivid green arthropods with meter-wide dragonfly wings, froglike eyes, and writhing tails. The scientists watched from the natural blind of the honeycombs as one fandancer hefted a rock in its tail and hurled it at the stalks. The impact startled the scorpflies into the air, and the 'dancers launched into pursuit. Literally launched—after running up to top speed, they leapt skyward, thrusting down with their broad fans for extra lift. Spreading their fans wide to slow their descent, they managed to take several scorpflies from the air before drifting back to the ground.

Safira gasped with ecstasy, while Marc was struck dumb with awe. "Do you realize what we just saw?" Safira crowed when she caught her breath, never mind that it spooked the 'dancers. "We've just witnessed the first phase in the evolution of vertebrate flight on Cybele!" She laughed hysterically. "This is...this is history! This is the kind of moment a naturalist lives for. That we would be here to witness such a key moment in evolution...oh, my...." She babbled on in Swahili for a bit, most of it gleeful profanity, and then just gave up talking and assailed him with hugs and kisses.

Marc had tried to return to a professional distance, with limited success due to the decades of seductive skill that Safira happily wielded against his defenses. But that had been casual play compared to this. Equally overwhelmed by the thrill of this discovery, they found themselves overwhelmed by each other as well. The joy of the experience evolved into joy at sharing it, at sharing each other, and they delineated that joy with their bodies until the slow-moving sun sank below the horizon.

"Ohh, Marc," Safira sighed at length, when her body was too tired to continue its more eloquent communication. "The greatest wonder of this day is that you were here to share it with me." And then she spoke sweet disaster. "I love you, Marc. I always saw things to love in you—your brilliance, your passion, your tenderness. But they weren't fully formed—you were too much the child. But now...now, love, you're all I saw you could be, and I can love you unreservedly.

"Oh, Marc, I longed for this. That's why I let you join me out here. It's so hard sometimes, being hunted, being hated. I needed someone who could love me, who could join with me out here, match my passion for the work, and give me the strength to fight on. And I knew you were the one, my golden love," she gasped, stroking his blond hair. Then her lips stopped speaking and began exploring him, probing his every contour with a scientist's attention to detail. Marc sobbed his lifelong love for Safira while silently wishing he'd never been born.

The lake shimmered like satin. Seeking the cause of the odd metallic sparkle, Safira had sampled the water and found it teeming with extraction nanites, the kind used to mine seawater for its dissolute material wealth. "But how?" Marc frowned, gazing over her shoulder at the magnified image. "Those nanites weren't designed to operate independently of the submarine auxons, were they?"

Safira shook her head. "And they certainly weren't made to evolve. They're too small, too simple to have adaptive replication. They could only mutate through random error, so any meaningful evolution would take millennia."

Luckily, the loggers had camped in the adjacent forest, enabling the humans to make their own camp by the lake. It took most of the day to solve the puzzle. The nanites, it turned out, were not autonomous. A breed of submarine auxons descended from aquatic probes inhabited the lake. These cyberfish manufactured the nanites within their bodies and released them into the water, where they gathered dissolved elements and were then reabsorbed by their host species. "Amazing," Safira beamed once this became clear. "It's like termites' symbiosis with their digestive bacteria—only outside the body."

"Somewhat too efficient, though," Marc cautioned. "They've extracted so much material that the lake can barely support organic life."

"But the cyber-ecology's in good balance," Safira replied. "Plenty of piscivorous heliraptors around; and I saw the ripple of a cybarracuda on the prowl."

"But what about the *real* ecology? The lake's natural ecosystem's been all but exterminated. Who knows how many species lived in that lake before? Or how many other species fed on them, or were fertilized by organic remains flowing out of the lake?"

Safira frowned. "Now you sound like the government. Like the hunters."

He took a breath. He had to do this delicately. If she realized too much, she would bolt and make things harder. "When I see things like this, Safi, I wonder if they have a point. I mean, look at all the wonders we've seen the past few days. The unique forms that life—biological life—has taken on this world. How many species have the auxons already competed to extinction?"

"No species lasts forever, Marc. Extinctions are only to be expected when different branches of life come into contact."

"But the auxons' Lamarckian evolution lets them develop faster than organic life can keep up. And they have abilities no biological species has ever possessed. They've got an unfair advantage in the competition. I mean...I just, I can see the government's point. This is such a young biosphere, with so much untapped potential. Those gliding fandancers—with the auxons around, do you really believe they'll have the *chance* to evolve actual flight? Is it...." He pulled back, softened his approach. "Sometimes I do have doubts whether it's really right to, to allow all the extinctions the auxons have caused."

Safira stroked his hair, her face wistful. "Oh, Marc. Remember that time in Sumatra? You were so hurt when that baby orangutan was taken by a tiger...especially knowing that we had bred the tigers as well as the orangs. You felt so responsible. But do you remember what I told you?"

He nodded, and spoke with lowered eyes. "That our responsibility ends with correcting the damage we caused in the past, and avoiding further damage."

"That's right. Nature doesn't belong to us, Marc. No, it's not ours to exploit and destroy, but neither is it ours to nursemaid and cultivate like a garden. Nature is larger than we are, and can take care of itself without our arrogant meddling." She wasn't so much lecturing him, Marc realized, as reflexively restating a long-practiced argument.

"But we sent the auxons here. Gave them the ability to evolve."

"And designed them to cause minimal ecological damage. But then they were threatened, and had to breed and defend themselves to survive. When our programming conflicted with those imperatives, they discarded it as maladaptive genes are always discarded. When they came into competition with native species, they did so not because of humanity's will, but *in spite* of it. They've evolved beyond our jurisdiction!" she insisted.

"But we made them strong, durable, adaptable," Marc countered. "Made them able to function without food or water or air. Gave them tools more potent than any tooth or claw. Let them build defenses so strong, nothing natural could break through them. Safira, they're competing because of evolution—but they're *winning* because of us. Doesn't that make us responsible?"

"So what do we do? Consciously exterminate a whole, unique category of life? Correct an accidental evil by committing a deliberate evil? How does that moral equation balance?" She shook her head sadly. "Yes, I regret the loss of the native life. You know I cried as hard as you about that baby orang. But I didn't try to kill the tiger who was simply following her instincts. Whatever responsibility I bore for her existence did *not* entitle me to end it!"

Marc was reluctant to continue, but he felt he must. "But if the whole biosphere is in danger of extermination—"

"Absurd!" she snapped. Then she sighed, breathed deeply and hugged him. "I'm sorry, love, it's not you I'm angry at. But you can't really take that claim seriously. Those fools, they claim to be defending the native life, but they have no faith in it. They've forgotten that life manages to survive in the harshest conditions, no matter what the universe throws at it. Cybele's life will adapt, will find new ways to thrive. There may very well be a mass extinction event, but such things are normal on any world, and a new evolutionary phase always follows. And who can imagine what that next phase might hold for a world where bio-life and cyber-life coexist? Marc, we have no right to narrow the possibilities. And bottom line, no matter the cost," she added with passion, "we have *no* right to deliberately exterminate any species, period!"

Marc sat quietly for a time, not wanting to argue further, not knowing how. "A lot of people out there don't agree," he finally said. "You...we've got most of Cybele's population against us. I don't see how we can win. I just...don't want you to get hurt."

Safira smiled wistfully. "Marc, my dear one. If I pulled back from a just fight because I feared getting hurt, could you love me as you do?"

It was painful to meet her eyes. "No," he breathed with utter sincerity. She would fight on until she was broken, and he adored her for it...but still he knew he had to bring her down.

The lake's heliraptors proved too numerous and hostile for the loggers' comfort, so the troop moved on. Two of Cybele's 32-hour days passed before they came upon the majestic sight of a city-hive. It gleamed like a fairy-castle of diamond and quartz, bearing the clean-lined polish of late-21st-century architecture, but with the comfortable asymmetry of an organic structure. The feral city-builder auxons still followed their innate construction protocols, but had adapted to the survival needs of wild creatures as opposed to the creature comforts of civilized humans.

The town-sized hive bore few doors, and those were auxon-sized openings obscured within the maze of towers, roadways and non-functional streetlights. The city was walled with high diamite ramparts, with only hidden tunnels allowing ingress. The once-fashionable colorshift dyes followed no aesthetic rules, functioning merely to regulate temperature or absorb solar energy, changing to follow the sun across the deep indigo sky; yet that simple functionality gave them a special beauty.

And the whole magnificent structure was thoroughly dead. From an adjacent hill, Safira and Marc could see that the hive's streets were littered with city-builder corpses. "EMP bombs," Safira said with soft, tearful fury. "The hives are easy, sitting targets. Fish in a barrel. No-fuss genocide. *Cowards!*" She allowed herself the skyward shriek, then indulged her rage no further, instead coolly deploying a camera to record the atrocity. The *necessary* atrocity, Marc reminded himself.

The loggers seemed subdued at the mass carnage, but they were a pragmatic lot. They soon found an entrance and filed inside, unhesitant to exploit a ready-made redoubt. The casual way they gathered corpses for consumption made Marc queasy, but Safira narrated it as a hopeful thing, the beginning of the city-builders' rebirth as a large, new generation of loggers. "Imagine what evolutionary variants might arise as loggers absorb builders' experiences and adaptations," she said into her recorder. "A whole new species could soon be born from Galadriel's womb."

This time Marc heard the engines first. *Sorry, Safira,* he thought with sad relief, recognizing aircars as well as drones. *Galadriel will have no more children.*

The loggers were the next to react, their agitation alerting Safira. "Shit, not again!" she snarled, leaping for her pack and the plasma rifles.

"Safira!" Marc protested. "Those aren't just drones. There are people coming."

She looked up and out, recognizing the silhouettes of several police aircars accompanying the small fleet of drones. Her grimace of despair was gone almost before Marc saw it. "Come on. Under cover. Come on!" she called to the loggers, adding gestures and whistles. Galadriel joined her in corralling the troop, and collectively they took cover beneath a large plaza that sloped between two buildings. A place like this, cut off from the sky, defied the standards of this architectural period, but the mutant city planning now served the loggers well. Of course, another EMP bomb would've finished them; but the collateral radiation precluded the bombs' use while Safira and Marc were present.

"Galadriel!" Safira called, gesturing curtly toward one end of the underpass. Shortly, the loggers began erecting a barricade from city-builder corpses and plasticrystal secretions. "This leaves the drones only one way in," Safira explained, "so we can pick them off more easily."

"What's the point?" Marc urged. "They've surrounded the whole hive by now. And *we* can't eat the builders. It's over, Safira. There's no way out."

"We'll find one. Tunnel out if we have to."

Marc shook his head. "They can track us wherever we go."

"What makes you so sure?" she taunted with an encouraging smile.

The smile vanished in an eyeblink when her wristcom spoke to her. "Take his word for it, Dr. Kimenye," it said in a heavy, but not unkind male voice. "You're broadcasting loud and clear."

Safira gaped at the instrument. "Governor Berdahl?"

"A pleasure to speak to you again, Safira," said *Anansi*'s former captain. "I only regret the circumstances. Please surrender quietly, old friend. You can't evade us now, even if you abandon your wristcom. And then you couldn't take your notes, or stir the public to your cause."

"There would be other ways."

"And I'm sure you'd find them. You're as resourceful as they come. But your current resources can't bring you escape," Berdahl said in a tone of simple reason. "They can only delay the inevitable."

"I'm not the only one out here, protecting the auxons," Safira countered defiantly.

"But you're the inspiration. The cause would wither without your strength, your passion. Besides—we infiltrated your support network weeks ago. We've shut them down. Those other few dedicated naturalists scattered around Cybele, protecting other auxons—soon they'll have no choice but to come in from the cold."

A pause. "I don't believe you."

"Then how do you suppose we're talking now? How else could we have gotten a hard virus into your wristcom to reactivate its transceiver?"

"Impossible. The supplies are scanned for nanites." Yet Safira had already begun tapping commands into her wristcom before she spoke.

"Nanites, yes. But you've shown us that the lines can be blurred—that machines can behave like living things. We simply turned that around. We engineered an organic `hard virus.' Actually, more of a bacterium—a native protozoan to which we gave an affinity for certain trace elements in certain ratios, elements such as those you'd find in a wristcom's circuitry; and to feed on those elements and lay down waste products along certain specific paths...like those that, for instance, would re-connect severed transceiver circuits."

"Richard, that's a rather implausible story," she scoffed, still tapping out commands. Marc suspected this was more than denial, was perhaps some sort of delaying tactic. Her next words, though, left no more room for that thought. "The only person on Cybele with the necessary expertise for that is right here by my side—*on* my side. Isn't that right, Marc?"

His silence was confession enough, even without the guilt he knew he must be radiating. Finally the silence grew too long, and he had to look up. Her gaze seared him.

He struggled to think of something to say. He'd been too afraid of this moment to plan for it. "You, you have to understand, Safira. I didn't do this to hurt you. I admire and respect and... and truly love you.

"Which is why it hurt me so much to see you out here helping to perpetuate the crime against nature our forebears committed. To see you blinded to the devastation, and to our own culpability for it."

She merely looked at him stonily. "Yes," Marc continued, "I've seen how remarkable the auxons are. But they're just *too* strong, too capable for organic life to compete with. They're killing Cybele, and I can't stand by and watch that happen.

"The thought of betraying you to do it...Safi, it devastated me. But...you yourself taught me that you have to do what has to be done, no matter how hard or painful. I...I had to remain true to what I believed in."

No reply. No fury, no tears. She was a sculpture of icy dignity. "Safira, I never expected that...that we'd fall in love. I tried not to let it happen, I *knew* it'd hurt you so much worse. But...but then it happened anyway. And I just couldn't tell you, I didn't know how. I...." He floundered. At least if she'd railed and screamed, he could've stood up to it, justified himself with righteous anger. But she remained silent, so that the more he strove to explain, the clearer it became that he was really trying to convince himself. She was so bitter that she gave him nothing, not the dignity of self-defense, not even the right to see her pain.

"I had to do this," he finished weakly. "It was bigger than you or me. I'm sorry, but it had to be done."

The long silence that followed was finally broken by Berdahl's voice. "Safira...don't be too hard on Marc. Nobody here feels good about what's happened, the way colleagues and friends have been pitted against each other.

"But we don't blame you for that, Safira. Your fascination with the auxons is perfectly understandable. They are an amazing phenomenon, and it would be a shame if they were destroyed completely. Rest assured, some specimens of each species *will* be preserved, relocated to Attis, where they can—"

"Where they may not survive," she said flatly. "They've spent over a century adapting to this world, a living world. Uproot them to such a barren planet and they might not be able to adapt. Many of them, maybe most, would indeed go extinct."

"I thought you had more faith in their adaptability."

"Even cybernetic evolution has its limits. And even if they did survive, it's still wrong," she insisted. "If it's wrong to kill a hundred percent of a species, then how can it be right to kill ninety-nine percent of them? Or ninety? Or fifty? Or even one animal that doesn't threaten you and you don't need to eat? Where can you draw the line, Governor?"

"The line was crossed the moment the first Cybeline species was driven to extinction by our creations," Berdahl responded with conviction.

"We designed them *not* to harm native life. They evolved away from that on their own."

"Conveniently letting us wash our hands of all responsibility? No, Safira. However they behave, auxons are human technology. This is our mess and we have to clean it up."

"*Not this way.* You cannot be allowed to sentence whole species to death." She smiled faintly at something on her wristcom display.

"As we see it, Safira, that's what you're doing. And you can't be allowed to continue. I'm—" Suddenly he broke off. Marc heard another voice speaking urgently in the background. "Safira, what have you done?"

"You reactivated my transceiver, I used it. The past few minutes have been beamed out all over CybeleNet." Somehow, the discovery that Marc's betrayal had been exposed to all of Cybele brought him no more shame than he already felt. "As your monitors will have read by now, my supporters are coming. You've arrested my volunteers, but the people who believe in what we're doing are still out there. They will no longer stand by while you commit these crimes."

"That's it," Berdahl said angrily, "move in now!"

"Not advisable, Governor! I'm armed!"

"I'm not sending in drones, Doctor, but live people. We can stun you and take out the loggers without ever getting in a stun pistol's range."

"How about a plasma rifle?"

A moment of shock. "You wouldn't kill humans to save the auxons!"

"I will do what I must to stop a horrible crime!" she said with sorrow.

"And the people who are coming to stand with you? Will they be armed too? Are your convictions so unshakable that you'd allow this to escalate into open warfare? My God, there are only three hundred adult humans on this planet! The whole settlement could be at risk!"

"Don't you think I realize that?! Do you think I'd do this, any of this, if I had a choice? Just *turn around,* Richard. Don't force this on me."

"Every day the auxons live kills another species. We *will* not do to Cybele what we did to Earth!"

"Put it down, Safira."

Marc's voice lacked the conviction appropriate to the threat...but the stungun in his grip compensated. Safira whirled on him, her eyes lit with fury, and for a moment he feared her hatred would translate into plasma flame. "It's over," he urged when the moment passed. "You can't win."

"Neither can you," she hissed. "Can you be sure I won't convulse and fire if you stun me? Can you be sure the loggers won't avenge a fallen troopmate?"

"As long as you're safe...as long as you're stopped from this madness...I'll risk it."

"The madness is yours! I'm defending innocents against murderers. I can't shirk that duty." Her eyes gleamed with something other than rage. "Even now, Marc, even with all the hate I have for you...the thought of killing you shreds me inside. But I no longer have any choices."

She laughed bitterly. "I suppose this is why we shouldn't take sides in nature. There's no right or wrong out here; there's just *need.* When two animals, two species fight to the death, they're both driven by the same needs, the same forces. Morality and choice don't come into it—only blind necessity."

She laughed, though it was half a sob. "The hell of it is, I *know* you can't back down any more than I can. We're both fighting for the same causes, just interpreted differently. We're both doing what we have to do...and so we have no damned choice at all."

Their guns and eyes remained fixed, unwavering, upon each other. The moment stretched like steel wire toward its breaking point. But then Marc shook his head, lowered his weapon. "No," he breathed. "No, Safira. We're reasoning beings, not slaves to instinct. Even when the circumstances go beyond our control, we still *choose* how we react to them. Saying we're prisoners of the situation is just a cop-out.

"If this turns bloody, it will be *our* choice, *our* fault. It's not inevitable. We can all just back down. Go home. Talk this over, find another way."

"There is no other way," came Berdahl's voice. "Species are dying too fast."

"We have to leave nature to itself!" came Safira's words on his heels.

"You're right—you're *both* right in what you're fighting for. But you're fighting too hard. Too inflexibly. Life survives by adapting! By making compromises with its environment! We have to compromise too—have to bend before we break."

"What do you propose?" Safira was businesslike, suspicious.

"Um...give me a moment." He thought faster than ever before. "Okay. Extinctions happen, all right? They're part of nature, the result of competition, of changing conditions. So maintaining a perfect status quo, keeping the roster of species unchanged, isn't a realistic objective.

"The main concern here is that the whole biosphere may be endangered. Safira, you're probably right that some life would remain untroubled by the auxons, but there might be nothing left but microbes. And the nanites might take care of those eventually.

"Anyway, the point is: instead of erasing the auxons from the biosphere, let's just make sure they don't wipe it out. Let's allow them to live, to compete. If they should compete another species to extinction, *c'est la guerre.* We only intervene if a whole ecosystem is threatened with collapse. That way the auxons and Cybelines can both live."

"It won't work!" Berdahl countered, but with honest regret. "The auxons are too adaptable, too capable, their defenses too strong. They've won *every* competition with the native life. The fix is in, Marc."

"So we even the odds. This is where you have to compromise, Safira. To save the auxons' lives, you bend some on their untouchability. We used a hard virus on your wristcom, we can use it on them. Reprogram their instincts, restrict their behaviors. Not enough to make them our robots again...but enough to limit the destruction they can cause. Enough to diminish their performance, weaken their defenses.

Maybe even cut out their Lamarckian adaptation so both sides are playing by Darwin's rules."

Safira was thoughtful, but far from pleased. "But do we have the right?"

"Why not? We're part of nature too. That means we can't pretend it belongs to us—but it also means we have as much right as any species to have an effect on our environment."

"But only where our own survival is concerned."

"There's more to us than survival, Safira! We have the power of choice. The effect we have on other species isn't a random matter, it's something we *decide*. Something we're *responsible* for. So if we take responsibility for the world and the species around us, it's not so wrong. We just have to be responsible *enough* to interfere only when we have to, and otherwise trust nature to manage itself."

Again, the silence stretched, but without the earlier tension. "Not an easy balance to maintain," the governor opined. "But worth a try, isn't it, Safira?"

Long moments of thought. "I still don't like it."

"Nobody will," Berdahl said. "It means letting native species die out *and* restricting the auxons' right to live according to their nature. It stinks coming and going. But would you rather start shooting?"

She gave way without weakening. "Promise there will be no more exterminations. Melt down the hunter drones. Release my colleagues and work with them to implement the plan. I will remain out here with my charges until I know they're safe."

"Agreed. I'm calling the retreat even now." A sad smile underlay his next words. "I hope it's not too long before I can have you over for dinner again. I've missed our talks. Good luck, Safira."

And then Safira and Marc were alone with the loggers once more. But Marc realized he was more alone than any of them. "Safira...."

"Thank you," she said simply, distantly. "You've prevented a tragedy. Cybele owes you a debt. Now go the hell away."

He took a breath—then let his lungs keep it. He had no more defense. "You did what you had to," she continued, too matter-of-factly to be absolving. "No matter the cost. I taught you that. You learned it well. And when the time came, you unlearned it before it ruined us all. You backed down and found a compromise Cybele can live with.

"But you're too good at compromise, Marc. You couldn't choose between your feelings for me and your mission to betray me, so you tried to have both. You dodged the hard choice—and now who has to pay for it?"

"Both of us, Safira," Marc said simply. "Believe me."

"Maybe. But we both have only you to blame. You'll have to live with yourself—but fortunately I won't. I can't speak to the future, Marc...but for now, you no longer exist in my life."

Head lowered in total agreement, Marc slowly rose and strode toward the sunlight. He gave her one last glance. "I guess we all do what we have to do."

She never acknowledged him. She was alone with the loggers now.

Aspiring to Be Angels

The naked dead man in the airlock was the first clue that this wasn't an ordinary metasapience incident.

Arkady Nazarbayev reflexively moved his big, armored frame to shield Emerald Blair from the sight. He knew she would have to become inured to such things in the course of her training, but it was hard sometimes to think of her as an apprentice Troubleshooter rather than a surrogate daughter. As foolish as it was in their chosen line of work, he always wanted to protect Emerald from having to witness death up close.

But Emry would have none of it. As soon as he began to move, she sensed his intent and pulled herself around his bulk. Her light, formfitting EV suit gave her more agility than his heavy symbot armor afforded, even in the microgravity of the Iwakura Research Institute's docking hub. She stiffened briefly before burying her emotions beneath the hardened façade she'd developed in her years on the streets. "Damn," she said. "I've heard of forgetting to check your suit first, but this is ridiculous." She looked over the man's rather well-built form and sighed. "And he had *so* much to live for."

"Emerald. Show some respect."

"What, like you weren't thinking it too?" Arkady simply glared. "Sorry."

A cursory scan suggested the obvious mechanism, death by anoxia. Which didn't begin to address the *why*. Arkady took the body across into *Hermes*—who kept station a few dozen meters away from the docking hub as a quarantine precaution—and asked the ship to perform an autopsy while he and Emerald went below.

The airlock doubled as a lift between the hub and the Institute module of the dumbell-shaped habitat, an independent facility orbiting a dormant, midsized comet in the Outer Main Belt. It was just the place for the kind of AI research that went on here—plenty of carbon as raw material for the tech, plenty of water ice to sustain the personnel, and not many authorities around to quibble about the ethics of dabbling in metasapience. But that hadn't kept them from screaming for help from the nearest Troubleshooters when something went wrong, as it inevitably did.

And yet the institute had fallen silent by the time they arrived. On the way down, as the lift pressurized, Arkady made one more attempt to reach someone over IRI's internal comm system. The only reply was a cackling, borderline-hysterical male voice. *"We're not in tomorrow. Please come back yesterday! By then the wall should still be up."*

"Identify yourself!" Arkady called, knowing it was futile. "Who is this?"

"You know! Everything I can say, you already know. We're all connected, us waves in the hologram. Doesn't matter. We're less than real! Why are you talking to me? I don't exist!"

The voice dissolved into desperate laughter before the channel cut out. Emry looked up at Arkady, eyes wide. "What the vack is going on here? It's supposed to be the metaminds that go crazy, not the creators. They are doing cyber work here, right? Not modding themselves?"

"As far as we know," Arkady told her.

"And why do people keep experimenting with metaminds, anyway? These things always go crazy. *Always.*"

"Except when they go catatonic, or just crash." He sighed. "Those are the easy ones."

"But they keep trying anyway. It's just so...cruel."

Arkady spread his arms in a shrug. In the symbot, gestures had to be broad. "They keep dreaming up new theories—figure *this time* they've finally cracked the problem. Make a stable superbrain, bring on the Singularity at last—it's the Holy Grail to this type."

"Typical. Don't care who gets hurt, so long as they can prove how smart they are." With the lift now pressurized, she reached up for her helmet seal.

"Wait," he said. "Something's affecting the people here. Best stay suited up for now."

Her hand froze, but she still complained. "Aw, come on, it's stuffy in here."

"Live with it. I *know* you know better than to take off your helmet in a potential contagion scenario." Maybe no one had ever succeeded in creating a viable brain more brilliant than the greatest human geniuses, but Emry's father's people, the Vanguard, had modded their minds and bodies to the pinnacle of human potential.

Not that you'd know it from her recent performance. "If *you* were smart, you'd have left me in the ship," she muttered. "Or back at Ceres."

"Not an option. This is your last chance, you know that? No more slacking off, no more sabotaging yourself. You step up now, or you wash out. And we both know you have nowhere else to go."

Perhaps that was unfairly harsh. Emerald Blair had the physical and mental advantages to excel in any career she chose. But she was wild and undisciplined, a former delinquent searching for redemption, and only the Troubleshooter Corps had given her a true sense of purpose. It had seemed like an ideal match. The Corps wanted its operatives to be charismatic superheroes that the diverse and fractious peoples of the Belt would celebrate, rather than a transhuman paramilitary they would distrust. With her exceptional strength and endurance, her aggressive sex appeal, and her knack for witty repartee, Emerald had been a TSC recruiter's dream. She even looked like a classic superheroine, with tumbling red-gold locks, huge green eyes, and curves as ample as her muscles.

Yet beneath that flawless surface was a deep well of insecurity, the impulse of an orphaned child to fear she wasn't good enough to be accepted. For nine months, Emerald had performed superbly—if perhaps taking more readily to the physical challenges of TSC training than the intellectual ones—but when she had finally, inevitably stumbled, it had shaken her confidence badly. In the weeks since, she'd begun living down to her own expectations, slacking off in her training and entering a spiral of self-sabotaging behavior. Arkady had convinced Director Villareal to let him take her on as a provisional apprentice two months early, hoping that more personal guidance could get her back on track before it was too late. He hadn't intended to bring her into a situation this dangerous, but he had been the only responder in range of IRI's distress call. He prayed that bringing Emerald along would not prove a fatal mistake—either to her or to someone else.

Once the lift reached the bottom, they found the corridor outside occupied only by a honey-haired woman who slumped against the wall like a rag doll, staring vacantly forward and making faint, staccato noises. Emry knelt before her and tried futilely to get a response. "Triage," Arkady said, leading her down the hall toward the louder sounds of people in distress.

Another woman came through a door and intercepted them, her dark skin covered only with water from the still-running shower inside—plus various pins and clips with which she'd crudely pierced or pinched herself all over her body. Her head was roughly shaven, her skin scalded from the shower, and a few of the piercings still bled. "Input!" she cried, flinging herself against Arkady's armored chest. Water dripped down the front of his symbot and trickled along the corridor in search of Old Man Coriolis. "Stimulation! You must feed it. Give me sensations!"

"Sorry, honey, you're not his type," Emry said.

The woman winced. "Voice, it hurts!"

"Sorry," Emry said more softly. She *could* get a little shrill.

But the woman had turned to her, clutching her shoulders and shaking them. "No, give me more! Anything! It hungers! Give me something to feed it!"

Arkady moved in behind the woman and administered a sedative from the medical unit in his gauntlet. She whirled around to face him, eyes growing panicked as the drug kicked in. "No, no! Don't shut me down...if nothing else to feed it...devour me...leave nothing...."

Emry caught her as she slumped. "Okay, *that's* not at all creepy."

A bullet struck Arkady's armor. He spun, the symbot triangulating the source, and shielded the women with his bulk. "See to her!" he told his apprentice, striding forward as the quiet whirring of a Gauss pistol heralded more bullet hits against his second skin.

He found himself in what looked like the institute's lounge, deserted save for the shooter, a panicked, black-haired young man wearing some kind of complex visor over his eyes, and an unmoving body, also male, its blood pooling to antispinward. Cause and effect. Arkady raised his arm, deploying the wrist-mounted shock laser.

But he hesitated. Even through the visor, the man seemed more terrified than murderous, and he couldn't hurt anyone else at the moment. "No!" the shooter cried, firing a few more ineffectual rounds. "Stay back! I won't let you take me!"

"Please, sir, calm down! I'm not here to hurt anyone. I'm Medvyéd. The Troubleshooter. You've heard of me, yes?"

The man shook his head. "No, you're with her. You're part of her." He gestured at his visor. "Don't have this, so you're part of her. Keeps me safe. Keeps me from seeing the truth, only the safe illusions."

"Can I have one too?" It was Emry, easing her way into the room. She was keeping her distance from Arkady, watching him warily. "Can you keep me safe from him?"

Good girl, he thought. *Enemy of my enemy.*

But Emerald Blair had never made a convincing damsel in distress. Even when trying to look meek and afraid, she couldn't cloak the toughness that had kept her alive and intact growing up on the streets of the Belt's worst habitats. Arkady had spent ten months earning her trust, and still he'd never seen her truly let her guard down.

"No," the shooter said, pistol shakily coming to bear on her. "You're with her too. All stimulation and seduction, all body. She feeds through your body!" Shots fired, bounced off Emry's close-fitting (perhaps too close-fitting) EV suit. She kept advancing, aware that it would take more than this man had to penetrate TSC gear—or to do much damage to the Vanguardian physique beneath hers.

But the visored man just grew more panicked. "No! Keep away! The body!" At a gesture from Arkady, she slowed. But the shooter took in a sharp breath. "The body. The body! I'm so stupid!" The gun tilted back, the man's mouth opening to receive the barrel. "Discard the body. Don't need it. Just dead meat."

Arkady debated whether to fire. The shock laser, the tangle-gel, any nonlethal round he fired might convulse the man's muscles enough to send a bullet through his brain.

But Emry didn't hesitate. She let out a piercing scream and charged the shooter, moving frighteningly fast. He reacted instinctively, jerking the gun back toward her. But she'd knocked it aside and punched the man's lights out, sending the visor flying, before her shriek had stopped ringing in Arkady's ears. It was no wonder her mod-gang nickname had been Banshee.

"Good thinking," Arkady told her once the shooter was in restraints. "That scream would scare the hell out of anyone."

"Who was thinking?" she replied with a smirk. "I just like to scream."

He sighed. "Don't sell yourself short, Emry. You have a natural instinct for helping people. No matter what, when you see trouble, you try to fix it. I brought you out here to remind you of that."

"Oh, yeah? Then how come I always end up hurting people?" She glanced back at the unconscious shooter. Unlike most of the opponents she'd faced as a gang member and an apprentice, he was an ordinary person with no augmentations beyond the basics necessary to survive in space. Despite her best efforts to gauge her blow, she'd broken his jaw in several places.

But a few hours in a medbed would fix his jaw. Arkady knew her concern was for the injuries that were harder to repair. "No one expected you to go easy on Deema just because you were sleeping with her."

"But I didn't have to sabotage her chances just to prove how unbiased I was!"

"She sabotaged herself by trying to cheat off of you. You did the right thing by not helping her."

"I went too far. It backfired."

"And she went too far in her reaction. She betrayed your confidence, violated your privacy."

"I betrayed her first. She was just showing everyone who I really am. Someone who'd throw her own girlfriend in front of a stroid just to get ahead."

"You and Deema are the only ones who see it that way." He shook his head. "You blame yourself, she blamed everyone but herself. That's why she wasn't Troubleshooter material—and why you are."

She turned away. "I thought this was a rescue mission, not a therapy session. You coming, Arkady Changxievich?"

Reluctantly, he let it drop. He locked the disarmed man in the lounge and found another empty room where the two women would be safe. Then it was a matter of wading into the chaos and trying to sedate or isolate the staffers one by one before they caused any more harm to themselves or one another. Of those who were at all coherent, several more objected to being locked away without stimulation.

"Whatever this madness is," Arkady said after a time, "it's shared. Maybe a drug tailored to attack a certain part of the brain?"

"Can't be that tailored," Emry replied. "We got everything from drooling rag dolls to homicidal paranoids."

"So what's the common denominator?"

"Not our problem, boss. Let's just lock 'em up and let the doctors worry about it."

"What doctors? Who's going to take jurisdiction way out here? It's not like Iwakura will take responsibility for this disaster. And we can't take these people anywhere civilized if we don't know what's infected them or how." He clasped her shoulders. "'I don't know' is not an acceptable answer for a Troubleshooter. Our job is to find solutions when nobody else can or will."

"Then you tell me, Papa Bear," she said, turning away to resume their sweep of the corridor. "You're the teacher."

Arkady sighed. "Teachers look forward to being surpassed by their students. If you'd just—"

"Hello?"

The voice came over the institute comm channel. A soft female voice, the calmest one they'd heard yet. "Hello," Arkady replied.

"You're Troubleshooters?"

"Yes! Medvyéd and...my apprentice, Emerald Blair. Who is this?"

"Come to the cleanroom."

"Is that where you are?"

"Yes. I was here when it started. It's safe here. Please find me."

He tapped into the institute database for directions. "We're on our way. What's your name?"

A pause. *"Alice."*

Emry snorted. "Vackin' frabjous. What's a Mad Tea Party without an Alice?"

En route to the cleanroom, Arkady and Emerald got the autopsy report from *Hermes*'s shipmind—and Emerald almost wished they hadn't. The cyber had discovered an invasive smart gel wrapped around the dead man's brainstem, piercing it with tendrils that had apparently altered his brain activity. It seemed to Hermes like some kind of interface material.

"Interface?" Arkady asked. "With the metamind, perhaps?"

"It seems a reasonable conjecture, but I can't prove it here." While Hermes's memory capacity and processing speed were far beyond a human's, his intellect and imagination were, of course, not fundamentally greater. They would get no oracular insights from him.

The cyber was, however, able to confirm an Alice Neal among IRI's staff, a 22-year-old grad student from Vestalia. At least this one was sane enough to know her own name.

Arkady's suit sensors were soon able to confirm traces of the smart gel in the environment and on the outside of their suits. Emry ruefully acknowledged to herself that she'd been stupid to try to doff her helmet.

They had to pass through a decontam lock to get into the cleanroom. "Must be why Alice was safe," Emry said.

"Probably. But don't assume anything."

The cleanroom computer demanded they leave their EV suits in the lock, in case something escaped the decontam process. It was a standard binary model, not a sapient neural net, and thus impermeable to negotiation. Arkady chafed at taking off his symbot in a crisis, but Emry was relieved to strip to her light armor. Her augmented metabolism ran hot. Although the generic design of the armor was a frustrating reminder that had yet to earn her championym and costume.

She had been playing with names and designs for months, narrowing the list down to "Redhot," "Green Blaze," and Deema Jayesh's suggestion of "Firegem." Nothing had excited her more than the prospect of being reborn with a new identity, a hero at last.

Until Deema had revealed Emerald's true colors to her—and then to the rest of Solsys. Emry had proven through her own actions that she was no hero. She would never truly leave the Banshee behind.

Finally, the inner door slid open. Alice Neal stood on the far side of the pristine, white-walled chamber as they entered, her gaze wary but hopeful. Though she had a year on Emry, she looked more grade school than grad student—dainty and girlish with enormous brown doe eyes, a ragged, unflattering haircut, and loose, drab clothes. Yet her manner was quiet and subdued. When Arkady asked "Ms. Neal?" she simply nodded, keeping her distance. Suspecting she might be in shock, Emry held back. Though Arkady significantly outbulked her even without the symbot, he was still the more reassuring of the two. Emry tended to come on pretty forcefully.

Arkady took his time questioning the eerily quiet young woman, asking about the institute's work and her role, in hopes of drawing her out. "My thesis is on sapience as an adaptation to its environment," she finally said, her eyes not quite meeting theirs. "You understand why intelligence plateaus at the human level?"

"I believe so," Arkady said. "Emerald?"

She met his gaze and sighed. Of course he'd turn even this into a test. She knew the basics; in fact, she couldn't get away from them. Troubleshooters periodically had to clean up metasapience experiments, of course, but she'd known some of their victims growing up, children damaged by failed attempts to broaden their minds. Her gang had helped them escape the experimenters, given them a family that didn't exploit them, supported them as they struggled to function. It had made her ashamed of the Vanguard in her genes, in her brain. Strength was one thing; anyone could have it by getting the right mods or donning the right gear. It let her help people, not lord it over them—or undermine them to get ahead.

So there was an unavoidable undercurrent of emotion beneath her clinical recitation. "The neurological Goldilocks Zone," she said. "We're as smart as we are for the same reason we evolved on Earth instead of Mars—because that's where the conditions are balanced just right. Intelligence needs flexible minds, imagination, pattern recognition...but too much of any of that makes us unstable. Too much imagination means schizophrenia, too much patterning means paranoia. That's why there's no Singularity, no infinitely rising intelligence." She took a breath. "Because too much brain is always a liability." Arkady sighed.

"Basically," Alice said, ignoring or missing the subtext. "More fundamentally, it's a question of complexity. Our brains are complex enough to have the level of controlled instability they need to function on a sapient level."

"Controlled instability?" Arkady asked.

"Like walking. You're constantly off-balance...but you catch yourself and make it quasi-stable. Consciousness is like that: unstable enough to get you places, but not so much that you lose control."

"But if you make the brain too complex..."

"It becomes too unstable to function. It goes mad or retreats into catatonia. Too much is going on at once and the system simply crashes. It's not so much that there's a fine line between genius and insanity as that genius itself represents the dynamic transitional zone between sanity and chaos—an upper boundary on coherent thought." Alice paused. "That's the conventional view, anyway."

"And you had a different one?"

Alice looked down at her feet. "Professor Hayami does. I've simply built on his work." At Arkady's prompting, she went on. "We believe the Goldilocks Zone analogy is truer than you think. One AU is the optimal zone for life around this star...but around a hotter star, it's farther out. The zone differs depending on the environment.

"The professor's theory is that our level of mental complexity is the optimal one for functioning within a universe of this complexity: a universe of four dimensions, four fundamental forces, a certain value of *c*, and so forth. Our internal activity is in balance with the external inputs we must process and comprehend. The reason a more complex mind collapses is because its internal complexity is not balanced by sufficient external complexity. For a metamind, existing in our reality is like extreme sensory deprivation. Without enough external stimulation to balance its internal life, the mind becomes starved for input. Like a starving body consuming its own muscle mass, the starved mind feeds on itself. Its own memories, imaginings, fears become its entire reality, rendering it delusional, psychotic. Memory and cognition suffer as brain pathways go unstimulated." Her eyes went unfocused. "Imagine if that never ended. Imagine if it were all you'd ever known. Imagine being trapped in a reality that's simply not...not *real* enough to nourish you. Existing on our level is sheer torture for a metaconsciousness. It's no wonder they go mad."

"So...what?" Emry asked. "You wanted to make the universe more complex? Maybe unroll a couple extra dimensions?"

For the first time, Alice met her eyes. Just for a second, her face lit up with a mischievous smile, making her plain features suddenly pretty. But then it was gone, her vivid gaze drifting off into space somewhere. "We're not there yet," she said. "But Professor Hayami believed there might be a way to bridge the divide. That a metamind might be able to function in our universe if it were given...an anchor. An interface."

"Interface?" Arkady asked. "The smart gel."

Another nod. "A human mind—a system teetering on the edge between the mundane outer world and the hypercomplex inner reality of a metamind. Perhaps human imagination could bridge the gap and allow the metamind to ground itself in our reality. Perhaps human imagination could, in turn, interpret its thoughts into something comprehensible on our level."

Emry stared. "So you created a hard virus that infected everyone's brains?"

"It was designed to interface with a single volunteer," Alice said, taking a step forward. "Implanted in the spine, the metacyber would form in symbiosis with the volunteer's neural network, learning to experience the world through human perceptions and insights. As it grew steadily more complex, the volunteer's mind would adapt to it, and together they would learn to coexist. The cyber would make the human superintelligent, and the human would keep the cyber grounded and focused."

"Oh, shit," Emry breathed. "So of course the whole thing got blown to vack."

Alice took another step closer, her eyes dancing. "It wasn't enough. The demands of such a complex consciousness are intense." Another step. "It hungers for input. For stimulation. The volunteer could only give it so much. Food...sex...pain...passion...joy...despair...fury... laughter...cruelty...love...it wanted all of it at once, and more. It made her design...a new interface. Made her use it to add... new sources of input. One anchor isn't enough. It needs more. More complexity than one human brain and its associated senses can provide."

Now Alice plodded toward them at a slow, but deliberate pace, eyes gleaming. Her body moved jerkily, as though something else were puppeteering her. Arkady stepped back. "*Bozhe moi,*" he said, crossing himself. "You were the volunteer."

The lopsided smile that appeared on Alice's face was far less appealing than the previous one. "And now so are you."

Arkady's hand shot to the back of his neck, which glistened with the residue of the gel that, judging from the inflammation there, had already forced its way in through his pores. He whirled. "Emry, run! Stay away! *Run!*"

Her impulse was to go to Arkady, to try to save him. But for once, she let thought overcome impulse. Or perhaps it was just obedience. Arkady was one of the few who'd ever earned it from her. All the others were Troubleshooters too.

Emry retreated into the decontam lock as fast as she could, knowing it was probably too late. Alice must have released the hard virus from within her own body. It could've been coming out with every breath, accumulating on them bit by bit until it gained enough mass and collective processing power to act. She could feel the tendrils of the smart gel crawling on her skin already, and she couldn't risk wondering if it was her imagination. She ordered her light armor into nanohazard alert mode, but the status response in her retinal HUD was erratic and full of failure warnings. The gel had already overwhelmed its defenses. *Punking generic piece of shit!* she thought. Emry dove into the emergency shower, stripped off the treacherous garment, and began to scrub as thoroughly as she could.

But before long, the desperation driving her motions became something else: a sensual excitement, a hunger for stimulus. All her senses were going into overdrive. The intensity was painful, yet she craved still more. *Holy vack, I could get into this if it weren't driving me insane!*

She fought it as best she could, curling into a ball and squeezing her eyes shut. She focused on her breathing, tried to remember the mantras that Overload, poor little Daniel, had used when his augmented perceptions had made the world a living hell for him. But of all her friends in the gang, he'd been the one she'd kept the most distance from, afraid of overwhelming him with her loud, passionate presence. Peacefulness had never worked for her. Not since the peace of her childhood had been destroyed, a casualty of those who thought their power gave them license to ruin others' lives through random violence. She'd been fighting ever since: fighting the father who, for all his power, had failed to save her mother; fighting to survive on the streets; then fighting for its own sake until she'd nearly become the thing she hated most. Ever since, she'd been fighting her past, fighting her guilt.

"Deema, I made a point of treating you the same as everyone else!"

"Yes – you made a point *of it. You went out of your way to flare me up in combat training, in the exam..."*

"You shouldn't have asked me for help in the first place!"

"Then you should've just said so! Not deliberately fed me the wrong answers!"

"I thought you'd check them first, not just use them! I was trying to make a point!"

"So you'd rather treat me like a child than a partner? Damn it, Emry, I trusted you! And you used it against me, just so you could prove how self-righteous you are!"

Deema Jayesh had been the one judged unworthy of the TSC as a result of her cheating, but in Emerald's eyes, she was the one who had failed. She had betrayed a friend over a point of pride. Deema had spent her entire adolescent and adult life training to become a Troubleshooter, striving for it longer and with more commitment than Emry had ever spent on any pursuit in her life. And with one selfish act, Emry had destroyed her lover's dream. How could she ever call herself a hero when she was capable of that?

The memory of her pain blurred with the humiliation she had felt weeks later, when Deema had gone to the press with the details of Emry's sealed juvenile record as the Banshee, founder of the infamous Freakshow gang. Which might not have been so bad if Emry hadn't lost her temper at the mob of reporters besieging her and nearly injured one of them, worsening the scandal and the embarrassment she was becoming to the Corps.

All because you lost control! she chastised herself. She knew far too well how dangerous she could be. Who knew what damage she could inflict if she succumbed to this madness? *Get a hold of yourself, Emry. Don't give in to it!*

"That's impressive."

Involuntarily, Emry's eyes snapped open. Alice stood before her, unconcerned as the shower drenched her clothes. In the doorway behind her, Arkady was on his knees, mumbling incoherently. His eyes stayed fixed on Alice. In Emry's own vision, the girl burned even brighter than her amplified surroundings. Emry tried to wrest her gaze away and finally succeeded.

"A strong mind," Alice said, and she could hear it in her head. "You're like me. Higher than the others. Closer to the next level." Emry strained to shove the voice out of her mind. She trembled and heaved an involuntary sob. She felt Alice stroking her hair, cradling her head against her hip. "It's all right. You'll understand soon. Of all of them, you're the one most likely to understand. Most likely to survive. But you have to stop fighting."

Never. She tried to pull herself away, reached out to her mentor. "Ar...ka...dy...."

His murmurs went on without interruption. She realized he was praying.

"Don't worry about him," Alice said. "He's having a religious experience. You see, we think we may be becoming God." A pause. "We're sorry if that sounds vain. But don't you think that maybe we've had it backwards? If consciousness is an emergent property of life, arising from sufficient complexity, then might not God be an emergent property of consciousness? Perhaps all our tales of gods have merely been an expression of the potential we had within us. The prophecy that creates the reality. In the beginning was the Word, after all."

Emry tried not to listen. She couldn't help but listen, but still, the bulk of her focus was elsewhere—gathering itself to power a single, extended, primal scream. It broke the spell enough to let her lash out at Alice and knock her aside. Scrambling to her feet, she staggered toward the door. It wouldn't open, so she dug in her nails and began to force it, the edges of the metal crumpling under her fingertips. "Sorry, sister," she grated out. "I'm an atheist."

Alice rose smoothly to her feet, a beatific smile on her face even though her left arm hung limp and broken. "Call it what you like, then. But we've tapped into something higher. Just listen, feel it, and you'll understand." She reached out her right hand. "Please, Emerald. We need someone else who can understand. The others feed us...but they aren't with us. All we have is us."

Emry finally tore open the door and began to run. The last thing she heard before she passed out of earshot was, "You have no idea how lonely we are."

She ran without knowing where she was running. Eventually, through the torrent of sensation surging within her mind, she thought of *Hermes*. If she could get to the ship, maybe he could cure the hard virus. Assuming it only infected human minds. But she had nowhere else to go.

If only she could find the lift. Emry strove to focus through the overload. Multiple images lay cluttered atop each other, as if she saw through many eyes...ears...she saw noise, smelled colors, heard pain. Her senses blurred together to the point that it was hard to remember the difference between them. There was just one great wash of perception sleeting through her, feeding *it* through her.

But she fought it. *Remember who you are. You are...*

It wasn't easy. She'd spent so long trying to figure that out, wandering from life to life, role to role. Failing at everything she'd ever tried, because none of it had meaning for her.

She thought she'd finally figured it out when she applied to the Corps. The one thing that had felt truly meaningful to her was helping others. She'd been so certain that was her true purpose. But now she was failing even at that, hurting her friends instead of helping them. So why even keep trying? Why not just surrender to the tide?

"Don't sell yourself short, Emry. You have a natural instinct for helping people. No matter what, when you see trouble, you try to fix it."

Arkady. He was still out there. He needed her. And so did all these others. She was all they had. That gave her a responsibility to do all she could. But how could she trust herself?

"You blame yourself, she blamed everyone but herself. That's why she wasn't Troubleshooter material – and why you are."

With her heightened clarity came understanding of what he had meant. Yes, she could make mistakes. She could be defeated. But there was no shame in that—only in failing to try. Only in abandoning the responsibility that came with power, like the Vanguard, her father, Deema, and so many other superhumans had done. Troubleshooters had failed before. They had died before. But the ones who were worthy of the name were the ones who had never stopped trying, who kept getting back up no matter how many times they stumbled. That was what it meant to be a superhero: never giving up the good fight, no matter what. So long as she focused on that, she knew exactly who she was.

I am Emerald Blair.
I'm a Troubleshooter.
I solve the unsolvable.
And I look damn fine doing it!

With herself as a reference point, she was able to begin reassembling the world around her. She recognized where she was, identified the path that led to the lift and *Hermes*. She made her way surely, swiftly. She was naked, but she strode as though cloaked in full Troubleshooter livery. In her mind, she blazed green.

Others blocked her way. Alice's drones, the mind vampire's thralls, they hurled themselves at her, screaming and gibbering. She tossed them aside, her strength dwarfing theirs.

But one clutched her from behind, and she found herself pulling her blow even before she consciously registered that it was Arkady. With her senses heightened, she'd subliminally known him by scent, by the sound of his breath. It delayed her enough to let him get a secure grip. Without his symbot, he had a fraction of her strength, but he had height, mass, and experience on her. Once he robbed her of leverage, the fight was over.

The throng parted, the gibbering thralls falling quiet, sinking to their knees, and gazing in adoration at Alice as she came forward. "Fight her, boss!" Emry cried. "Arkady! *Medvyéd!*"

She'd hoped that invoking his superhero persona would work for him as it had for her. But he'd never placed the same importance on it that she had. "No, Emry," he sighed in her ear, unmoved. "Love her. Pray to her."

"What was that First Commandment again, Papa Bear? She ain't your vackin' God!"

"I am who he needs me to be," said Alice. "They all reflect in me and I in them." She gave Emry an apologetic smile as she reached up and stroked her cheek. "That's why you can't fight me, Emerald. Your strength is my strength."

"No. You're not like me! I wouldn't make these people suffer. Wouldn't make them kill each other!"

Alice's eyes lost focus for a moment. Emry couldn't look away from them. She was fixated by every striation in the girl's irises. "We're sorry for that. We didn't mean it to happen. They are part of us, after all. But it wasn't for nothing. We're convinced now—we've tapped into something bigger than anyone's imagined."

Emry scoffed. "God."

"Or something else, if you prefer a more concrete definition. Think about the metaminds that don't crash or go insane. The ones that simply retreat into themselves, into intense activity with no outside interaction."

"Yeah, and then they burn themselves out, so what?"

"That's what we've thought. But what if it's something more? You were on the right track before. If metaminds are too complex for the universe, make the universe more complex. Or move to one that is already. There must be metaminds out there, somewhere, in a spacetime with more dimensions, greater energy density. Or perhaps some hypercomplex domain of our universe. A manufactured region of inflationary-era spacetime, or perhaps a Matrioshka brain of nested computronium Dyson shells powered by a star, could have the necessary complexity. There could be a network of hypersapience out there, waiting to be discovered. Maybe some metaminds find it on their own, or are contacted by it, brought into it. Maybe they live entire lifetimes in that brief surge before they burn out. Maybe they're even transferred and live on. Maybe we've already succeeded in creating the mind of God without realizing it.

"Don't you see, Emerald? This interface could connect us to the greatest minds in the universe. Reveal whole new layers of cosmic truth to the human mind. This experiment must not end."

"No matter how many people have to die for it?" Emry spat.

"The cost is high, I know. But isn't it worth the risk if we're on the verge of breaking through to a higher level of consciousness?"

"There's no higher level, sister! There's just craziness and oblivion. Make a mind too big and it falls apart under its own weight. That's all there is to it."

Alice's endlessly intricate eyes gazed into hers imploringly. "Why do you resist the idea? Your mind has so much potential. You could rise as high as any human ever has, yet you reject it. You resist exploring your own possibilities."

Alice's hands clasped the nape of Emry's neck, and flashes of memory burst into Emry's consciousness, bringing with them emotions as vivid as if she were living the experiences anew. She went through years of grief, rage, pain, and guilt in what felt like moments yet seemed like it would never end. When it faded, she was drenched in sweat, gasping for breath and crying uncontrollably.

"I see," Alice said. "The crimes you committed. The damage you punish yourself for. You've worked so hard to atone, but can't believe in that success because you hurt a lover in the process. All you feel is the guilt. You don't believe you deserve to become anything higher."

How could she have processed so much so quickly? The metamind within her, insane as it was, must be truly amazing to decipher Emry's neural coding at all, let alone translate it for a different brain. But still, it was fallible, imperfect in its understanding. That gave her hope, and she grinned fiercely.

"You're wrong, honey. I am trying to make myself something more. More responsible. More ethical. Better able to help people, protect them. Because that's what I have to do first, before I can *deserve* to be more powerful. Because I've seen what happens—seen it from both ends—

when people think their power or their brilliance gives them the right to throw other people's lives away. It's not enough to improve our brains and bodies. That just makes us worse if we don't improve our hearts first.

"You say you're my reflection? You feel what I feel? Then feel it, Alice," she snarled. "*Really* feel it. Take a good, long look at what I've been through—not just the crimes and the pain, but what I've done since, who I am now. Face it all. *Then* ask if it's worth letting innocent people die just so you can prove a scientific point!"

She saw Alice look within. Through their link, she felt the girl reviewing the memories the metaconsciousness had mined from her head. She caught echoes of the perceptions, the emotions that went with it—not as potent as before, but longer, deeper. If this was just the echo of her loss, her guilt, she could only imagine what Alice was enduring.

But she didn't stop pushing. "Now, Alice—look at your own memories. Look at theirs. *Feel* what you've been doing to them. To your colleagues. To your *friends*." Alice's pupils dilated, and Emry could hear her heart racing. "That's right, honey. I'm not talking to that thing inside, I'm talking to Alice Neal. Don't look at it from some abstract height, feel it like a human being. Whether you've tapped into something higher or not, that's the only level these people will ever know, so that's the one that should matter.

"Of all the things I've done wrong in my life, none of them feel as bad as hurting my friends, letting down my family. And you know what? That's a good thing. Because it makes me want to keep trying to do right by them. And maybe that's what matters most.

"You want to raise yourself up, Alice? Then ask yourself: how can you become more than you are if you start by throwing away your humanity?"

The surge of emotion and sensation in the link grew overwhelming. All around them, Arkady and the others were screaming, passing out from the overload. Arkady's grip released and Emry fell forward, unable to catch herself. She looked up at Alice, the only one still standing. In her perceptions, the girl still burned, now brighter than ever. Yet the glow was flickering, like a flame in the breeze.

Finally, Alice turned to her. Tears pooled in her eyes, but her mouth bore a sweet, gentle smile. "Thank you, Emerald. I know what I have to do now."

Alice knelt down and tilted Emry's head up by her chin. Her lips pressed against Emry's for the briefest of eternities. Then, slowly, silently, she made her way to the airlock lift. The doors slid open before her and she stepped inside. Emry reached out for her, trying to speak, trying to stop her. "It's the only way," Alice told her. "We—I can't shut it off. It's too much a part of me." She didn't seem to think that was a bad thing.

She tilted her head, suddenly looking far older and wiser. "It's okay, you know. I believe we have tapped into something. Maybe it will save us. Transfer us to its domain. And maybe someday you'll be ready to follow."

"And what...if you're wrong?" Emry gasped.

"Either way, we won't be alone anymore." Then something changed. In Emry's mind, something seemed to step back, to relax its grip. And Alice gave a sweet, wistful smile, suddenly looking more human—and more angelic—than she had all day. "No. It's more than that. If I'm wrong, I've still learned more in a day than most scientists do in a lifetime. And if I'm right...." She smiled wider as the doors began to close. "How much would you risk, Emerald, to get all your questions answered?"

The doors sealed, and she could hear the pumps and motors as the airlock chamber rose toward the dock. Soon, she felt the chaos in her mind subsiding, the craving for input fading. Then there was a burst of overwhelming sensory feedback—and she was alone again. The monster feeding on her from within was finally dead.

And she wept for its absence.

Arkady recovered better than the others. He and Emerald had gotten the briefest exposure to the madness. What he could remember was harrowing, disturbing, but given time and prayer, he knew he would recover. He wished he could be as sure about the others.

But Emry, somehow, seemed more at peace than ever. It was a relative thing, of course; her energy was as overwhelming as before, but a little less at odds with itself. *She's entitled,* he thought. The sidekick had saved the hero, and maybe much more.

"But I still lost the girl," Emry countered when he told her that back on *Hermes*.

"No, Emry. You did better than that. You convinced the bad guy to become the hero. That's the greatest victory there is." He smiled. "I think you've earned your championym today. Have you decided?"

Her gaze turned briefly inward. "Green Blaze."

"Are you sure? That's basically just your name."

"That's kind of the point. It's about knowing who I am."

He gazed on her with satisfaction. "Then who am I to argue? Although we need to talk about your uniform designs. Plunging necklines and body armor don't exactly mix..."

Emry had other concerns for now, for she insisted on taking responsibility for returning Alice Neal's remains to her family. IRI had begun demanding the body for study, but as it turned out, there was nothing for them to examine; *Hermes's* medical scan found no remains of the metacyber in Alice's brain. There were traces of its compounds in her bloodstream, but not enough to account for its likely mass. *Hermes* suggested that it had somehow jettisoned itself into space, perhaps to prevent its remains from falling into unscrupulous hands like IRI's. But Arkady had to wonder how it could have done that with so little damage to Alice's tissues.

"Do you suppose...maybe she was right?" he mused after hearing the ship's report. "About tapping into something higher, living on in some other form? A galactic metamind network, or maybe...."

"Hell, no," Emry said. "Don't give me false comfort, Papa Bear. There's nothing higher. The poor girl was delusional. Too much mind just drives you insane, and that's it."

"Then what was that burst of interference on *Hermes*'s sensors just before she died?"

"The metamind was broadcasting all over the station. When it started to go, the signal became static, that's all." He made an uncertain noise, and she stared at him. "Don't tell me you of all people are buying into her babble about becoming God."

He shook his head. "No, not about God." *But about the potential of the human soul to become something greater?* Still, he chose to cast it in secular terms for Emry's benefit. "I just think every problem has a solution. Comes with the job." That got her attention. He clasped her muscular shoulder. "Knowledge is power, and power is only as good or as bad as the intent and judgment of the user. That's what you taught Alice today, I think. What you *showed* her.

"You have to admit, Emry: it was your superior mind that let you hold on to sanity. And you saved the day with your intelligence, your reason, not just your muscles."

"It wasn't that," she countered. "I got through to her heart. Her humanity. That's what really matters."

"Oh, Emry." He carressed her shoulder. "Can't you see, my dear girl, that it's both? You were smart enough to know that compassion was the key to reaching her. And you were smart enough to see that your own mistakes were something you could use constructively—

something that you, and she, could learn from. And that's something even more important than intelligence. That's *wisdom*.

"And that—Green Blaze—is why you will be a fine Troubleshooter."

For once, she had nothing to say. Arkady took it as a good sign.

Twilight's Captives

In Madeleine Kamakau's long experience, one could learn much about a society from its angry mobs. The focus of their protests could illuminate its values, its priorities, and its degree of unity or division, while their character and tone could reveal much about its rationality and stability. Now, as she followed her escort through the main thoroughfare of the small Daikoku colony, Madeleine observed that the protestors lining its curbs were orderly, civil, and self-disciplined, almost embarrassed by the deep anger they had come here to express. The dense air filtered the light of the setting K-type sun to a melodramatic blood-red, evoking the familiar footage of the firelit riot that had already become an interstellar flashpoint, and yet these people who had lived through that riot resisted the urge to succumb to the same fury once again. Nevertheless, their chants and placard animations left no doubt that they felt violated to the core by what the Nocturne League had done here. *"No negotiation!" "Don't make deals with darkness!" "Give us back our babies!"*

Inwardly, Madeleine ached for them. It had been well over a subjective century since the war in Chryse Planitia had taken three of her children, but at times she still felt the grief as though it were fresh. She vividly remembered the terror when her fourteenth child had been kidnapped to undermine her peacemaking efforts among the Martian states. And she still lived with the pain of that day, half a century ago at the start of the warp era, when she'd returned from a months-long diplomatic mission to find that her latest husband had divorced her in absentia and taken their two children. She knew every flavor of the anguish, loss, and rage she saw in these parents' eyes, and then some.

Yet if that flame were allowed to spread, it could spark an interstellar war that would only kill more children. Madeleine could not, *would not*, allow that.

Daikoku's governor, Sato Leiji, met his people's eyes supportively. "Our League clientship has been trouble from the start," the younger man told her with quiet intensity. "So many rules they insisted we follow—just excuses to impose extortionate penalties, gain control bit by bit. But we never expected it to go this far. Interpret the rules differently and they steal your children?" he went on with rising volume. "Burn your houses, kill your families?"

This was a dangerous time to play to the crowd. "I'm sure no one is assuming the loss of life—either human *or* Aksash'sk—was intentional," Madeleine countered, using a tone of gentle implacability developed over more than a century of motherhood and politics.

Sato calmed under her gaze. "Certainly, it was a tragedy. But the Aksash provoked it."

Madeleine's Denzeuur colleague, Rabnaara Vutiiri, flipped his head up and over on its swanlike neck to face the governor. The quadruped's pear-shaped body was front-back symmetrical, and the vertical symmetry of his head let it function either side up. To human eyes, it was a disarming trait, and Rabnaara used it cagily. "That's one way of looking at it," he observed in his soft clarinet voice. "But every point of view has its flip side." He blinked his loris-like eyes and waggled the sunburst of whiskers around his broad, lavender-furred face. Madeleine smirked. Denzeuur were subtle, shrewd people, good at putting others at ease...and off their guard.

Sato faltered a bit. "Even if the Nocturnes had a case about our alleged violations, it wouldn't justify kidnapping. Or precipitating an incident that claimed lives. The *Akisu* are the criminals here."

Madeleine's gaze subtly chastised him for the racial slur, the Japanese word for "sneak thief."

"Who did what, and why, is a matter for our investigation," she replied. "But it would surely be a crime to let our anger spark a war."

One protestor stepped forward: a tall woman, bronze-haired with epicanthic green eyes. "Is that all you see? Some cold exercise in galactic strategy? Are our children just variables in an equation to you?"

"Claire..." the governor cautioned. "Ambassador Kamakau, Mediator Vutiiri, this is Claire Takeuchi-*san*. Her Shannon-*chan* is one of the prisoners."

"I'm sorry for you," Madeleine said sincerely.

Claire was unmoved. "Of course you are," she scoffed, looming over the ambassador. "The pain of a small colony out in the boondocks matters *so* much more to the Planetary Commonwealth than your vital trade arrangements. What do you plan to do? Buy peace with our children's lives?"

"There's no reason to believe their lives are in danger," Madeleine tried to reassure her.

"You face down an Axe charging you with bloody claws and tell me that. You watch your house burned down, your *daughter* get ripped from you by those claws, and tell me that!" As she went on, the crowd grew agitated. Reluctantly, the governor nodded to the guards to escort her away. "This isn't some diplomatic puzzle, this is about *family!*" Claire called out.

"Don't sell our children!" a protestor cried in sympathy. The crowd readily picked up the chant.

Rabnaara stroked Madeleine's back, seeking calm as much as offering it. "Don't listen to her. If she had any idea how many children you've raised...."

"It's all right, Rab." Madeleine understood how the young mother felt. Modern medicine and relativistic starflight had brought her through more than two centuries with her Polynesian features unlined and her meter-long hair still shimmering black, save for the well-cultivated white streak emerging from her left temple. But outliving one's great-great-grandchildren made one feel one's age.

The Denzeuur who met them within the Nocturne League compound (dimly lit as a symbolic compromise between nocturnal and diurnal negotiators) was larger, longer-furred and brighter-hued than Rabnaara, looking just a bit too perfect and engineered. Madeleine recognized that this was a native of the species' birthworld, Toraam. "I am Mufii-kalaa, Senior Negotiator, native to the argosy *Holy Reciprocity,*" the Toraau declared in a bass-flute voice.

Mufii and Rabnaara greeted each other with ritual grooming, but Madeleine sensed veiled tension in Rab's body language. The Toraau had chosen to become asexual, factory-grown organisms, anathema to the family-centered value system of Rab's far-flung colony, Taarzerek. And to Madeleine's own, come to that, but she had more practice remaining objective.

Despite her extensive experience with xenosophonts, Madeleine felt an instinctive chill when the Aksash'sk emerged from a shadowed doorway. They were fearsome beings, theroid pack-hunters built like raptor dinosaurs with bulbous fishy eyes, a spiked fin cresting the bristle-haired skull, and a snapping-turtle beak with snake tongues writhing from the corners. Madeleine wondered if her heat pattern was as disquieting to the Aksash'sk's infrared vision. Well, maybe their tongues would savor the scent of the Cybeline flower in her hair.

The lead Aksash'sk stepped forward. "Rha Tak Ch'kihha," Mufii introduced him, rendering the barks and snaps with their approximations in Denzeuur phonetics. "Senior Arbiter of the High Business Council of Aksash." A specialist from the homeworld. Not regular League? It was sometimes hard to tell where Aksash left off and the League began.

Ch'kihha's tongues waved forward to probe Madeleine's breath as the human introduced herself. Not that Madeleine Kamakau needed introduction—Mother of the Mars Republic, Midwife of the Planetary Commonwealth, bringer of warp cages to the Nocturne League, moderately acclaimed poet and linguist, written about in countless history texts and still around to correct most of the distortions...or cultivate the ones that suited her. But there was nothing an Aksash'sk negotiator loved more than overconfident prey across the table. So Madeleine gave her name with unaffected modesty.

Once the introductions were made, Ch'kihha lowered his head in submission to an unseen superior. "May the Higher Powers bless this exchange and bring satisfaction to all parties," read the translation text in Madeleine's retinal HUD, supplementing her own interpretation of the language. "May both sides gain profit and enlightenment in equal balance."

They sat on cushions around a low table, accommodating Nocturne anatomies as well as Daikokujin customs. "First," Ch'kihha opened, "we express profound regret at the loss of life on both sides. The Nocturne League exists to promote balanced exchange and satisfaction, thus to eliminate the causes of conflict. Know that we are committed to understanding how the process failed here, so that such failures will not recur."

"We have confidence in that commitment," Madeleine said smoothly, "and share it. We look forward to working together to discover what caused this tragic misunderstanding and to arrive at a peaceable resolution."

Ch'kihha's tongues swept across his eyes—the Aksash'sk equivalent of a blink. "Your offer is gracious, but the Arbiters' Branch is thorough and efficient. We are prepared to present our findings now."

"Excuse me," Madeleine replied. "It was our understanding that this was to be a joint investigation."

"Daikoku is a signatory to the Nocturne Code of Mercantile Ethics and Standards," the Arbiter declared. "We have the authority to investigate and punish Code violations."

Sato bristled. "This isn't a business deal! Petros and Midori Makarios died in that fire—and their boy Teruo is still missing! Is he one of your prisoners, or did you murder him too?"

"The fire was started by human agitators resisting our punitive action!"

"My people were *defensively* armed with whatever was available, including arc welders and other tools. The fire would never have happened if *you* hadn't decided to steal our children. Let's not forget—Nishimori Kenji's death came at Aksash claws! A death so brutal there was no way we could reverse it with the resources we have here."

"We defended ourselves," Ch'kihha hissed, his tail lashing with suppressed anger. "The first kill was yours."

Madeleine turned to Sato. "Is this true?"

Some regret showed through his anger. "It wasn't deliberate! We...the Aksash are from a Jovian moon. Their bones are more fragile. And then the fire engulfed the...the body...and there was no chance for revival. Kenji-*san* was no killer. He was a father fighting to protect his little girl from creatures who wanted—"

"You've made your point, Governor," Madeleine told him, softly but irresistibly.

Mufii-kalaa's head craned forward. "Agreed...recriminations for the past cannot help us build a better future. We of the League seek balance in all things. There is blood enough on both sides of the ledger, so let us call it balanced and close it for good."

"Very wise," Rabnaara purred. "We should focus on the future. On our children, who are our future."

"Thank you, Rabnaara," Madeleine said. He'd expressed her thoughts perfectly. "The children are the real issue here. Our first priority is to verify the safety of the hostages and assure—"

"*Hostages?!*" Ch'kihha was on his feet, neck thrusting toward her. Madeleine yelped and fell back off her cushion. "How dare you? *Taking* what someone already has, to offer in trade for more of what they have...." He growled disgustedly, his claws twitching. "It is unbalanced! Shameful! Do you take us for barbarians?!"

Ashamed of her moment of panic, Madeleine strove to regain her center along with her seat. "Forgive...my misunderstanding, Arbiter. No offense was meant. But then...."

"We acted in the children's interest," Ch'kihha went on, anticipating her question. "Rescued them from the criminal irresponsibility of their own community. Now, raised by our finest brooders, they will have the best of care, education, and opportunity."

"Call it what it really is," Sato challenged. "Slavery, pure and simple!"

"In fact, your children have a noble destiny before them," Mufii-kalaa interposed. "We do not blame the Daikokujin for your failure to understand our Code and abide faithfully by its wisdom. Adjusting to alien values can be difficult and confusing.

"But human children raised within the Nocturne League will be able to internalize our principles and relate them to our human clients in terms they can appreciate. The children of Daikoku will be the bridge between League and Commonwealth, bringing a new era of understanding and peaceful commerce."

"That's a commendable goal," Madeleine said carefully. "Surely many would volunteer for such a project."

"The proposal was made," Ch'kihha said. "Our terms were rejected."

"They amounted to the same thing," Sato protested. "Separating us completely from our own children!"

"While we salute your high ideals," Rabnaara said to the arbiter, "your choice is regrettably based on a misunderstanding. The effect of separating children from their families cannot be positive."

"The commitment of the Taarzeuur to their system of genetic bonds is well-known," Mufii-kalaa replied. "But the wise being adapts to each situation, reversing where needed."

"In general, a sound philosophy." Both Denzeuur grew smoother and more polite with each sentence. Madeleine could tell they despised each other. "But my esteemed counterpart from Toraam has perhaps forgotten that there is...asymmetry...in matters of family. Parents cannot reverse themselves if it takes them away from their young."

"Guiding the development of a new mind is a task of unmatched importance and delicacy. Surely it is best pursued by highly qualified personnel. These children will be in the hands of Aksash'sk brooders, a sex solely dedicated to the nurturing of young, and of Toraau educators with centuries of practical experience."

"Children need more than skill and experience," Rabnaara insisted, his whiskers gone rigid. "Take away the bond of family and you destroy a part of them."

"Does the mere fact of contributing genes to a child automatically make one an expert in childrearing? If so, how could there be abused children, neglected children, children raised without proper moral guidance?"

"How can there be love when offspring are made to order in a lab?"

Madeleine laid a hand on Rabnaara's arm, halting his achingly civil tirade. "Gentlebeings," she addressed the room, "I don't think any of us intended this first meeting to be an intensive debate. Perhaps we should adjourn to absorb tonight's discussion and prepare our cases."

Ch'kihha made a thoughtful sound in the back of his throat. "You will download our findings for review. After sufficient time for study, we will reconvene to clarify any confusion."

"Meanwhile," Mufii-kalaa injected, "we will take your concerns about the children under consideration." In the wake of the negotiator's prior statements, the concession highlighted the Denzeuur knack for compromise.

"Yes," seconded Ch'kihha after a moment's thought. "You have a right to be reassured of your children's well-being. We will prepare for discussions on this point."

Now if only Madeleine could decipher what it meant. Might they be willing to negotiate the children's release after all? And if so...what price might they demand?

The human young were still huddled in their chamber when Ch'kihha entered the brooders' compound at the side of his alpha, Rha Kef Kh'tlau. The alpha was small for a female, but her taut, golden-skinned frame was adorned in the finest kilt and jewelry, making her dominance clear to all who viewed her. Ch'kihha had been uneasy about bringing brooders and cubs into this dangerous situation, but Kh'tlau had not wanted to show fear by splitting the pack. She had also insisted that the human children belonged in the care of Pack Rha, not some obscure Leaguer pack in the outmarches. As always, Ch'kihha deferred to his beloved alpha's judgment.

Sh'thai, the senior brooder, approached them with a drooping neck and tail. She was larger than the males and females whose seed she carried to term. Her body hair was thick and soft and her fingers unclawed, the better to handle the cubs she reared. "They still do not let us near," she said to Alpha Kh'tlau. "They must have been so neglected, with no brooders to care for them. How can we help them heal when they fear we will eat them?" She absently shooed a cub away from the four mammaries on her belly.

"Perhaps," Mufii-kalaa ventured, "my argosy should take them. There are many Denzeuur there. We can pronounce their speech, and their children are usually comfortable with us." Mufii and the Aksash'sk spoke in their respective dialects of Nocturne Trade Language, differing only in phonetics. "And if the goal is to teach them the ways of the League...."

"The goal," interposed Kh'tlau, "is to teach them the Holy Code. Better done where the Code was born than among mere followers."

"Ahh, but the majesty of the Holy Code is such that it glows as warmly even far from the hearthworld. And seeing it in action—"

"Would expose them to alien ways. Confuse them. They must know the pure Code before they face the chaos it would tame."

Mufii hesitated. "Of course. I unwisely assumed that, since generations of our kinds raised in the argosies have matured without such confusion, these human children would necessarily do the same. Thank you for...reminding me of the wisdom which springs from the hearthworld alone."

"Still," Sh'thai mused, "Mufii-kalaa can speak their language, and thus perhaps could reassure them."

Kh'tlau peered skeptically at the Toraau, but finally gestured approval. "Do it."

"As always, we Leaguers are at your command," Mufii replied before moving into the humans' chamber, seeming quite eager to retreat. Ch'kihha admired the enthusiasm with which the negotiator followed orders.

The human children seemed to benefit from Mufii's visit. Before long, some snuggled against the Toraau, while others made those staccato pant-hoots they used for social bonding, baring their omnivorous teeth. Kh'tlau bore the aggravating sound, studying the children solicitously. "We should take them to Aksash now. Severed from their past, they will adjust better."

"That would provoke a fiercer response," Ch'kihha cautioned.

The Alpha growled in assent. "Yes. I fear them, Tak," she confided, rubbing her side against his for comfort. "Undisciplined, violent creatures."

Ch'kihha entwined his tongues tenderly with hers. Kef had fought her way from runt to Alpha through sheer force of will, and she never showed weakness to anyone save Ch'kihha and the brooders who'd raised her. He cherished her trust. "Our wars were fiercer," he reminded her. "We are more implacable."

"That is how we ended war! Once committed to peace, we never let go. These half-foragers lack our constancy. They end their peaces as easily as their wars." She barked in contempt. "And what is their peace based upon? 'Equality'—a random assignment of tasks with no regard for innate suitability. 'Charity'—the free sharing of plenty with nothing in return. As unbalanced as taking by force! It must surely collapse back into savagery. And they may drag us down with them. Look how they've disrupted the League already!"

Ch'kihha shook once, convulsively. "Sapients' blood on good Mercantilists' claws...this is much to atone for. We dare not revert to what we were."

Kh'tlau's thick tail lashed against his, and Ch'kihha tried to wrap his own tail around it, soothing its convulsions. "We must bring them Holy Mercantilism," his matriarch and mate went on. "The way of true balance can tame their souls, as it tamed ours. Can't it?"

"Of course," Ch'kihha reassured her, clasping her hands. "The Higher Powers command peace throughout the universe. All will bow to their loving wisdom in time."

Shannon Takeuchi, at the venerable age of eight standard years, had found herself accepted as leader and spokesperson by the younger children. So she strove not to cower before their fearsome captors or the perpetual dark. Still, it was a relief to cuddle up against the Denzy's soft purple fur. "Why are you on their side, Mufii-*san*?" she asked, peering up at those big round eyes. "You're nice. You should take us back home."

"I'm on your side as well," Mufii told her. "Take it from a Denzy..." and Mufii's head flipped over to address a boy opposite her, "there's more than one side to everything."

The children laughed. "How do you do that and still see right-side-up?" seven-year-old Nishimori Hiro asked.

Mufii blinked. "The sky is up. My feet are down. It's not so hard to keep things straight when you turn onto a new path. You just have to keep track of yourself. If you all do that, you'll do fine in your new lives."

"But we want our old lives!" Shannon said. "We don't wanna live with the Axes."

"They're scary," Hiro whined.

"I understand," Mufii assured him. "Sometimes they can scare me too. They even scare themselves." The children reacted with disbelief. "Yes, they do. That's why they try very, very hard to be good and just and peaceful. They developed a wonderful Code for living in peace. They saw that fighting comes when one person has something another doesn't have—when they're out of balance. But if one takes what the other has and gives nothing back, the imbalance continues and causes more fighting. So the only way to stop fighting is to create balance: for everything you take, you give something back. For every wrong you do, you must do something to set it right. The people who lived by this Code instead of fighting found they were happier and richer, and so they convinced others, until eventually they'd all stopped fighting."

"I don't believe that," one boy challenged.

"It's true. They fought because their instincts drove them to—but they didn't really like it, because they also have an instinct for order and efficiency. War is messy and wasteful, so they were glad to give it up when they found a better way.

"Tell me—in the weeks you've been here, have any of them tried to hurt you?"

"No...I guess not," Shannon admitted. "But the other ones did. Took us, fought our parents. My house burned down."

"And who saved you from that fire? Who healed your burns?"

She looked away. "The Axes."

"They only tried to help you. They feared your parents weren't giving you the attention you need or helping you learn the right things. They tried to change things, but your parents refused. When they came to rescue you, your parents fought back and hurt them." Mufii paused before continuing. "It...was your parents who started the fire."

Some of the children were crying now. Shannon was confused, distraught. Mufii held her closer. "The brooders only want to help you. Give them a chance. Their whole job in life is to take care of children's needs."

"You mean," Hiro dared, "they have to do what we say?"

Mufii's whiskers waggled. "I mean they'll protect you and guide you and always be there for you. They'll never ignore you or send you away because they have 'more important' things to do.

"And they'll teach you the way of peace, so that when you grow up you can bring it to your people, so they'll always treat each other right and not start any more fights."

"You mean we can see our parents again?"

"In time. When you're all grown up and they can't boss you around anymore."

Mufii stood, gingerly dislodging the children. "Let me bring Sh'thai, the head brooder, in here. You can start to get to know each other."

"*Hai*," Shannon finally conceded. "But could you get them to turn up the lights?"

"They'd like to, but it'd hurt their eyes. Mine, too." Mufii stroked her hair soothingly. "Trust me. Once you get used to it, you'll find the darkness very comforting."

"Is there any real chance the Makarios boy is alive?" Madeleine asked Sato as they neared the *geshuku* where the diplomats were lodged.

"We can only hope. The local wood burns very hot. But we found Teruo-*kun*'s DNA in the ruins, and no clear traces outside. We've made repeated demands to know his status, but they won't answer. I believe they killed the boy and are trying to cover for it."

"There are many reasons for keeping silence," Rabnaara observed. "Especially in a negotiation."

"Negotiation!" The disbelieving echo came from Claire Takeuchi, the protestor from the embassy, whose presence in the *geshuku*'s entranceway was decidedly not a startling coincidence. "So you admit that you're negotiating with the Axes. Using my daughter as a bargaining chip."

The Denzeuur pulled back reflexively from her anger. "Rabnaara didn't mean that," Madeleine reassured her. "He was simply making an observation about Nocturne motivations. We have to understand how they think if we're to find a solution to this crisis."

"Oh, of course. Madeleine Kamakau's legendary rapport with nonhuman cultures. No one relates to them better—so no one's more likely to give in to their agendas." She turned to Rabnaara. "Except maybe a scavenger who's better at dodging and retreating than standing up for a cause."

"Claire, you're angry; that's understandable. But it won't do any good if you turn it against those who are here to help you."

"'Angry?' I don't know where my *daughter* is, what's being done to her. Can't you understand that?!"

"I understand being a mother, Claire."

"How long ago? A hundred fifty years or more? Oh, I know all about your life story. My husband's always telling Shannon about the exploits of his great-to-the-eighth granny." Satisfaction shone in her eyes as Madeleine's quiet poise slipped for the first time. "That's right, *Ambassador*. We're family. Your own flesh and blood is in Aksash claws. So what are you going to do about it?"

Madeleine refused to let her shock show. She'd learned too much discipline over decades of delicate interactions with unfathomable minds, whether children or xenosophonts. She wouldn't give Claire the satisfaction of breaking that down.

No. Best not to think of her in that way. Claire was family, after all. And certainly a part of Madeleine's soul screamed for her to liberate her flesh and blood from danger. She wanted to reach out, to share those feelings with Claire and help her work through them.

But an audience was forming. These people were on edge, yearning to *do something* that might slake their rage. If she showed sympathy with Claire's desire for action, it might be the pebble that started the avalanche. She had to play this like a professional.

"Right now, Claire," she said with a calm that was pure façade, "I'm going to get a good night's sleep. Then I'm going to talk to the Nocturnes and find a way to bring our children back peacefully. I'm sure the last thing any of us wants is more blood on our hands."

That scored points with the crowd. They were genuinely ashamed of regressing to violence, even Claire. But her descendant recovered quickly. "Of course nobody wants that. The question is, how much will you sacrifice to avoid it?"

"Easy, Claire-*kun*," Sato urged. "I promise you, we will get Shannon and the others back. We won't surrender them, for any reason."

"You can't make that promise for the Commonwealth, Governor."

"They're only here to arbitrate. This is our world, and our crisis to solve. I'm watching out for your interests, you know that." Sato turned her around with a gentle hand. "She's right about one thing—you should try to get some sleep. All of you." His sympathies may have lain with the crowd, but he had no desire to see more chaos erupt in his community.

But as Sato led Claire away, she turned back for a parting shot. "Go ahead and get a nice, cozy sleep, *obaa-sama*. Why not? This is just some abstract problem in interspecies relations to you. You've been living with aliens so long you've forgotten how to be a human being, let alone a mother!"

Once they were alone in the lift, Madeleine sagged against Rabnaara. "That was cruel of her to say," he fluted, stroking her shoulders.

"She's young, angry. And she loves her daughter desperately. To see me so stoic about...." She took a shuddering breath. "I can't blame her for hating me."

Rab nuzzled her in commiseration. After a moment he met her eyes and asked, "Now that you know...does it change anything?"

"No. My family or anyone else's, I'm here to get them back." She recovered her balance as they exited the lift. "But it means Claire is family too. I should've handled it better."

"I felt you were admirably controlled. You could hardly have anticipated this."

"Are you kidding? I've had twenty-six children, starting more than two centuries ago. I've been estimated to have over four *million* direct living descendants."

Rabnaara showed his admiration openly. "I pray the Mother and Father will let my line be so fecund."

She grew wistful as they entered their suite. "But maybe it's been too long since I was a mother. I keep meaning to go back to it...but the one time I tried, on Taijitu, it didn't work out." The rejuvenation treatments for her reproductive system had been the easy part. But in her eagerness for motherhood, she hadn't chosen her husband well, and he'd proven unwilling to share her with her diplomatic obligations. "Maybe Claire's right. Maybe I've grown too detached from family, from humanity. Forgotten how to care for my own."

"I can't believe that," said Rabnaara as he knelt on his futon. "You left for your heirs' sake, so they could finally take leadership of the clan as they deserved. And ever since, you've worked for the safety and enrichment of your extended family throughout human space."

She smiled—his admiration of her as a maternal figure was endearing. "But at what cost?" Settling in against the slope of his warm, furry torso, she told him, "I miss it, Rab. I miss motherhood so much. But everybody's always coming to me with another world to explore, another bridge to build, another fire to put out. I'm kept too busy being everyone else's mother."

Madeleine grew quiet, thinking. "But I made a beginner's mistake tonight," she admitted. "Calling the children 'hostages.' I was unthinkingly defining what they'd done as a terrorist act."

"That's how many see it."

"But I should've known better than to judge. There are even human precedents, like the Ottoman Empire's *devshirme* system." She sighed. "I guess I'm as scared for the children as anyone else is. And it's affecting my judgment."

"Don't worry." He stroked her hair with a knobbly palm. "You're...not the only one whose reputation for tact suffered tonight."

She smiled sympathetically. "You and Mufii-kalaa...that was practically a brawl."

"The Toraau have no love of family. A child is simply a replacement you order when an old cog in the machine goes away or dies. I wish they'd altered their genes more, because I'm ashamed to be related to them at all."

"And here I thought you were so good at seeing every side of a question."

Rabnaara met her gaze frankly. "Just because Denzeuur are good at sudden changes of direction doesn't mean we abandon our basic goals. We're circumspect with other species as a survival trait, but within our own kind, conflicts can be more overt."

Madeleine nodded. The Denzeuur's one asymmetry was between the legs: reproduction at one end, elimination at the other. Their ambivalent sense of bodily direction created confusion between the two functions and a set of sexual hangups that dwarfed even the human variety—and commensurately intense conflicts between the sexual mores of different Denzeuur societies. If anything, it was amazing that the Denzeuur worlds were able to coexist as Nocturne League clients at all. Perhaps the Code really worked as advertised.

"Luckily," Rab went on, "since we never developed hunting instincts or weapons, we never redirected them into warfare."

"No...you settled for espionage, sabotage, blackmail, poisonings...."

"I never said we were saints. Just that we don't make as much of a mess as you predator types."

"Armchair sociobiologist," Madeleine teased. "There's more to it than hunting, you know," she went on more seriously. "What would you do if someone tried to take Dilaasi or little Kuuvaara from you?"

Rabnaara paused—not because the answer was elusive, but because it was so potent. "Anything I could."

"The Aksash'sk badly miscalculated. Maybe it's a symptom of their segregation of gender roles—the ones making and enforcing the decisions aren't the ones rearing the children."

"Isn't that somewhat judgmental?"

"Frankly, Rab, I feel judgmental. I hate what they did. If I were still as young as Claire, I'd hate them for doing it." She sighed. "I wish she could understand—I feel the same things she does. But this whole tragedy happened because passions got out of hand, because we let our mutual fear and tension drive us to strike out.

"There's too much at stake to give into those tensions. I can't let myself make any more mistakes."

"Remarkable," Rab fluted. "You can decide whether or not to be fallible? What an extraordinarily useful talent your evolution has blessed you with."

She laughed and snuggled up against him. Life without children was lonely, but it meant a lot to have such a friend.

"An exchange of students is an admirable idea," Madeleine told Arbiter Ch'kihha the next day. "Certainly we could institute such a program. But shouldn't it be a balanced exchange, with both peoples enrolling students?"

Kh'tlau hissed in frustration. "You bleed our words of meaning! Your minds are like your eyes, seeing only the surface!" It was common enough for the Alpha to join the negotiations at this phase, but Madeleine couldn't help thinking that it had gone more smoothly without her.

Ch'kihha issued an untranslated bark, causing his matriarch to subside—a reminder that, although she led the pack, diplomacy was his domain. "We have explained this," the Arbiter said. "The exchange was balanced. The Daikokujin's persistent violations demanded punitive response. The League's sanction was at once appropriate and ultimately constructive. Rejecting their judgment can only bring imbalance and renewed danger."

"The only thing we're guilty of is trying to become self-sufficient," Sato insisted. "They kept manufacturing new 'regulations,' reinterpreting their Code to keep us dependent."

Kh'tlau hissed. "We do not twist sacred law on whims. You misunderstood it, complained when corrected, then willfully defied it."

"Translation can be an inexact science," Mufii-kalaa interjected. "However, there were clear instances of defiance on the Daikokujin's part."

"We resisted their efforts to impose import quotas, to force us to buy things we didn't need. We're too busy building a world to have much time for luxuries. But they pressure us to waste resources and effort on pointless trade."

"Pointless!" Kh'tlau exclaimed. "You are intractable. No wonder you have brought us to the brink of war!"

"*We* have?"

"Governor." Madeleine's soft voice overwhelmed the shouts. The others quieted instantly. "It seems to me that commerce isn't always about material needs. The League worlds could exchange information and manufacturing patterns by laser if it were that simple. Physical trade between the stars is more about the intangibles—the value of the rare and exotic, the skills and perspectives of individuals, or the power of trade itself as a form of cultural expression. In human cultures, like Imperial China, trade has often been the basis of diplomacy. The material profit or loss has been considered secondary to the maintenance of good relations.

"To the Aksash'sk, peace is secured by a bond of interdependence in much the same way. Like Earth's Iroquoian peoples, they see the severing of trade ties as a severing of diplomatic ties, a breach of trust—practically a declaration of war."

That gave Sato pause, but only for a moment. "I know my Earth history too, Ambassador. China's trade was not just about 'diplomatic ties,' but about exacting tribute and submission to the Emperor. That's what the Nocturnes want from us—acknowledgment of their dominance. Oh, the early argosies gave no hint of it. But once they got us comfortable, then the higher officials came in and started treating us like imperial subjects. There's a deeper agenda at work here, and we can't afford to overlook it."

"The governor has misinterpreted," said Mufii-kalaa. "The argosies have always faithfully represented the intentions of the League authorities and the homeworlds." The negotiator seemed to be trying to assure the Aksash'sk as much as their Commonwealth counterparts. "The League is not an empire, but a system for cooperation between worlds. A stable relationship requires a commonly accepted set of guiding principles. Naturally, we in the League always seek to clarify and promote those principles."

"Tell me," Rabnaara ventured, "have argosies in the past ever...confiscated the children of a client people?"

"Each client relationship requires unique solutions," Mufii responded smoothly. "There is precedent for offering convicted criminals rehabilitation through our interstellar labor exchange."

"But these aren't criminals," Sato protested. "They're innocent children."

"In this case," said Ch'kihha, "the intent was to penalize the parents. And to protect the young from their...negative example."

Sato barely held his anger in check. "What gives you the right to decide how *our* children should be raised?"

"Children belong only to the future. We have taken them under our care so they may bridge our cultures and create a better future. Few penalties bring such honor."

Madeleine leaned forward to catch the arbiter's gaze. "That will bring small comfort to parents whose children have been wrenched away without their consent. Speaking as a mother, I know—that pain will override all objective appraisals or abstract future gains. Even if your charges against the Daikokujin are proven, Arbiter...the price you've exacted is simply too high. It's a loss we can never accept."

"So should we have asked what price they would find convenient? If they could accept it, what would be the point?"

Rabnaara interposed. "This is not the forum for a debate on punitive philosophy. What matters is the well-being of the children. Should they be harmed to punish their families?"

"How often must we say," Ch'kihha sighed, "that they are in the securest care?"

"No doubt the finest you are able to provide. But even your fine brooders lack the necessary experience with human children to guide their proper social and emotional development."

"Then the Planetary Commonwealth should provide experts on human child care. We would welcome this."

"These children have a right to their heritage," Madeleine countered. "Daikoku is a branch of an ancient culture in which ancestral ties have profound significance."

"They will be allowed to learn of their ancestral culture. But they will be raised in Nocturne culture, to provide a bridge between us. They will share in our identity, our heritage. Must culture be dictated by genetic lineage alone? If that were so," Ch'kihha said, "then I would be a holy warrior against Mercantilism, for that is the precedent of my bloodline."

"I have a proposal, Ambassador Kamakau," Mufii-kalaa interjected. "We have among us one of humanity's most experienced and celebrated providers of child care—yourself. Although you gained your experience in a more...informal way than, say, a Toraau caregiver, you no doubt acquired a wealth of practical knowledge over decades." Madeleine forgave the slight. "And today you are a recognized expert in interspecies relations, renowned for your ability to empathize across species lines and build common ground.

"I suggest that you would make an ideal consultant for this project. If you join with us in the care of these children, you can ensure that they receive the proper socialization and care. You can help them develop the skills to negotiate across species and cultural lines. And you can keep Daikoku and the Commonwealth assured that the children are well off. You, Ambassador, could play a key role in building a lasting peace between our peoples."

Madeleine found herself at a loss for words. Rabnaara came to her rescue. "We...request a recess to discuss this proposal."

"You can't be seriously considering this," Sato said. "Letting them keep the children?"

"I am not about to accept that, Governor. But if I agree to consider the possibility, they might let me see the children, determine their well-being. This is how negotiation works—give a little, get a little."

"You're not used to dealing with Aksash. To them, business is a sublimation of hunting instincts. And once they take a bite out of their prey, they pursue it relentlessly. Give them a little and they'll never back down from taking it all."

"Are our instincts really so different? And have we never overcome them with reason?" She put a hand on his shoulder. "You know I have as much reason as you to want your children back. But making sure they're safe and well right now is just as important."

"Madeleine...." Rabnaara led her aside as Sato pondered. "What do you plan to say to them?"

"I'll agree to consider the possibility, if they'll let me see the children. It'll be their chance to sell this *devshirme* project—they won't pass that up. First rule of sales, get the customer in the door."

"And you will get to see the children and reassure them that everything will be all right."

The very thought of it brought relief. "That's what matters most. All this maneuvering, interstellar politics...the children don't care. They need someone to hold their hands and tell them they'll be safe."

"They need someone to mother them."

"Exactly."

Rabnaara made an intrigued sigh. "The one thing you miss the most ardently. And you could have it without losing the challenge of building interspecies bridges. How marvelously convenient."

Madeleine frowned. "Rab, I'm not saying I'll accept their offer. I just want to visit, reassure the children."

"And once you get in the door, how hard will it be to resist the sale?" He whispered in her ear, whiskers tickling her face. "Could the children be in better hands than yours? Surely if the Daikokujin knew a human they could trust were looking after their children, it could put them at ease. They might even let you take responsibility for them—oh, with visitation rights, of course, but you could raise them and love them like your own. Be surrounded by two dozen raucous, needy children, always getting into trouble, never giving you a moment's peace—what could be more heavenly?"

Madeleine laughed—more out of nervousness (and the tickling) than humor. Rab was right—that would be just like old times, simpler times, and she might just sell her soul to have it back. And if Rabnaara could see that, how much clearer would her feelings be in infrared?

"You're right, Rab," she sighed. "I'm not...I'm not a mother anymore. Someday, but not now."

"Kamakau has forgotten what it means to be a mother!" Claire's words provoked an angry rumble of agreement from the cluster of parents around her. "She's selling our children to preserve her precious good relations. Well, I'm not going to lie back for that!"

"But what's the alternative?" a distraught father asked. "I *killed* a sophont, Claire. I don't want to go through that again."

"Nobody does, Hideaki. Nobody did before. But we still did what we had to when our children needed us.

"And you know what? They *still* need us. And what are we doing? Being *patient*. Talking it out. Sitting around placidly like good little civilized people while our *babies* cry out for us! Well, I for one am fed up with being civilized!" She could feel the crowd's energy building, feeding her as she fed it. "I say we go in there and take our children back!"

Some of the faces were clearly reluctant, but the pressure of the crowd kept them silent. Only Hideaki spoke in dissent. "Isn't there another way?"

"Don't worry. They know now that we're stronger. They'll back down once they see how determined we are! That we won't let anything stand in our way until we get our sons and daughters back home!"

Now the momentum was surging. Claire hardly had to incite them; they were pulling her along with them, caught up in a tide of relentless action. It frightened Claire, but she embraced it—because the surge would carry her to her precious Shannon.

Madeleine had devised an alternative proposal: to consider the Nocturnes' offer in principle, provided that Rabnaara could visit the children and ensure their well-being. As expected, the Aksash'sk balked, but it was merely the first round of haggling. Rabnaara sensed that Ch'kihha was willing to accept, but the arbiter, under pressure from Kh'tlau, insisted on concessions in return. Madeleine would bend where she could, but she considered most of the demands unacceptable.

Rabnaara's outward placidity masked his concern as he watched the other negotiators haggle. Both the human and the Askash'sk were sincerely striving to hold their predatory natures in check, yet they could not break the impasse. Their instincts told them that combat with fellow predators was a life-or-death affair in which backing down could be disastrous. Their biology might drive them to war despite their firm belief that it must be avoided.

But as Mufii-kalaa blithely deflected all of Rabnaara's proposed compromises—or rather, offered competing compromises that gave greater advantage to the League—the tension in Rabnaara's own neck reminded him that conflict was not the unique province of meat-eaters. He could barely stand being in the same room with the sexless Toraau—let alone other Denzeuur offshoots such as the Riitha'el, who had bred their females into subservient animals, or the Shaakrethal, who pretended to asexuality and ostracized anyone whose sex became publicly known. Perhaps he had no business being judgmental. The Nocturne League had done a remarkable job maintaining peaceful trade relations for over a millennium. What was their secret? Had Taarzerek kept itself isolated too long? Was his own failure to find a resolution a consequence of some intrinsic xenophobia within his own beloved people?

An angry outburst from Kh'tlau shook Rabnaara from his reverie. "This is futile! You humans have no protocols, no hierarchies, just unstructured talk! And you spread your disorder to the League. Tensions between worlds that traded peacefully for centuries. Peoples once well-behaved now drawing punitive measures. Never has the Nocturne League seen a more turbulent time!"

Rabnaara craned his neck forward, fascinated. "Pardon me...only since the human contact?"

"An influx of new ideas is bound to be disruptive," Mufii-kalaa observed. "Perhaps you should be more careful as you race to seek out new life." An oddly direct criticism. A Denzeuur would rarely make an open strike—unless it were a diversion from something more important.

Before Rabnaara could ponder it further, a subordinate Aksash'sk male burst in, barking agitatedly. The League party moved to meet him and they conferred too softly to hear. Kh'tlau snarled, threw a poisoned glance at Madeleine, and dashed out, her packmates close behind. Mufii remained to interpret. "I fear we must recess. A group of Daikokujin has stormed the Embassy. It would do much to restore good faith if you could help us stop them."

Shannon wasn't scared of the Axe-ashes anymore. Not the little ones, anyway. Kids were pretty much kids all over. And the big mommy ones weren't so bad, with their velveteen fur and no claws and all...but mommies were always intimidating. In a good way, though, she guessed. The way Sh'thai watched over her and the other kids as they played together made her feel safe, like her own mommy had before.

She was Sara the *Triceratops*, and an Axe-ash boy was a wily *T. rex* hunting her, barking playful taunts Shannon couldn't understand. She'd picked up a few Nocturne words, but not enough for conversation yet. But the game was pretty simple, though the Axe-ashes seemed puzzled about why she was sticking her fingers out from her forehead.

But then there was a lot of noise, and the door broke in, and it was confusing after that, but she saw humans! But they were fighting, like that night with the fire, and the other kids were running, hiding behind Sh'thai and the other brooders. But some were caught in the middle and couldn't get to safety.

Some new Axe-ashes ran in, led by an angry one in a pretty kilt and jewels. The dressed-up one batted some humans aside, not caring if her fancy clothes got messy. Shannon's mom always complained when she acted like that. But then the dressy one grabbed little Sandip and barked loudly, holding her claws near his throat. He cried, but the Axe didn't care.

Her *T. rex* friend yanked her to the ground behind him. It hurt, but she knew he was trying to protect her. Then she saw what was charging toward them—the vivid bronze hair, the big, strong body—it was Mommy!

And Mommy had a look in her eyes like Shannon had never seen before, and she had a wiresaw, its thin glowing blade poised over her head. And she started to swing it down at the *T. rex* boy. Shannon cried out and threw herself in front of him, and....

"STOP!!"

Everyone froze, shocked into silence.

Madeleine Kamakau had cried out in rage.

Even those few who didn't know her reputation were stunned. It was as if an ancient, sleeping power had been unleashed.

"How *dare* you?" Madeleine demanded, her voice low again, but far from gentle. She strode up to Claire Takeuchi and yanked the wiresaw from her unresisting hand. "Bringing weapons into a nursery. Putting your own children at risk."

She whirled on Kh'tlau. "And you. Let him go this instant." Even before her implants could translate the words, the Alpha's arms fell nervelessly to her sides, and Sandip ran to his parents. "How could you? Hiding behind children. Using them as pawns."

"You tell 'em!" a human called out hesitantly, seeking to recover some of his indignant confidence. "They started this." Others chimed in. "That's right!" "They killed Teruo Makarios!"

"*Enough.*" Madeleine's gaze scalded them, not with fury but with overwhelming *disappointment*. They bowed their heads like misbehaving juveniles. "They started it, so you finish it, is that it? They kill one of your children, so you get to kill their children, and that makes it *right?*" She took a breath, and continued in a more controlled tone, capturing their gazes. "Feels so easy, doesn't it? A nice quick fix, an eye for an eye, balance the ledger. Simple, seductive.

"But what about the other side? What stops them from feeling the same, doing the same right back? And then your children retaliate against their children, and back and forth and back and forth...." She shook her head, crying freely. "You may as well murder your own babies and cut out the middleman!"

Claire let out a sob, and fell to her knees as the realization of what she'd almost done sank in. Madeleine wanted to rush to her side, but sometimes a mother just had to let a child live with her pain. "Both our peoples are supposed to have learned this by now," she went on. "How could we let ourselves forget so easily?"

She looked around, taking it all in, the whole crisis in microcosm. "This has gone on long enough," she realized. It was time to go to the heart of the matter.

Madeleine's eyes locked on Sh'thai, recognizing a kindred spirit. "Are you the head brooder?" she asked in Denzeuur Nocturne.

"I am. Rha Fith Sh'thai. And so are you, it seems."

"Madeleine Kamakau. I was sent here to resolve this matter. But this is my first real chance to do so. Let the children go, Sh'thai."

"I cannot. This is a matter of League policy, interstellar relations....It is not my responsibility."

"Isn't it? Look at what just happened here." She gestured to Shannon, to Sandip. "Look at whom those policies and relations have put in danger. This is where it all begins, Sh'thai. All the rest—commerce, politics, diplomacy—they're merely things that we do to try to make a better future for our children. How can we put them above the children themselves?"

She clasped the brooder's hand with her own. "We mothers have always been the ones who suffer when our precious babies are sent out to die. But we have the power to do something about it. Because it's not governments and armies, churches and embassies that really make history—it's *families*. The characters of the people who lead those institutions, the values that guide them and define the civilizations they build, they're all shaped in childhood. Everything else is an aftereffect—family is where it all begins.

"Everything that happens to people, Sh'thai, is a mother's responsibility. Whether our civilizations go to war is up to us, right here, right now. After all...what gives anyone else the right to make that decision for *our* babies?"

The two mothers stood eye to eye for a time. At last Sh'thai turned. "Children! Go with your parents. I will miss you, but please go home."

"No!" Kh'tlau cried. "This is a state matter!"

"Quiet!" Sh'thai cuffed her, once. It was hardly enough to sting, but the Alpha was stunned. "You would lecture your teacher? The human children are in my care. That makes it my decision, by law and custom. And it makes them effectively your packmates. Do you wish to offer an excuse for threatening your own brother's life?"

Kh'tlau was chastened. "But Mater," she pleaded. "They are a threat to our order."

"Then deal with them, as any good Mercantilist would."

"We *tried!* But they were unruly and had to face discipline!"

"A discipline poorly chosen. It intrudes upon my purview, and I declare it void. Find another."

Ch'kihha stepped forward, placing a hand on his Alpha's shoulder. "Kef...let it go. The Code is meant to prevent conflict, not create excuses for it. Somehow the laws have failed us here."

Kh'tlau glared at him in astonishment. "We cannot submit to them!"

"We submit to Sh'thai. And to practicality. All things must be negotiable if peace is to be won."

Kh'tlau hissed, but her posture was acquiescent. "The Council will not approve."

"That's the Council's business," Sh'thai said. "I will not see the humans pulled apart again."

The Alpha slunk off, frustrated, but chastened. Ch'kihha followed, seeking to comfort her. They swept by Sato, ignoring him as he called out, "Teruo-*kun*? Has anyone seen Teruo Makarios?"

The children's replies were uniformly negative. "Are you sure?" He came up to Sh'thai. "You must tell me. Where is Teruo Makarios?"

The brooder was slow to answer. "The boy...died in the fire," she finally confessed. "A terrible loss. At least his parents were spared the grief of outliving him."

Sato was somber. "I never really expected it, I suppose. But I had to hope."

Madeleine shared his grief; but her gaze fell on Claire, who had engulfed Shannon in her arms, begging for forgiveness. Madeleine's approach drew her attention from her daughter's reassurances. "I was a fool," she rasped.

Madeleine knelt and touched her shoulder. "So was I. You were right...I've been thinking too much like a diplomat instead of a mother. I...." She blushed. "The world I grew up in is gone, and I don't fit in anywhere else. I figured if I was going to feel like an alien anyway, it might as well be among aliens. Maybe I've lost touch with my humanity."

"No...no, you're a better mother than I could ever be. I caused all this," she sobbed. "I incited the crowd, I almost...almost...."

Madeleine didn't let her finish. "You were in pain. And I treated you like a, a rabble-rousing politician instead of a fellow mother. Instead of family."

Shannon looked at her. "Are you my *obaa-san* Madeleine?"

"Yes," Madeleine smiled tearfully. "Yes, I am."

"Don't be sad. I'm okay now. And we were okay before. We were playing dinosaurs, and learning Nocturne, and it was scary at first but it was kinda fun. Here." Noticing that the flower in Madeleine's hair was coming loose, Shannon pushed it back into place. Madeleine let the tears come and wrapped both her descendants in her arms.

Rabnaara watched Madeleine's family reunion with a tender sigh, but his whiskers drooped as Mufii-kalaa approached. "The hearthworld will not accept this easily," the Toraau told him.

"You will convince them," the Taarzeuur said.

"Indeed. Should I?"

"You should," Rabnaara went on in their shared ancestral tongue. "For certain truths are best kept hidden."

"Such as?"

"It's truly astonishing," Rab said, "that cultures as different as Aksash, the disparate Denzeuur worlds, and the rest could all coexist smoothly under a single, rigid set of economic regulations."

"The Code is unequalled in its wisdom."

"A single wisdom, for all worlds? And you must admit, it does seem much less effective these days."

"Yes, since the human contact."

"Since the League gained warp cages," Rab added. "Before, a client world would see a League argosy only every decade or two. The different populations rarely met one another. Contact was mostly mediated through the League.

"And the merchants themselves spent their lives hurtling between stars, isolated by distance and time dilation from the cultures whose goods they traded in. The sharing of information was gradual, tempered by time and distance, so the worlds could absorb, adapt, or ignore new ideas as they saw fit.

"But then came warp cages. Suddenly worlds were weeks apart instead of decades. Separate cultures were thrown into direct contact. Officials from the hearthworld could visit the client worlds and see the Code in action.

"But to their shock, they found that each world interpreted the rules to suit its own culture. Orthodoxy was threatened. And the client worlds were increasingly undergoing ideological collisions and disruptive relations."

"But the same diversity existed before. Clearly the Code must have been able to regulate it."

"Except the defenders of orthodoxy were back on Aksash, expecting the Leaguers to pass on their doctrines unchanged. But the Leaguers were living in their own worlds at their own pace. The rules of commerce were not a divine abstraction to them, but a pragmatic reality.

"Let us speak plainly for once. The League reinterpreted the Code for each world, didn't it? That's why the Daikokujin feel the rules have been changed. First the argosies came and adapted the rules to local culture, as they had always done. Then the homeworlders came in, preaching a conflicting orthodoxy, leading to the mutual perception of bad faith. On how many other worlds has this happened?"

Mufii-kalaa's guard finally dropped. "The hearthworld Aksash'sk have been taken aback by the disorder, responding with a stricter enforcement of orthodoxy." The Toraau's whiskers twitched bitterly. "For centuries, the League enabled coexistence at a comfortable, mutually profitable remove. Now the hearthworld seeks to turn our smooth-running trade network into a regulated state. Our operations and our autonomy have been compromised enough as it is." Mufii met Rabnaara's gaze intently. "If the truth were revealed, the hearthworld would brand us traitors, maybe disband the League. Our whole way of life would be destroyed."

"Then you have an incentive to convince them to accept this outcome. As long as that happens, I see no reason why this information should become known."

"And how should I convince them?"

"If you are any sort of salesperson, you already have some ideas. Besides, your brooder Sh'thai has managed to salvage something for them. Haven't you, Sh'thai?"

The lurking brooder came forward openly, looking as sheepish as a wolf could manage. "Yes, I know your classical language," she admitted to Mufii's stare. "In a lifetime of teaching, I've learned a few things. Though apparently not stealth.

"Do not worry about your precious League secret. My allegiance is to the next generation, not the one in power."

"Where is Teruo Makarios?" Rabnaara asked.

She stared for a time, but she made no attempt at denial. "He was on the brink of death. Our nanotes have kept him alive, but they have needed time to adapt to his anatomy. The healing is slow. How did you know?"

"No good negotiator surrenders everything she holds. But why did you conceal his survival?"

"To spare the other young from worry and fear at his condition. Because they did not know, I saw an opportunity—a way my pack could still achieve its purpose to build a bridge between our cultures.

"But more...it was a brooder's sentiment. Every day I have kept vigil at his side, watching him fight for life. He is strong and brave, and I could not bear to lose him. Besides, he has no one left alive to love him as I do. Does he?"

Rabnaara cast a long look at Madeleine, who still clutched her descendants close to her. "No," he answered wistfully. "There is one who would cherish the opportunity...but she has other duties. We need people of wisdom and compassion to preserve the peace in these tenuous times."

"You surprise me," Mufii said. "Didn't you say that human children must be raised by human caregivers and communities? This boy will not even have other children of his kind."

"It is...not an ideal situation," he breathed, eyes still on Madeleine. "But ideals are never fully realized. I will arrange what assistance I can, Sh'thai, to help you raise a healthy human child without revealing his presence." His whiskers twitched unhappily. "It is a risky experiment to subject a lonely child to." *And Madeleine will never forgive me if she learns what I have done.* "But I am not a predator, believing I can pounce on the universe and wrestle it into obedience. We scavengers must make the best of what little it grants us."

Mufii appraised him. "You may be a true Denzeuur after all."

"More than you will ever be." Rabnaara eyed his counterpart more coolly. "Make sure the boy is tended well."

"Of course. Our common future may ride upon him."

He stared at Madeleine until her gaze rose to his, forcing him to look away. He couldn't meet her eyes...not yet. "His future is just as important," he told Mufii. "Never forget that."

That big Axe is there every day, watching me from the dark. She talks to me, even though I don't answer. She says she wants me to get well. But I saw what they did. People said they were bad, and Mom and Dad told me not to listen. But then they killed Mom and Dad.

Maybe they only want me to get well so I can run and they can hunt me down and kill me. So I pretend I'm still sick. I pretend so well it even fools the machines.

But what if the Axe really does want to help? Sometimes she sounds so nice, even with the barking. But I saw what happened when people trusted them. I just want them to leave me alone.

But I can't stand being alone! I'm lost and afraid and I need...someone....

Maybe I should try to trust them. But I don't know if I can.

No Dominion

A lot of people think homicide investigation is easy these days, now that you can just interview the victims.

Generally, they're right, at least in the industrialised world, and increasingly elsewhere as death prevention becomes more affordable. The majority of homicides anymore are crimes of passion or stupidity, committed by people who don't stop to think about emergency cerebral oxygen supplies and secondary circulation pumps. Typically, you just have to wait until the victim wakes up and ask who killed them.

(I know you're wondering, why not call it attempted homicide, then? Some people do. I don't. I've died myself, and let me tell you, reversible or not, there's nothing impermanent about it.)

But those aren't the cases I get called in for. The local cops can handle those. For a victim like Isabelle Warner, a specialist has to be summoned. Which is part of what makes it difficult right there. Homicide used to be so common that every city had experts on hand within minutes of the scene. That's still true in places where death prevention is a luxury reserved for the rich, or where governments still think keeping the death rate up is better population control than limiting the birth rate (as if that ever worked before). In a place like Onogoroshima, though, a killer's trail can have hours to cool before an expert can arrive.

Of course, they sent me the full sensory record of the crime scene, which I studied in depth on the flight in from Brisbane. "Crime scene" was a misnomer in this case, since the site of the murder hadn't been identified. This killer had been smart—an exception to the rule. Onogoroshima was an arcology complex in the Philippine Sea, one of many such artificial islands springing up around the world these days—compact, self-sustaining greenhouse ecosystems that accommodated tens of millions of residents apiece without placing heavy demands on the Earth's biosphere. Onogoroshima itself was a huge artificial atoll with a freshwater lake in the center. Enclosed and protected from ocean winds, the lake had slow and turbulent currents that resisted prediction. So our victim could've been dumped from just about anywhere on the eastern shore and drifted an unknown distance and direction before she was discovered by an early-morning boater.

I viewed the scene as the local cops had experienced it, sharing everything they'd seen, heard, felt, and smelled. Isabelle Warner was a tall, attractive woman with strawberry-blond hair, no less than thirty-five years old. Her file said she was sixty-five, born 1993. Her killer had stripped her naked and wrapped her in a white sheet before setting her afloat. There were no obvious signs of sexual assault, or of any assault aside from a diffuse burn mark on the back of her neck. That was odd. Generally, if you wanted to kill someone these days, you had to destroy the brain past any possibility of regeneration, then eliminate any backup memory and cognitive implants. So smart, premeditated murder tended to be a messy business. To see an assault this subtle was unusual for me. It looked like the work of a surgical laser tuned to focus underneath the skin. The killer had probably targeted her backup oxygen supply and memory chips as well as her brainstem, but hadn't destroyed the gross structure of the brain. It was a risk for a killer; natural anoxic damage could be repaired if caught within six to eight hours, and Isabelle was found inside that margin. Memory, skills, and identity would be lost, but the survivor could develop a new personality. But maybe that was enough for this killer. Maybe Isabelle had seen something or known something she shouldn't have. Some killers don't mind if their victims survive, so long as their memories don't.

Still, with the murder scene unidentified and the evidence washed away by the lake, I'd have my work cut out for me. If I didn't piece this together quickly, the killer could disappear, adopt a new identity (in the more conventional sense), and be free and clear to kill again—maybe permanently this time.

But I wouldn't let that happen. I had enough death on my conscience already.

I was met at the airport by a nervous, hopeful man I immediately pegged as the lead investigator. "Detective Chief Inspector Craig?" he asked. "Tamara Craig?"

"That's right."

"Hi. Welcome. Assistant Inspector Istfan Majid. Call me Steve."

I shook his hand. "Inspector." He blinked, but didn't react beyond that. He seemed a pleasant enough man, a bit heavyset but fit, probably fortyish. Warm, brown skin, a few shades lighter than my own. No wedding ring, but he probably had little trouble finding dates. Still, I wasn't here to socialise.

Majid offered to take my minimal luggage—a classic gentleman. I indulged him; I didn't want anything slowing me down. He offered to show me to my hotel, but I asked to go straight to the victim.

"We're in luck," Majid told me in the pedicab as we rode into the arcology proper. "The perp underestimated how well-equipped Ms. Warner was. Made sure to fry all her cerebral implants, but missed what was in her blood."

My brows lifted. "Genetic memory?"

Majid nodded. "She's really on the cutting edge."

Nearly a century ago, an experiment with flatworms seemed to show that memory was stored in RNA and could be transferred from one organism to another. But the experiment had been an unrepeatable fluke—pardon the pun—and later research showed that memory worked in a completely different way. But decades later, nanotechnologists had begun researching the possibilities of engineered DNA as a data storage medium, and in time they made junk science into reality. Now it was possible, with the help of transcriptor biochips, to have your memories redundantly recorded in DNA packets that travelled throughout your bloodstream, an extra backup in case something happened to both your brain and your primary backup chips. But it was barely out of prototype stage, only recently approved for human use and still quite costly. Had Warner had reason to take extra precautions against death?

"So she'll recover her full memory?"

"Most of it, probably," Majid said. "Though it'll take time to retrain the neural pathways, to assimilate a whole lifetime all over again. It could be weeks, maybe a month or two before she's lucid enough to tell us who killed her. If she even remembers. The DNA encoding isn't instantaneous, apparently."

I nodded. She wouldn't remember the murder itself, which would be a mercy for her, if an inconvenience for us. But hopefully her memories could point us to the most likely suspect. "Any way of reading the memory traces from her bloodstream?"

He shook his head. "No more than with any other kind of backup memory. Otherwise people could steal each other's memories just by punching them in the nose."

"Right. Good point." Personal memory encoding was too subjective—not discrete data files, but a web of associations unique to each brain. The engrams would only make sense to her own brain once it reassimilated them and fit the pieces back together in the right pattern. Human memory and personality weren't something you could copy and transfer like software files; that was one sci-fi conceit that remained a fantasy. Survival of the self still depended on survival of the brain; technology could supplement and protect it, but never replace it. And so, humans remained mortal, and murder remained a crime.

I knew I should look into getting a genetic memory upgrade myself; given my speciality, I could justify the expense. But I hadn't gotten around to it yet. There were some painful memories I wouldn't mind losing.

But then, those were the very memories I could least afford to forget.

Isabelle Warner was slowly coming back from the dead. She was on full life support, but her blood was flowing again and she looked less like a corpse. The doctors were taking care to restore oxygen to her tissues gradually to minimise ischemic damage. That could be repaired, but there was no point in doing more damage than necessary.

Takeshi Ozaki, the grey-haired medical examiner, grunted as he, Majid, and I looked her over. "Not much to see here," he said. "So busy saving a life they don't bother to preserve any evidence."

I gave him a sour look. "Your job would be easier if they just plain died."

"Damn straight."

"So what *can* you tell me?"

He looked to Majid. "Cause of death was what you thought, Steve. Laser probe to the base of the skull. Someone didn't want to make a mess."

"But there were burns on the skin," I said. "We're not talking about an act of surgical precision."

"No. Someone trying to be surgical, but failing. There's collateral damage to the surrounding tissue."

"Their hands shook?" Majid asked.

"Maybe. But most of the collateral damage preceded the targeted destruction. I'd call it hesitation marks. He hasn't killed before, not this way at least. Some of it came during, though, so yeah, there was some shakiness."

"Emotion," I said. "The killer cared for her. Didn't want to damage her beauty. In their own way, they cherished her. Wanted to honour her in death. Hence the ritual quality. The killer didn't just wrap her in plastic and dump her, but swathed her in a pure white sheet and set her afloat on the lake."

"Just one problem there, DCI Craig," Ozaki said. "Nobody's had sex with her, consensual or otherwise, for at least two weeks."

"Maybe we're not dealing with a 'he'?" Majid suggested.

"Lesbian sex leaves traces too," Ozaki told him.

I looked over her body. "No signs of a struggle?"

"Nope."

"Any drugs or foreign nanotes in her system?" Ozaki shook his head. "Then she knew her attacker. Let them in, let them get close."

"Let them take her clothes off," Majid added.

I threw him a look. "If you were the killer, and she was willing to get naked for you, wouldn't you wait until after you rooted her?"

"Oh. Damn, yeah. So first he kills her, then he strips her." He frowned. "But not to rape her. Just to…why? To humiliate her?"

"Then why wrap her in a sheet? Why remove her clothes, yet try to preserve her modesty?" In an old mystery story, it might have been done to make her harder to identify. But now we had genetic testing, biometrics, phones in our heads, traceable biochips and nanofibers throughout our bodies…it just didn't add up. I shook my head. "Maybe it's part of the ritual. We'll find out when we get the killer."

"One more thing," Ozaki said. "There's evidence that she may have died once before."

"Violently?" I asked.

"Natural causes," he said, his tone apologetic. "Signs of a brain aneurysm, almost completely healed."

"How long ago?"

He shrugged. "No way to be sure without an autopsy. Anywhere from three to six years ago. There's nothing about it in her medical records. But they're pretty sparse. Nothing from before she came here four years ago."

"And have you considered checking elsewhere?"

"We've been trying," Majid said. "Nothing's turned up yet."

I didn't like it. There could be any number of reasons for that, from a dark, hidden past to sloppy data-handling practices. I hoped the reason for her murder could be found closer at hand.

The only physical evidence we had besides Isabelle herself was the sheet she'd been wrapped in. It was a dead end. The outside had been washed clean by the lake, and the inside bore no fingerprints and no DNA besides Isabelle's. The killer had worn gloves and possibly even a surgical mask. The sheet itself was a standard type, synthesised from a fabricator of the sort found in most of the hotels and stores in the arcology complex. We couldn't match it to the specific fabricator unless we knew which one out of thousands to test.

There was no way to track her movements either. She'd put her neurophone on private mode several weeks ago, making its location untraceable. And Onogoroshima didn't have video surveillance in most places; it was redundant since most people had cameras in their clothes or eyeballs, and not in great demand since there was little violent crime here. Any resident might have video of Isabelle with her killer, but unless we could narrow down just where and when the murder took place, we'd have to subpoena and search the private videos of over twenty million people. Even if we could narrow the number, no judge would consider such a subpoena unless the victim died permanently.

Isabelle lived and worked on the local university campus, a bioengineer working on a project to modify methanotrophic bacteria and integrate them safely into the ecosystem. "Methane's twenty times more potent a greenhouse gas than cee-oh-two," explained Rosa Manzano, a cute, diminutive Filipina who was Isabelle's colleague and roommate, as she led us toward their apartment. "So the more of it we can scrub out of the air, the more carbon-producing humans the planet can safely support."

"Isn't that just a stopgap?" Majid said.

"There's no magic formula for the atmosphere," Manzano said with a flip of her short, brown hair. Nearly everything about her was what they used to call "perky," though her perk was subdued under the circumstances. "It evolves like everything else. We can't go back to the way things used to be, even if we killed off most of humanity—which, well, isn't so easy anymore. Thank God," she added, crossing herself. I looked away uneasily. "So we need to find a new equilibrium, one that works for humanity *and* the Earth. It's about stability, not nostalgia."

"Is this research critical enough to require advanced memory security?" I asked. "Such as a genetic memory backup?"

Manzano frowned. "It's important, sure, and Isabelle's a valuable part of the team. But there are people working on this all over the planet. It's not like she had some unique knowledge worth killing for or something. I mean, I knew she'd gotten the upgrade, and she convinced her insurance to cover part of it because of her work, but it's not a requirement."

The researchers' apartment didn't reveal much about Isabelle. It wasn't spartan; on the contrary, it was cluttered with all sorts of trendy art, gadgets, and clothes, all the latest things. But Isabelle's half of the apartment contained nothing but the latest things. There was no evidence of a life nearly seven decades old, no family photos, no childhood toys or heirlooms, nothing.

"Yeah, that's Isabelle for you," Manzano said when I pointed this out. "She's always looking forward to what's next, what's new. Always looking to the future. Me too. It's why we're in this job. We've got a long future ahead of us, so we'd better make it a good one, right? But Isabelle's even more…" She frowned. "Is? Was? Will she be the same person after this?"

"No," I said. "You're never the same."

At Manzano's worried look, Majid threw me an irritated glance and told her, "Of course it's a traumatic event, and it will take time for her to heal. But she should recover her memory and her familiar personality almost completely. It helps having friends and familiar surroundings to reinforce the memory pathways."

"Old memories would help too," I said. "Does she keep anything in a storage facility? Possessions that aren't this recent?"

Manzano shrugged. "She didn't bring anything with her when she came here. And she generally just recycles her old stuff when she gets tired of it. If it's not new, she's not interested."

"People who look to the future are generally running from something in their past," I said. "Did she ever talk about her life before you knew her?"

"Never," Manzano said after a moment's thought. "Whenever I brought it up, she changed the subject back to me." Her cheeks coloured adorably. "It's easy to get me to talk. I kind of monopolise our conversations, and she lets me."

"What about the present?" Majid asked. "Does she talk about her social life? Friends, coworkers, lovers?"

"Oh, I know pretty much all of them. We travel in the same circles."

The list of names Manzano proceeded to give us wasn't very long. Lack of serious commitments at Isabelle's age wasn't surprising in an arcology dweller. Universal death prevention was one of the incentives that drew people to places like this, easing the population burden elsewhere; but the tradeoff was a stricter-than-usual set of limits on childbirth. So a lot of the people who chose to emigrate here were career singles. Isabelle was a wallflower next to her roommate, though. They both attracted male attention about equally (female too; with childbirth out of the equation, arcology dwellers tended to be flexible about preference), but Isabelle was willing to defer to Rosa most of the time. While Isabelle wasn't chaste, neither was it surprising to Manzano that she hadn't had sex in weeks. "Well, except virtually," she added. "She's a lot more active there." Most people were, so that didn't strike me as immediately significant.

"And how about the two of you?" Majid asked. "Have you ever been…involved?"

She gave a nervous giggle. "Just casually, a few times. But only virtually!" she insisted. "As a game, you know. I mean, to see each other's real faces while we did it—that would be too weird."

"For you, or for her?"

"Both of us. We're friends! Coworkers! We'd be too busy giggling in embarrassment to get anything done." She shrugged. "Look, it wasn't anything serious. Even in virt, we mostly just giggled a lot and messed around. You can probably find the sessions in my database, I never bothered to delete them." She smiled at Majid. "Feel free to watch."

Majid blushed. I thanked her and led Majid out the door before he embarrassed himself any further. "What were you going for?" I asked. "That maybe she had an unrequited crush on Isabelle?"

"Just exploring all the possibilities. You said yourself, the killer cherishes her beauty. And it sounds like Rosa is the closest person to Isabelle."

Police-manual boilerplate: the ones closest to the victim are the most likely suspects. In my job, I run into so many detectives who've never dealt with homicide before and have to wing it based on half-forgotten courses and old cop shows. Well, I guess it's better than the alternative. "Majid, she's tiny. She couldn't carry Isabelle across the room, let alone to the lake."

"She could've had help."

"She didn't show a trace of guilt or defensiveness. No fear of being caught. Save your energy for when we find a more likely suspect."

He conceded the point. We walked in silence for a while, and I concentrated on running Manzano's list of names through the local databases I'd downloaded into my neurophone. Nothing jumped out, so I began running them against Isabelle's computer records. Then I noticed Majid studying me. "What?" I asked, minimising the text window on my retina with a thought.

"People don't only look to the future because they're running from the past. Sometimes it's just because the future is worth looking forward to."

"Is that what you think?"

"Tamara—DCI Craig—look at what we're doing. Just thirty years ago, even twenty, that woman back there would've been in grief, devastated because she'd never see her friend again. Now, death is just a temporary setback. So yeah, I can understand looking forward to what comes next."

"People still die, Majid. People who don't come back. That's the reason for what we're doing. Remember that."

"I do," he said. "I remember that we have a chance to prevent it, not just punish it. If you ask me, that makes our job even more important."

"It's just as important either way. Murderers need to be punished." I turned away and went back to the name search.

But his gaze stayed on me. "Tell me, DCI Craig. What are *you* running from?"

Surely he didn't expect an answer. It was hard enough to relive *(the blood, the flames, Jason screaming)* without talking about it.

Fortunately, I didn't have to dwell on it for long, since the search turned up a hit. "Interesting."

"What?"

"Russell Takizawa. Manzano called him a passing acquaintance, but his username shows up on the same virt sex site Isabelle used, and at a lot of the same times she was online. They must've been virt sex partners pretty regularly."

Majid nodded. "Manzano said he dated Isabelle two or three times, only got to first base, but then she broke it off for no apparent reason."

"It seems he sent her a lot of calls and mails that she didn't answer." I sorted through the files in my field of view. "She had him spam-blocked…even set up a warning cordon." That was a do-it-yourself restraining order; if his neurophone came within fifty metres of hers, she would be notified and he'd get an automatic mail warning that the police would be called if he didn't leave the proscribed zone. That explained the privacy block on her locator signal. "What do you want to bet it wasn't her idea to meet in person?"

"He liked her in virt, she turned down his invitations, so he cracked her personal data and tracked her down, pretended it was their first meeting."

"But then he let something slip that clued her in that he was stalking her, and she couldn't get away from him fast enough."

"But he could shut down his locator signal too. Get close without her knowing."

I called up a map. "I'm getting a location for him now."

"If that's not a fake signal," Majid said.

"We'll soon find out."

We broke into a run. The memory of Jason's screams followed behind me, accusing me. But Majid was wrong. I wasn't running away from them. They were what drove me to hunt murderers so relentlessly.

Because I was a murderer too.

Russell Takizawa was exactly where his locator said he was—until he spotted us. Then he ran. His locator signal shut off a moment later, but we'd called in backup and already had him surrounded. We tracked him down the old-fashioned way, with eyeballs and feet.

"Look, I didn't do anything to her!" Takizawa insisted later in the police station's interview room. "How could I? I couldn't even get near her."

"You could cut off your locator signal easily enough," I told him.

"So I could do what, sneak up on her? Then I'd just scare her off even worse. I didn't want that."

"And what did you do to scare her off before?" Majid asked.

"Nothing! I don't know! All I did was ask a few questions and she just went nuts on me. I was just trying to patch things up, not hurt her."

"Then why did you run from us?"

"Are you kidding? The way she kept threatening to sic the cops on me? As soon as I heard she was dead, I figured she'd try to pin it on me the minute she woke up."

"So what did she have against you, exactly?" I asked. "What kind of questions did you ask her?"

Takizawa looked away, his nervousness belying his words. "The usual. Just the questions you ask anyone when you're trying to get to know them. Where are you from, where'd you go to school, what were your folks like. She didn't like to answer those."

"Yeah, we got that. But you kept prying, didn't you? You don't like to leave well enough alone. You don't let privacy keep you from finding things out about a woman."

He sank in his chair. "Okay. I admit it. I know you're not supposed to track down your virt sex partners if they don't invite you. But it's not a crime. And we really hit it off in there. We made a connection. It was more than just sex. The way she talked about the future…it was inspiring. I got the feeling she was part of something important, part of making the world better. She wouldn't say what exactly, but there was just this air about her that she was doing something special. I wanted to be connected to that. To her. But she kept saying no."

"So you ignored her wishes," Majid said, "hacked her private info, and approached her under false pretenses."

"Yeah, I didn't tell her we'd met before. I didn't want to scare her off. I was going to tell her eventually, once we'd..."

"Made virtual into reality?"

Takizawa glared at Majid. "Not like that. Once we'd gotten close enough that she'd understand I wasn't a creep or something—that I was inspired by what she did, who she was, and wanted to share it with her."

"But something tipped her off before you were ready," I said. "Did your 'questions' get a little too pushy?"

He sighed. "Maybe. Okay, maybe I don't like not having answers. I'm a googler. So's half the human race. I wanted to know more about her, to get close to her, but she wouldn't open up. So I searched. I didn't get any hits on her name more than four years old, so I put her picture online, looked for matches. I didn't get anything definite. But then a guy mailed me. He wanted to know about Isabelle. Said he was an old friend looking to get back in touch. Wanted to know where to reach her."

"Did you tell him?"

"Sure. Seemed harmless enough. Next time I saw Isabelle, I mentioned the guy, asked how it went. She went ballistic on me! Accused me of invading her privacy, stalking her, all sorts of things. I tried to explain, but it just freaked her out worse. She put that cordon on me and stopped answering my mails. I haven't seen her since." He blinked rapidly several times. "And when I heard what happened to her, I couldn't even go see her. Hell, I don't know if she'll even remember me."

"Maybe you'd like that," Majid said. "If she lost her memory of what you did to her and you could start all over again."

"God, no! We had something. A real spark, intangible, you know? Take away her memories, that changes who she is. She might as well be really dead then. And what about her work? That knowledge in her head, that's our future! I couldn't jeopardise that."

His expression hardened. "You want to find the guy who did this, find that old friend. His name's Charles Trendler. It was after I gave him her address that she freaked out." He winced. "Oh, God, maybe this is my fault. How could I have been so stupid?"

"We only have your word this Trendler even exists," Majid said. "You've already admitted you're capable of lying when it suits you."

"Hey, I have proof. The mail's still in my database. Just like I have proof I was nowhere near Isabelle that night." One of the first things he'd told us was to check his jacket's memory. The garment had recorded video and audio of his visit to a nightclub that evening.

"You're a pretty good hacker. You could've forged the video."

"Maybe. But I was in a public place. Find the other people there. They'll have vids too, and I'll be in them. They can't all be forgeries."

Takizawa's lawyer arrived then and made him shut up. As we left the interview room, Majid asked, "So what do you think?"

"I think he's a creep and at least a borderline stalker. Whether he's a killer...well, we have some alibi evidence to check out."

"I don't know," Majid said. "He sounded pretty...idealistic."

"Majid, this whole arcology is full of idealists. Easy enough to perfect the act."

Majid was quiet for a moment, fidgeting as we walked down the hall. "You know...just looking into someone's past doesn't make you a stalker. Sometimes it's out of concern."

I caught the subtext—he wasn't talking about Takizawa. I pulled him into an empty room. "What do you know?" I asked with heat in my voice.

"Don't take that betrayed tone, Craig. I saw the way you looked me over like a suspect when we met. Trying to figure me out. It's what we do. We're as nosy as Takizawa, we just do it for the law."

"What...do you...know?"

He sighed. "What's in the public record," he said in a gentle voice. "The car crash. You and your son. You didn't have any kind of death prevention. The doctors were able to bring you back within an hour, but your boy was too far gone." Silence for several moments. "I'm sorry."

"It's not your fault."

He caught the emphasis on the pronoun. "It's not yours either, Tamara."

"The hell it wasn't! I was a stupid Luddite. Thought it was wrong to tamper with God's design, outlive our Biblical threescore and ten or some such bullshit. I don't even remember exactly." I didn't have a backup to reload once they regrew my brain, so a lot of who I used to be is gone forever. Good bloody riddance.

"A lot of people feel that way. You were entitled to make that choice."

"For me? Maybe. But for my son?" I took a deep, shaky breath. "I thought I was giving him a moral life, securing his place in the afterlife. But all I did was make sure that a six-year-old boy had no chance to live the life *he* was entitled to.

"Idealism's nothing admirable, Majid. If all you care about is an abstract ideal, that can make it easy to sacrifice real live people to it."

I hated the sympathy in Majid's eyes. "So you're the one murderer you can't bring to justice...since nobody blames you but yourself."

"This is justice. It's penance. I stop other killers."

"And punish yourself by isolating yourself from other people. How can you fight against death if you refuse to embrace life?"

I met his gaze coldly. "Because it takes one to know one. It's what makes me good at my job. And it's time we got back to it."

Takizawa's alibi was inconclusive. His video footage showed him at the nightclub, but hanging around in the dark areas in the rear while everyone else's eyes and cameras were focused on the strippers onstage. Checking the other patrons' data storage showed us a lot of medically enhanced flesh, but no faces or voices in the audience that could be unambiguously identified as Russell Takizawa.

Charles Trendler turned out to be a 73-year-old resident of Pittsburgh, Pennsylvania. The most recent photo showed a man who actually looked his age, with gray hair, wrinkles, age spots, the works. He looked frail and weak but did nothing to prevent his deterioration. Another Luddite. There was no record of him leaving Pittsburgh, and when we contacted him, the signal was routed through a North American server. He had no implants, just an old-fashioned handheld phone, and he asked to conduct the interview by texting, saying he was in a public place and preferred not to discuss such grisly matters aloud. It made for a slow interview. I THOUGHT THE WOMAN IN THE PHOTO MIGHT BE MY WIFE, SARAH, he told us. SHE DISAPPEARED FIVE YEARS AGO. I'VE BEEN SEARCHING EVER SINCE.

I asked if it had been Sarah. He said no, and I asked how he could be sure. I SPOKE TO THE LADY, he said. I REALIZED IT WASN'T HER. THE WAY SHE SPOKE, THOUGHT... AFTER DECADES TOGETHER, YOU JUST KNOW.

I asked Trendler if he'd mentioned Russell Takizawa to Isabelle Warner. He said he had explained how he'd learned of her through Takizawa, and that Isabelle had grown upset when he'd mentioned how long and how well Takizawa claimed to have known her. SHE CALLED HIM A STALKER. SAID HE'D INVADED HER PRIVACY, SPIED ON HER. DIDN'T BLAME ME, SHE SAID, BUT I APOLOGIZED ANYWAY AND LET HER GO. DIDN'T HEAR FROM HER AGAIN. A pause. SUCH A TRAGIC LOSS.

"Haven't you heard?" Majid sent, verbalizing it for my benefit. "She's expected to make a full recovery. Send."

HER BODY, MAYBE. NOT WHO SHE WAS.

Majid told him about the genetic memory. The pause was so long we thought we'd lost him. "Mr. Trendler?" I sent.

PARDON. OVERCOME WITH RELIEF.

Why would it affect him so strongly? "One more question," I sent. "About your photo. Do you object to longevity treatments? Send." Majid threw me a look.

A PERSONAL CHOICE, he said. I DON'T JUDGE OTHERS. I'M JUST NOT INTERESTED IN LIVING LONGER THAN NATURE INTENDED. I exhaled sharply at that.

After the call, I began a Web search on Sarah Trendler. "I have to admit, it's looking pretty bad for Takizawa," Majid told me. "Maybe you were right."

"I'm not so sure," I told him. "A lot of it doesn't add up. We know the killer had to be someone she trusted enough to let him get close. But she wouldn't let Takizawa anywhere near her."

"Maybe something changed," he said, playing devil's advocate. "He convinced her to patch things up. He does have a sincere way about him. Like you said, it could be an act."

"Speculation. And we still haven't explained why he'd strip her and not rape her. I think maybe we have it backward—stripping her wasn't about her body, it was about her clothes."

"The killer wanted to remove any recording devices, sure," Majid said. "But why strip off everything? Who keeps data storage in their panties?"

"You'd be surprised how much redundancy some people want. Maybe the killer didn't know where she kept her data, or in how many places. So he had to be thorough, take everything. But he couldn't stand to see her exposed, hence the sheet. That's not the act of a sexual predator."

Majid leaned forward. "Let's cut to the chase here, Craig. You were the one who liked Takizawa for this, but now you've suddenly changed your song. Don't tell me you suspect Trendler? What, just because he rejects longevity treatments? Because he reminds you of the Tamara Craig who refused death prevention for her son?"

"Don't question my objectivity, Majid. Or I'll bring up how you couldn't resist prying into Rosa Manzano's sexual dalliances with Isabelle."

"Hey! Now, that's—" He broke off, calming himself. "Okay. Let's not go there. But Trendler never came here."

"We communicated by text. We don't know how great the transmission lag was. It could've been routed to North America and back here."

"But why is Trendler a better suspect than Takizawa?" he pressed.

"I don't know that he is," I shot back. "But it really threw him to learn Isabelle would recover her memories. He claims he barely knew her—why be so 'overcome'?"

"Maybe he's just a compassionate guy."

"A man who doesn't believe in outliving his allotted time, and he's overjoyed that technology's brought someone back from her natural death?"

"You're saying Isabelle really is Sarah Trendler. That she disappeared, and now Charles tracked her down."

I showed him my search results. "Sarah Trendler, born 1989."

He studied the images. "It could be Isabelle. The hair is different, the nose..."

"Look beneath the surface." I called up her medical records. "She suffered a brain aneurysm five and a half years ago. The doctors brought her back, with partial memory loss. Her backup chips failed."

Majid's eyes widened. "That's a pretty good incentive to get genetic memory."

"Mm-hm. And she disappeared seven months later."

He frowned. "But wait. She trusted her killer. If she ran away from him, why let him get close when he found her again?"

"Maybe it wasn't him she ran away from. Or not everything about him." I sighed. "Here's a woman on the cutting edge of death prevention. She's pushing seventy and looks half that. She's determined not to go gentle into that good night. And here's Charles Trendler, a man just as determined to keep his appointment with the Reaper. If you were determined to live forever and had a husband just as determined to deteriorate and die, could you stand to stay with him and watch it happen? Maybe it wasn't hate or fear that made her leave him. Maybe it was love." I saw Jason's face again, that beautiful, terrified face in that last moment. I blinked away tears. "Maybe she couldn't bear to live with witnessing the death of someone she loved."

Majid's hand came into my field of view, holding a tissue. He made no further comment or gesture as I dried my eyes. "And maybe he couldn't bear to see her live on without him," he finally said. "Let's see where Trendler really was that night."

It didn't take long to confirm that Trendler's texts had actually originated from here on Onogoroshima. Facial recognition at the airport soon found a match for his photo—two, in fact. Not only had he arrived here the day before Isabelle was attacked, but he had just bought a return ticket—right after speaking to us—and was waiting in the airport at that very moment. A single call to port security ensured he wouldn't be leaving.

He didn't try to deny it. He knew that, now we had the name of Sarah Trendler, we could subpoena her records to verify that Isabelle Warner had her DNA. He told us where he'd disposed of the surgical probe and Isabelle's clothing, and what fabricator he'd used to make the sheet and the gloves. He didn't boast, didn't take any pride in his accomplishment. He was a sad, broken man, unhappy at what he'd had to do. But he was more unhappy that he'd failed.

"Why did you kill her, Mr. Trendler?" I asked as Majid looked on.

It was several moments before he answered. "Sarah and I were married forty-two years ago," he said. "We saw ourselves growing old together, eventually dying together, maybe living on in some afterlife if we were lucky.

"But as time passed, as science kept coming up with new ways to keep people young, Sarah gave in to vanity. It didn't matter to me how young she looked, but it mattered to her. And once she could stay young-looking, she began thinking that maybe she didn't have to die at her allotted time. She was tempted by every new breakthrough, every kind of brain protection and regenerative therapy and backup memory.

"But I argued against it. It wasn't natural. Look what technology has done to the Earth. The more we fight against death, against the natural cycle, the more we become a cancer overrunning the planet. We have to build whole new land masses just to hold all the people, now that they refuse to let go and die. It's selfish, it's irresponsible. I refused to be a part of it."

Trendler lowered his head, weeping now. "Then...she died. It was so sudden. I was devastated. But...it was worse when the doctors revived her. I asked them not to, but they told me she had a resuscitation request on file. She'd never told me.

"The...woman who came back...it wasn't my Sarah. She'd changed, lost too much. She was some kind of technological zombie. She claimed she still loved me, but I wanted nothing to do with her. So, she left."

"She did more than leave," Majid said. "She went to a lot of trouble to disappear completely. Did she have a reason to hide from you?"

"It wasn't like that," the frail old man insisted. "What I did wasn't an act of hate. It was an act of mercy."

"You'll need to explain that," I told him.

"I am dying, Ms. Craig. I suppose that's a sentence you don't often hear in these parts. I have terminal cancer and I'll stop being a burden on the Earth in a few more months." He paused to breathe. Even for him, it couldn't be easy to say those words. "I could get treatment, but I've lived a full life, and it's my duty to let my life end for the good of the planet. I have no regrets for myself.

"But I couldn't bear the thought of that...artificial person still walking around, desecrating my Sarah's memory. When I discovered she was here, I came to her, told her I was dying, begged her to join me in returning to the Earth.

"But she refused. She clung to this unnaturally prolonged existence, this selfish indulgence at the Earth's expense. She even begged me to join her in it. She claimed it was out of love, but she didn't know what love is. Love requires the willingness to sacrifice." He blinked, the tears coming more heavily. "So I...I decided I had to free what was left of Sarah. She wanted to meet me again, one last time, to say goodbye. I came prepared. I took her in my arms, and held her...and I raised my hand to her neck…and I set her free." The tears ran forth, but he gave a shaky smile.

I couldn't take his sanctimonious crap anymore. "Oh, don't even try! Don't pretend this was some act of moral responsibility. Don't think I don't know how that works. You make decisions for a loved one, force them to live according to the rules *you* think are best for them, but in the final analysis, you're only doing it to satisfy your own ego. Your own conviction that you can't be wrong! You tried to kill another human being so that you could feel self-righteous!"

I felt Majid's hand on my shoulder, and somehow it calmed me. Somehow, I let it calm me. I sat down again, facing Trendler. "You talk about responsibility, but you've got it backwards. Yeah, the world's overpopulated, but it got that way before we had death prevention. And since then, the birth rate's plummeted."

"Because of the draconian, unnatural laws the governments impose."

"No. If people didn't like those laws, they'd change them or just break them." I thought about Isabelle, about Rosa, about Takizawa. "The thing is, when you know you'll still be around in a century or two, you start to think more about the big picture, the long term. You take more responsibility for the future. People don't just go along with one child per couple because they get bribed with death prevention, they do it because they understand it's the right thing to do. Not just for themselves, but for others.

"And yeah, the arcologies are a stopgap. But the longer people live, and the longer their view becomes, the more time and incentive they have to figure out new solutions."

I leaned forward, catching his gaze. "You know what dying is, Charles? It's jumping ship. Washing your hands of the future because you won't be around for it. You don't save the world by dying, and you sure as hell don't save it by killing. You save it by taking responsibility for the people around you. Working to improve their future, not just stamping an expiration date on it. All your self-righteous talk about nature, it's just your excuse for giving up. And giving up doesn't help anybody."

After a moment, Trendler calmed himself and gave a small but confident smile. "It doesn't matter," he said. "Call it what you like, but I acted on my convictions. I didn't murder anyone, since my Sarah was already dead. And I will die content that my death has meaning. Maybe I'll even be reunited with Sarah somewhere beyond."

I met his smile with an even bigger, smugger one of my own. "Don't bet on it, Mr. Trendler. You're going to be in the care of Onogoroshima's penal system from here on. It's a very enlightened system. Big on rehabilitation. They treat the psychological conditions that turn people into criminals, help them become healthy members of society again. And of course, they take care of your physical health too. You'll get that cancer treatment—and even though your general deterioration is fairly advanced, I'm sure it can all be reversed in time. You'll have a long, long stay on this mortal coil, Charles."

The look on his face was priceless. I've never before seen anyone so horrified at being sentenced to life.

"All right," Majid said once we'd freed Russell Takizawa. "I admit it. Your past issues didn't blind you. They helped you recognise the perp."

"Bloody oath, Majid," I affirmed. "I'm good at catching murderers because I am one."

He caught my arm, stopping me. His grip was gentle but unyielding. "No, Tamara. You're a victim. You understand death and loss, you understand guilt, and that's valuable in your job. But there's a difference between understanding them and letting them define you."

I didn't object to the continued warmth of his hand on my arm. But I couldn't meet his eyes. "You don't know what it's like. I know I'll never forgive myself. So I accept that, and I use it." I sighed. "You think I'm a cynic, that I'm blind to how much better the world is getting. You're wrong, Majid. I believe in that better world. I'm determined to help make it happen. But I know I don't belong in it."

"Well, I think you do. The things you said in there, Tamara, those were the words of a good person. A person who truly understands how to make the world better. But there's something in those words that you're not hearing."

I frowned. "What do you mean?"

"You said that what matters in life is taking responsibility for how we treat each other. That our self-serving beliefs are no excuse for hurting each other."

Again, Jason's face burned in my eyes. "No. There's no excuse for that."

Majid clasped me by the shoulders. "Then doesn't the same go for how we treat ourselves? And isn't guilt just as bad an excuse for treating ourselves unfairly?"

I had no words to give in answer. All I could do was look into his eyes. "Maybe you can't forgive yourself," he went on. "But that doesn't mean you have to punish yourself every moment, does it? You did good today, Tamara. You got to look in a murderer's eyes and tell him he'd failed. You even saved his life, whether he wanted it or not. I think you're entitled to celebrate that."

I surprised myself by kissing him on the cheek. "I appreciate the thought, Ma...Steve. But there are other murderers to catch. And if I don't stay on the job, some of them might actually succeed."

"Well, we can't have that," he said, smiling. "But could I at least take you out for coffee?"

After a moment's thought, I nodded. "Sure."

We walked out with my arm in his. As the sunlight hit us, I really looked at him for the first time, and decided I could stick around for more than just coffee.

After all, I had plenty of time ahead of me.

Aggravated Vehicular Genocide

Arachne was a spiderweb spinning in space. Her strands were fullerene wire, cylindrical molecules of pure carbon a trillion trillion atoms long. The spin of the highly conductive web spawned a magnetic field megameters wide, which sucked in the hydrogen ions produced when *Arachne*'s vast lasers illuminated the cosmic gas in her path, then compressed them by the trillions into the silvery engine core at the center of the web. There, the dense, hot hydrogen was fired to still greater temperatures by reaction with minute specks of antimatter, producing a fulminous spear of high-velocity exhaust plasma that drove the vessel on her long, lonely flight through interstellar depths.

An hour ago, *Arachne* had been coasting at 95.1 percent of light-speed, her ramfield and lasers at low power, deflecting gas and debris away from herself, rather than pulling it into her belly. Her crew had slept soundly in her cryogenic embrace, and she had maintained her vigil over them, looking in to ensure their life signs remained stable, looking out to ensure their path remained clear.

Until something dragged *Arachne* to a dead stop.

Stephen Jacobs-Wong briefed the crew as best he could in the minutes remaining before the aliens docked. Cecilia LoCarno captained the ship, but Stephen led the colonists, so they looked to him as they sought to understand what had brought about their premature awakening one-point-six parsecs and two time-dilated years short of their intended destination, Gamma Leporis V. The crew was split up between three habitat modules in case of disaster, but those not physically with him listened via the intercom.

"Arachne woke the captain when she first noticed us slowing—and then noticed the alien ships," Stephen told them. "According to Captain

LoCarno, we went from point-nine-five *c* to practically zero in a matter of minutes." He strove to remain calm as he relayed this, to project that calm onto the crew. Brown-skinned and Asian-featured, Stephen had the kind of handsome charisma that made people naturally want to follow him. It had served him well in his efforts to organize this expedition, to convince these forty people to risk the journey to a destination as remote as Gamma Lep. But the thing about waking up from nine years in cryosleep was that you looked and felt like you'd been asleep for exactly that long. The crew looked up at him blearily, like a mass advertisement for intravenous coffee. Stephen felt much as they did, but he strove to keep his gaze clear and reassuring. His outright shock at what had happened did a lot to keep him awake.

"From the Doppler shifts she observed in the starlight," he went on, "Arachne thinks the aliens hit us with some kind of gravity beam. Like a huge tractor beam."

Haim Silbermann, the chief engineer, shook his head in awe. "The power expenditure must be incredible. Whoever they are, they *really* wanted us to stop."

One of the exobiologists—a small, delicate woman named Zena Bhatiani—asked a question. "Will we be able to talk to them?"

Arachne herself answered that one. "The alien computers established an interface with me several minutes ago," the ship reported over the intercom. "A translation program was initiated, but then terminated. This suggests that the computer recognized our language as one already in its database."

"Not too surprising," mused Silbermann. He was a stocky, bearded man in his robust seventies, just past middle age. "We've been broadcasting into space for centuries."

"Arachne, did you learn anything about them while you were interfaced?" Stephen asked.

"Only about their cybernetic designs and protocols. Nothing about the aliens themselves. They seemed reluctant to provide information."

"That's not good," said one of the crew—an opinion others echoed.

"We shouldn't jump to any conclusions," Stephen cautioned. "We don't know anything about them yet."

"We will soon," Arachne interjected. "They're sixty-eight seconds from docking."

"Zena, Haim, I think you should come with me," Stephen said with the tone of a suggestion and the authority of a command. "The rest of you should stay here. Arachne will keep you posted."

"Shouldn't there be more of us there, just in case?" someone asked. "What if they're hostile? I mean, they dragged us to a dead stop without permission, without a word. That's hardly a friendly act."

"Look at us," Stephen countered with a sardonic grin. "We're just out of cryosleep, we can barely stand up. If they're hostile, the best thing we can do is try not to antagonize them."

"Forty seconds," Arachne prodded.

Stephen nodded at Bhatiani and Silbermann. "Come on."

Arachne had no docking port *per se*, since an interstellar vessel headed for an uninhabited system wouldn't be expected to take on passengers. But there were maintenance airlocks on the habitat modules. The alien ship—which Arachne indicated was only one of numerous such vessels surrounding her—attached one of its own docking ports to the lock, after using some sort of gravity drive to match the ramship's rotation. The light emanating from the rear of the ships was not rocket exhaust, but seemed instead to be high-energy particle emissions from annihilation reactors.

Arachne's supplies did include stunguns for dealing with any hostile Leporian wildlife the colonists might encounter; but those guns were all in the landing craft, stowed hundreds of meters away from the habitat modules. So Cecilia LoCarno and the others had to meet their gate-crashers unarmed, and pray that they intended no harm.

The airlock opened and the first alien entered the ship, its long body barely able to fit in the lock. It was a tailed biped with an almost kangaroo-like build, but its arms were nearly as long and powerful-looking as its legs, with two fingers and two thumbs on each hand. Through its helmet, Stephen could see a long-snouted, blue-skinned head with a crest of bristly hair—or possibly some sort of sensory cilia—running from the "nose" to between its bulbous, chameleon-like eyes, which were sheltered under large, bony crests.

As a second alien began cycling through the lock, LoCarno steeled herself and strode up to face the lead alien. "I am Captain Cecilia LoCarno of the Human ramship *Arachne*, from the planet Earth. Identify yourselves, and explain your reasons for interrupting our voyage." Lanky, yet strong-looking, her severely cut hair gold tinged with steel, the captain radiated a confident authority which Stephen envied. But he'd seen the look in her eyes when she'd told him about the aliens and their gravity beams. Cecilia was as frightened as he was. This should have been thrilling—first contact with an alien civilization, a rare event in human history, an extraordinary privilege for an explorer. *So why,* Stephen thought, *does it feel like we're being pulled over?*

The alien remained silent for a moment, probably listening to a computer translation. Then it opened its mouth, revealing omnivore teeth, and began to speak. The translation emanated from its pressure suit's speaker. "I am Rillial. We are the Chirrn. We are the survivors of the vessel Lesshchi. Explain *your* reasons for destroying the vessel Lesshchi."

Four pairs of human eyes widened in shock; the aliens, now four in number, watched the unfamiliar anatomy curiously. "*What?*" Cecilia finally asked.

"Explain your reasons for destroying the vessel Lesshchi. Is there a translation problem?"

"No, it's.... There must be some mistake. We haven't destroyed any ships. We're colonists, not fighters. Besides, we've all been in cryogenic sleep until you captured our ship. The only person who could've done anything is the ship herself. And Arachne would have no reason to destroy an alien ship." *Unless she knew that ship posed some threat,* Steven thought, seeing the same realization in LoCarno's eyes. But Arachne had reported no such action.

"The Chirrn vessel Lesshchi," Rillial countered, "was destroyed by several high-powered beams of collimated light tuned to the ionization frequency of hydrogen gas. Do you deny that your ionizing beams are capable of pinpoint focus?"

"No," interjected Silbermann. "Um, I'm Haim Silbermann, the chief engineer. The, uh, the lasers can be focused. If the defense systems detect an asteroid or comet in our path, the lasers can focus to vaporize it before it hits."

"Haim!" LoCarno hissed, glaring at him.

Silbermann shrugged, then turned back to the Chirrn. "But...but we couldn't have destroyed your ship. The system checks for engine emissions and such before it locks on to fire. If your ship had been in our path, Arachne wouldn't have shot it. She would've vectored our thrust, tried to veer off."

Arachne spoke up. "Captain, I did fire on an obstacle shortly before the Chirrn captured us. But there were no emissions indicative of propulsive engines, and no indication of a lightsail. And I estimate the size of the object at twenty to thirty kilometers, which is far too large for a spacecraft."

Rillial's eyes swiveled to focus on LoCarno once more, but not before taking in all four humans. "The vessel Lesshchi did not have propulsive mechanisms as you would understand them. It was maneuvered gravitationally."

"But your ships have particle exhausts," Arachne observed. "No such exhaust was noted from the obstacle—which was far larger than your ships, in any case."

"The vessel Lesshchi was not a transport vehicle. It was our home. The Chirrn do not dwell on planets, as you do. We dwell in vessels which travel between the stars. Vessels which house thousands of Chirrn."

"Oh, Great Mother," Stephen breathed. "There is a translation problem. 'Vessel' doesn't just mean 'ship,' it means 'container.' Like something which contains an artificial environment. Cecilia, they're saying Lesshchi was a space habitat!"

"Correct," Rillial said. "Lesshchi was habitat to over eighty-eight thousand and seven hundred Chirrn. We survivors number less than three hundred fifty. All the rest—nearly eighty-eight thousand four hundred of my people—are dead."

"Eighty-eight...thousand people?" Stephen gasped. "And we...we killed them?" The shock overcame him in his weakened state. His legs folded beneath him, but Haim Silbermann caught him and held him upright. Yet the engineer looked none too steady himself.

The captain showed no reaction, silently meeting the alien's accusing gaze. Finally, she spoke. "I'll believe it when I see proof," she said coldly.

"Cecilia!" Stephen cried, stunned.

"And you shall see it," Rillial told her. "Your vessel will be towed to the site."

The captain nodded, then turned to meet Stephen's disbelieving gaze. In humanity's technically advanced society, where almost any physical evidence could be falsified, where only an expert forger or simulation artist could recognize a forgery or a simulation, the word of honor had become a precious commodity. Breaking one's word was a taboo on par with rape, and questioning another's word was a heinous accusation. It was the only way society could survive when illusion became indistinguishable from truth.

"I know, I know," Cecilia whispered. "But they're aliens. Who knows how they think?"

Stephen expected that beings so much more technically advanced would have an even greater need for honor. And if Cecilia couldn't trust them, how could she trust their evidence? It didn't seem to make sense.

Then again, Stephen realized, he couldn't blame her for not wanting to believe the Chirrn's accusation. He didn't want it to be true either.

Words of honor aside, perfect forgeries aside, there was still nothing quite as potent as seeing a thing before your eyes. And Stephen could only wish he didn't have to behold this sight.

The Chirrn habitat had been a vast, rotating cylinder constructed from an asteroid, apparently using the same basic techniques that human spacers had used for over a century. Now it tumbled and drifted erratically through space, the sheer size of the habitat making its wild motions seem slow, almost stately.

One end of the iron-nickel cylinder had been blown completely open, the ragged, melted edges a testament to the sheer heat and power of *Arachne*'s lasers. When the opening tumbled into view, Stephen could see the charred, lifeless remains of forests and fields; Chirrn-made lakes and riverbeds robbed of most of their water, with what remained glistening as ice; Chirrn cities burned, wrecked and devoid of light or movement. One city had been ripped clear through, its twisted, melted towers jutting from the open end of the mangled cylinder.

Stretching back behind the habitat was a long, expanding trail of debris, bits and pieces of an advanced civilization torn apart into randomness. Stephen tried not to look too closely at the debris. He knew some of it was organic. Some of it was Chirrn. Some of it was children.

Rillial stood behind the captain and Stephen at the viewport and spoke in a tone whose coldness was clear even through the barriers of mechanical translation and alien inflection. "Your beams hit near the southern end of Lesshchi and melted through in milliseconds. The air inside superheated instantly, cooking us by the thousands. The pressure hastened the rupturing of the hull, and the outracing air blew the southern end completely away."

Arachne spoke, her synthesized tones lacking inflection. Perhaps she was too shocked to simulate human speech mannerisms. "I fired at one end of the perceived asteroid," she explained, "in the hopes that the catastrophic vaporization would provide enough pressure to propel the remainder out of our path." There followed what for a cyber was a lengthy pause. "Now that I think about it, the asteroid's subsequent acceleration suggested a much smaller mass than I'd assumed from its size. As though it were hollow."

After a pause (for no one knew how to respond to that), Rillial continued its account. "Only those of us who were inside the infrastructure at the northern end were spared from the heat and the vacuum, but many of us were killed by the turbulence of the explosions and hull ruptures. Most of us who survived were already in our ships at the time; very few others were able to reach ships before death reached them." Rillial turned to spear the captain with its gaze. "Death for which you *will* be held responsible."

Cecilia glared at the alien angrily, but maintained her calm. "I agree this was a great tragedy...Rillial. But we did not do this knowingly. It was an accident."

"In space, accidents are usually fatal. To fail to guard against accident is intolerable negligence. Only a planet-dweller would claim accident as an excuse." Though it was hard to read the alien's emotions, Rillial seemed to say "planet-dweller" with considerable contempt.

But as Stephen stared out at the wreck of Lesshchi, he couldn't help but feel that contempt was justified. "Rillial..." he began hesitantly, "is there anything we can do to help you? To try to make up for what we've—"

"Stephen!" LoCarno warned sharply. She pulled him aside and spoke quietly, no doubt hoping the Chirrn translators wouldn't pick up their voices. "Don't say anything that would imply culpability on our part."

"But—"

"I'll make it an order if I have to. We have to think clearly. It's a horrible thing, yes, but we don't know what they plan to do to us. We don't want to say or do anything that would make it easier for them." She quailed at the expression in Stephen's eyes. "Don't look at me that way. I feel for them too. But my duty is to the passengers and crew of this ship, and to the hundreds of frozen embryos we're carrying. I have to place their interests first.

"What you were about to say could've been taken as a confession. And there's no telling what consequences that would have in their legal system. If they even plan to use their legal system, instead of just taking revenge. *We don't know* what they'll do. So we have to be on our guard, no matter what we may feel for their dead."

Stephen sighed heavily, but nodded. He'd been weakened by the cryosleep and the shock he'd faced upon awakening; but he was a leader, a pioneer, and he could accept cold realities. "Okay. So we need to find out what they plan to do next."

The next step, according to Rillial, would be a trial to determine the humans' culpability in the destruction of Lesshchi. The refugees proceeded to tow *Arachne* and her crew to the nearest intact Chirrn habitat. This took surprisingly little time—less than a day, in fact. Perhaps the Chirrn habitats travelled in packs; perhaps their ships gravitically accelerated *Arachne* to within a very small fraction of light-speed, time-dilating them by a factor of thousands; perhaps, for all *Arachne*'s crew knew, the Chirrn had hyperlight drive. Not only would the Chirrn tell them nothing, but they confined the crew in windowless rooms and blinded *Arachne*'s sensors.

Before towing *Arachne*, they had made her reel in the fullerene web and halt her rotation, leaving the crew in freefall. This gave the Chirrn guards a significant advantage, for their forms seemed finely adapted to life without weight. In microgravity they were sinuous and graceful—long, almost serpentine bodies sliding through the air, grasping handholds with fingers and toes, using their powerful tails and flexible spines to maneuver like cats twisting in midair. Now that contamination tests had proven it safe, the Chirrn had discarded their pressure suits, under which they wore only utilitarian vests; they had no sign of genitals in the usual place, so their sexes remained unknown. Behind their eye ridges, their bristly snout-hairs gave way to long, horselike manes that trailed elegantly behind them as they maneuvered in microgravity. Their skin colors were predominantly blues, often shading into violet or green. The manes seemed to come in all colors of the spectrum. Whether this was natural or cosmetic was unknown, for the Chirrn seemed unwilling to reveal anything about themselves to the humans they guarded.

Perhaps this was more than just reticence. The Chirrn made no secret of the fact that they blamed the humans for the deaths of their loved ones, the destruction of their homeland. It took barely an hour before a group of Chirrn guards snapped and attempted to beat their prisoners to death. Fortunately, most of *Arachne*'s crew had been raised in Earth's high gravity and were able to defend themselves against the lighter Chirrn until Rillial arrived to impose order. Still, three of the crew—including tiny Zena Bhatiani—had needed serious medical treatment. And though Rillial reassigned the guards, the alien leader offered no apologies. "For myself," Rillial told them, "I would have happily joined them in killing you all. But there must be law. The tribunal will judge you."

As soon as the humans were brought into the Chirrn habitat named Shilirrlal, they were subjected to thorough medical examinations, followed by a lengthy and unpleasant decontamination process—stripped naked, then collectively herded through a series of chemical immersion baths, uncomfortably hot "room-temperature" plasma bursts, nanotech "cleansings" of their respiratory and digestive tracts, and unknown other processes before finally being handed simple, ill-fitting garments which the Chirrn had synthesized for them. It was unclear why this was necessary, since the aliens' own tests had shown Terran and Chirrn biochemistry to be too different for infection to occur.

Then the prisoners were brought out into the open. Hundreds of Chirrn stood watching, fascinated by the sight of the humans, but remaining at a distance, as though they were somehow unclean. Stephen looked up to see a live image of himself and his crewmates on a large holoscreen in a nearby plaza. He realized that their decontamination must have been broadcast to the public. The entire procedure had been symbolic, to reassure the citizens of Shilirrlal that they would not be contaminated by the impure aliens. Stephen blushed fiercely. He wasn't modest about being seen nude, certainly not by aliens; but the knowledge that so many had watched the humiliating procedure made him ashamed, on behalf of the entire crew. He looked at Cecilia and saw her realizing the same things he had—but her expression was bitter cold.

Shilirrlal looked as Lesshchi must have before it was destroyed. Presumably it was a typical, asteroid-built cylinder on the outside; but inside, it was uniquely Chirrn. Everywhere, towers and terraces soared above the humans' heads, along with lattices stretching toward the central axis, climbed by vegetation and by Chirrn. It was an odd visual paradox; the architecture seemed to be striving for the sky, yet at the same time enclosed and introverted, for the sky was in the center of this wraparound world.

True to their kangaroid build, the Chirrn moved by hopping, keeping their bodies and tails horizontal as they leapt forward, assuming a vertical posture only at rest. They built large, to accommodate their long bodies and bounding locomotion. Stairways had only two or three steps between one story and the next; sometimes Chirrn would bound directly to a higher level, pulling themselves up with their arms like a cat leaping onto a high perch. Sometimes they climbed ladders and lattices with a brachiator's agility, grasping with fingers and toes.

A few hundred meters above ground level was a large, open framework forming an inner cylinder, the conduits over a meter thick and dozens of meters apart. Inside it, Chirrn soared in free fall from one tower, one terrace, one handhold to the next. Up ahead, Stephen saw a large globe of water jiggling through the air with small Chirrn swimming gaily through it. "Could that framework be generating some kind of antigravity field?" he asked Haim Silbermann, speaking quietly so as not to antagonize the guards.

"Well, there's no real gravity to begin with, just rotation. In the air, it's the Coriolis winds that shove you sideways and out, toward the ground." The bearded engineer peered at one of the conduits as they passed underneath it. "I'd guess the framework's somehow isolating the air in there, keeping it still. Maybe their gravity technology; maybe just magnetic or optical particle manipulation. Who knows?"

"Well, whatever the reason, it's beautiful," Stephen said as he observed four brightly colored Chirrn flying intricate patterns around each other in what could be a sport, a piece of performance art, a mating dance, or all of those. "This is what we destroyed, Haim," he breathed. Sudden tears blurred his view of the aerial dance.

There was a long pause. "I know," Silbermann finally said, almost too softly to hear.

Though Shilirrlal's rotation produced less than sixty percent of an Earth *g*, not all of the humans were able to traverse the Chirrn's high steps and climbing-lattices. The forty prisoners were taken up into the towering justice center via a cargo lift.

During their processing (Stephen wondered if "booking" was a fair analogy), they were provided with earplug translators. The devices were receive-only; presumably the Chirrn had their own earplug or implant translators already. "That's odd," Cecilia observed after they'd been confined. "They seem so isolationist, so disdainful of other races. You wouldn't expect them to use translators on a regular basis."

"I don't think it's all races they dislike," Zena Bhatiani told her. "They seem to have a specific bias against planet-dwellers. When the guards...attacked us...." Zena shuddered, understandably. Even after a day in a medbed, she still bore bruises and scars. "The things they said, the insults.... 'Ground-vermin.' 'Dirt-grubber.' 'Well-digger.'"

"'Well-digger'?" Cecilia asked.

"I guess like a gravity well. A planet." She tilted her head. "And maybe also because digging a well is something you can only do on a planet. Anyway, their use of translators suggests they do interact with other races. They just don't like ones that live on planets."

"That must narrow their list of friends a great deal," the captain said.

"I don't know. The number of humans who now live in space habitats instead of planets is close to a billion. And we've hardly met any aliens yet."

The discussion was interrupted by the opening of the cell door. An atypically stocky Chirrn, turquoise-skinned with a yellow-white mane, hopped into the large, austere chamber and surveyed the prisoners. "Are there any among you who are not of planetary birth?" was the being's first question.

Cecilia stepped forward. "Why do you want to know?" she asked.

"Are you of non-planetary origin?"

"No. I was born in Venezia on the planet Earth and proud of it. I also happen to be the captain of this group, so I'm the one you speak to. Now, just what have you got against planet-dwellers?"

The Chirrn looked around at the crew, ignoring her. "I am L'chellin. I have been assigned as your advocate for the tribunal. I advise you that it would be in your best interests to choose one not of planetary birth to speak for your crew. I repeat my query."

Cecilia moved before L'chellin, meeting its chameleon gaze firmly. "And *I* repeat, I'm the captain," she said sternly. "I speak for this crew, and you're going to have to accept it. Now, I asked you a question."

The alien made a sighing sound, its snout-bristles ruffling. "Very well. But you will have to live with the consequences of that choice."

"I'm waiting for an answer," Cecilia went on implacably. "We have a right to know—are we going to be tried fairly, or persecuted due to our origins? We need to know just how deep this anti-planet bias of yours runs."

L'chellin rotated its eyes back into its head, like a human pressing one's eyes shut in weariness. "We believe ourselves to be a rational people," it said. "Our civilization has thrived for over ten thousand years." (Later, Silbermann would point out that the translator was handily converting base-eight numbers into their base-ten equivalents—another indication that the Chirrn routinely interacted with other species, species with different numbers of fingers.) "But our... discomfort with planet-dwellers is deeply rooted in our history.

"Our primitive ancestors evolved on the planet Shayal. When the ability to enter space was devised, many of our ancestors left Shayal and became the first Chirrn, building their own worlds, which proliferated throughout the system of the star Roj.

"But those who refused to leave Shayal failed to learn the responsibility for their ecosystem that space-dwellers must learn quickly. In their sloppiness, they fouled Shayal, and came to depend on the Chirrn for support. Sadly, the Chirrn were subject to their rule, and were forced to submit to ever-greater demands." The advocate's recitation had the tone of a story learned in childhood and swallowed whole. "Finally, the Chirrn rebelled against the tyranny of the Shayaln. The wars lasted for many decades, bringing great death.

"Naturally, the Chirrn had the advantage. Their resources were greater, not limited to what a single planet could offer. They could block the Shayaln's sunlight, reducing their energy supplies. And the Shayaln were at the bottom of a gravity well, where they could be easily bombarded. But the Chirrn held back, out of compassion for their planet-dwelling cousins.

"However, the Shayaln's poor, isolated existence had twisted their morals. They showed none of the restraint of the Chirrn, attacking ruthlessly at every chance. Peace talks were used as opportunities for ambush. Medical ships were destroyed, biological weapons were used, against all laws and treaties." L'chellin lowered its head. "Finally, we reached the point where we could not tolerate coexistence with the Shayaln. Many argued that we should crush them utterly. It would have been easy to bombard the planet with asteroids until it was barren of life. But we had more decency than that. Instead, we chose to leave the Roj system forever, and live among the stars.

"It proved the best decision we ever made. It liberated us. We were no longer restricted to the orbit of a single star. We could discover the universe without leaving our homes."

L'chellin looked back at the captain again. "So you can understand that to live on a planet, to trap yourself within a gravity well and spend your entire existence in one place, is inconceivable to us. It would be the worst form of imprisonment. And, given what the Shayaln did to our ancestors, we feel it must twist beings' minds and morals beyond the point where they can be civilized. To us, planet-dwellers are dangerous savages who must be avoided at all costs." L'chellin tapped its hands against its brow ridges, as though symbolically hiding its eyes; this seemed to be a gesture of unhappiness. "And what you have done to Lesshchi only reinforces this belief."

"Now wait a minute, mister or Ms. or whatever you are—"

"I am currently male."

Cecilia blinked, but took it in stride. "I thought you were supposed to be defending us in this trial."

"Do you deny that your collimated-light projectors destroyed Lesshchi?"

"No. But it was an accident. We didn't even know what Lesshchi was until its survivors dragged us out of relativistic. We're sorry for what happened. Deeply sorry. We try to be a peaceful people, to respect all life. But accidents happen.

"So the question, Mr. L'chellin, is: do you accept that it was an accident, and are you capable of doing your best to persuade this tribunal of that fact despite their anti-planetary biases? Or is your role just a formality in a—a show trial whose outcome is already decided?" For a number of reasons, she had chosen to avoid the phrase "kangaroo court."

The Chirrn's eyes swiveled to focus on hers. "I take my duties seriously. No space-dweller who executes one's duties sloppily can expect to survive for long. My role is to participate in the search for the truth and the determination of justice. I will not allow myself bias in that pursuit."

Cecilia stared searchingly into those alien eyes, seeing nothing she could recognize...save for his unwavering gaze. "All right," she finally said. "That sounds pretty much like the role of the attorney in our legal system, so I can accept it. Now how much time do we have to work out a defense strategy...?"

Another translation glitch: in the Chirrn legal system, the role of the "advocate" was not to speak for the accused, but merely to advise the accused in legal principles and procedures; the defendants were expected to speak on their own behalf. This, L'chellin explained to Cecilia LoCarno, was why he had advised her to choose a non-planetary native as the crew's spokesperson; such an individual would be seen more sympathetically by the tribunal. But Cecilia insisted on speaking for her crew.

The tribunal panel consisted of six Chirrn who sat behind a long, raised construct not unlike a judge's bench. The tribunes were elected by the people, but would serve the approximate role of a jury. Before them in the center was the arbiter, who would ensure that proper procedures were followed; this individual filled some of the functions of both judge and bailiff. Along the sides of the courtroom were witnesses' benches, and the rear contained limited audience seating.

It seemed to Cecilia like a reasonable setup. She wondered if the Chirrn, like some human cultures, had gone through a period in their past when the courtroom had become an arena for combat between self-serving lawyers rather than a place to seek the truth. Perhaps the prominent position of the tribunes and the relatively subordinate role of the advocates was a reminder that the lawyers were there to serve the clients and the jury, not the other way around.

Perhaps in keeping with the diminished role of the attorney/advocates, there were no opening statements. The tribunal began with the arbiter briefly spelling out the basics of the case: the involved parties, the charges, and so on. It then proceeded directly to what was called the stating of grievances.

Rillial, as a representative for the aggrieved parties, spoke for the prosecution. The cobalt-skinned, mahogany-haired Chirrn (who, according to L'chellin, was "currently female") spent considerable time describing the exact details of the destruction of Lesshchi, including a listing of all the familial or clan groupings that had lost members or been exterminated in the event. Captain LoCarno objected to this as prejudicial, to which the arbiter countered that it was necessary and proper to identify the aggrieved parties in a legal proceeding, normally by name and family, but in this case only by family due to the sheer number of victims.

Cecilia offered no more objections and asked no questions—partly as a way of pointing out that she and her entire crew had been unconscious during the incident and thus had no perspective of their own to counter with. As Rillial continued her litany, her intense emotion barely hidden under her courtroom formality, Cecilia sat quietly, seeking to project an air of sorrow without guilt. Few others of the crew were able to maintain such reserve as Rillial spoke of the horrors that their ship's defenses had wrought. The Chirrn audience and witnesses were even more severely agitated, some seeming ready to attack the humans. So after Rillial's presentation, court was adjourned for several hours to give everyone time to calm down. (Apparently the Chirrn had no regular day/night cycle, since that was a planetary sort of thing; Chirrn slept when they had nothing else to do.)

When the tribunal reconvened, it was the defendants' turn to explain the circumstances under which they had become involved in the incident. This part was handled by Stephen. "My name is Stephen Jacobs-Wong," he told the tribunal. "Twenty-eight objective-time years ago, in the Earth year 2147, I organized an expedition to colonize the planet Gamma Leporis Five, which orbits the larger, yellow component of a binary star system twenty-nine light-years from Earth. An automated probe to that system had shown that planet to possess the right conditions to support terrestrial life forms, and had shown no sign of intelligent habitation of its land masses.

"Twenty-six objective-time years ago, we set out for Gamma Leporis in the hydrogen-ramjet vessel *Arachne*, commanded by Cecilia LoCarno. In addition to forty live humans and our colonization supplies, *Arachne* carries frozen embryos and genetic matrices of many terrestrial organisms, including six hundred frozen human embryos, which we would gestate upon settlement, using both artificial equipment and the wombs of our female members."

"You forty," one of the tribunes asked, "would raise six hundred young?"

"Well, not all at once. The embryos would be used gradually to boost our numbers and help us build a stable, diverse population base. We anticipate it taking two or three generations before all six hundred are born.

"Anyway, in order to minimize power and resource expenditure on our voyage, it was decided that all the settlers would make the journey in cryogenic suspension, and that *Arachne* would be provided with a fully sapient brain that would run the ship. The captain and necessary crew could be awakened if a crisis arose."

Ship's logs were produced as evidence that the entire crew had been in suspended animation at the time of Lesshchi's destruction. This was supported by the results of the Chirrn's own medical tests of the forty humans, which did show signs of recent awakening from cryosleep. Rillial countered that the accuracy of such tests was limited, especially with regard to a species never before encountered in the flesh, and that the same results could prevail if some or all of the crew had been awake before the "attack" on Lesshchi.

"I object!" Cecilia shouted. "There are no grounds for characterizing this incident as an attack, or an act of deliberate malice. The evidence clearly indicates that these events were not premeditated, and there is absolutely no basis for any contrary opinion.

"After all—you Chirrn don't exactly go out of your way to make contact with planet-dwelling races. We had no idea you even existed before these events. So how could we possibly bear you any malice, or wish to attack you?"

"Because you're dirtballers!" came a cry from one of the Lesshchi survivors. Rillial and the arbiter urged quiet, but this merely triggered more shouting from the embittered Chirrn. The arbiter ordered another recess to allow calm to return.

Upon reassembly, the head tribune, a garnet-hued male with a sherbet-orange mane, spoke. "This panel concedes that there are no legitimate grounds for the assumption of deliberate malice on the part of the crew of the starship Arachne. All defendants, regardless of the circumstances of their origin, are subject to protection from unfounded charges. This issue will not be raised again.

"However," the tribune continued, "there remains the charge of culpability due to negligence. This issue will now be debated."

"Pardon me, Honored Tribunes." It was L'chellin, who stepped forward diffidently. There was some muttering from the audience; apparently it was unusual for an advocate to speak to the tribunes directly. "I speak on behalf of a defendant who is unable to attend. The starship *Arachne* has asked me to file a motion that the charges against the humans be dismissed. Since Arachne herself was the only individual conscious at the time of Lesshchi's destruction, and since the defense systems which destroyed Lesshchi are part of her own person, she contends that she is the only one who should be placed on trial for that destruction."

This motion piqued the tribunes' interest considerably, and they pulled together to debate the question. Cecilia turned to Stephen and spoke softly. "I wonder why I didn't think of that. Arachne may just get us off the hook with that one."

"At the cost of her own freedom," Stephen reminded her. "Who knows whether they respect cyber rights here? If she's found guilty, Arachne may be reprogrammed or even killed."

"I know," Cecilia told him, placing a hand on his shoulder. "What I mean is, I'm gratified by her courage, her willingness to sacrifice herself for us." She frowned. "Though if our ship's convicted of a crime, what does that do for our chances of reaching Gamma Lep?"

Stephen threw her a disturbed look, but before he could say anything, the head tribune spoke again. "Though it is true that Arachne was the only conscious member of the expedition, it is also true that she is officially a member of that expedition's crew. Is that not correct?"

"Yes, it is," Cecilia confirmed.

"Arachne's actions were thus committed in service to her human passengers. This makes her passengers liable for her actions. It is a basic principle of Chirrn law that superiors are culpable for the actions of their subordinates."

"Honored Tribunes," spoke up one of the Lesshchi survivors/prosecutors, a deep-blue, grey-maned individual named Churrlaya. "Our studies of human law, based on their ship's records and on the signals we have recorded from their system over the past two centuries, suggest numerous precedents for this view in their own legal traditions. There are instances of war criminals being held culpable for actions carried out by their subordinates."

"Noted," the head tribune said. "Therefore, by both Chirrn and human legal precedents, the ramship *Arachne*'s motion is denied. She acted on behalf of the humans who stand before this tribunal; therefore those humans are the ones on which the ultimate blame, if any, will fall."

"Thank you, Honored Tribunes," Rillial said, one eye flicking around to leer triumphantly at the humans. "Rest assured, we will demonstrate the humans' guilt in this disaster."

"On what grounds?" Cecilia protested, taking full advantage of the rather loose procedures of the court.

"The grounds of criminal negligence."

"Honored Tribunes, there is no negligence here," Cecilia urged. "Just the opposite. As I will now show."

"Proceed," waved the arbiter.

"Consider the probabilities here. Two space vessels, each travelling its own course through interstellar space, each completely unaware of the other, just happen to follow intersecting courses—and what's more, both arrive at the point of intersection simultaneously. Given the immensity of space, what are the odds of such a thing occurring?

"As a species with over ten thousand years of experience in interstellar travel, you must appreciate even better than we do how immensely improbable it is for two vessels to meet with each other except by conscious design and careful maneuvering. According to your own records, which our advocate is now providing..." and as she said this, L'chellin handed a data crystal to the arbiter, "only seven such incidents have ever occurred in Chirrn history, and in all of them the two unrelated ships only passed within communication or sensor range, not within collision range."

Cecilia next called Haim Silbermann to explain the basics of *Arachne*'s laser defenses. "The beams are spread out into a conical shape by Fresnel lenses," the engineer explained, "in order to ionize the maximum amount of interstellar hydrogen. What happens is that the beam hits the focus node, a convex mirror at the focus of a parabolic dish. The mirror spreads the beam out across the dish, which then sends it out straight again, but wider than before. It then hits the divergent Fresnel lens and spreads out. But if the sensors detect an obstacle, the focus node can become transparent, letting the beam straight through, un-diffused and very powerful. It can be directed by the node at any desired target. And, of course, there are six of them."

"Why do we need such a defense system?" Cecilia asked.

"Well, to destroy space debris in our path. Or to give it enough of a blast to push it out of the way."

"But what if it weren't space debris? What if it were, say, an alien ship?"

"Well, that's very unlikely."

"Yes, it is."

"Still," Silbermann went on, bringing a grin to Cecilia's face, "the designers did prepare for the possibility. We didn't want to cause any...well, anything like what happened.

"The defense computers are programmed to scan for signs that an obstacle is artificial—like the reflection spectrum of diamite or aerogel or other synthetic hull coatings. Or for engine emissions, the radiation or particles you'd see from a fusion or antimatter rocket. Let's see, it also looks for the EM signature of a ship propelled by a particle beam. And of course it could spot a lightsail easily, from its reflectivity."

"And what happens if the sensors show the obstacle is artificial?"

"Well, we don't blast it. Instead, maneuvering thrusters are fired to turn the ship."

"But if the ship is travelling at ninety-five percent of lightspeed, you wouldn't have long to react before the obstacle reached you. If the object were twenty light-seconds away, you'd only have a second to respond."

"Well, our sensors can see much farther than that. And the computers can compensate for the time lag, extrapolate the true position of the obstacle. They're very fast. And at that speed, even a small change in direction would add up damn fast. We might not be able to clear the obstacle entirely, though; it might still hit the magnetic web. But odds are it wouldn't hit a laser or do any irreparable damage. Even if it did, we could probably limp along to our destination with a damaged web."

"So protecting the other ship is a higher priority than avoiding damage to our own."

"Well, of course."

Cecilia smiled again. "Of course. Honored Tribunes, we've established that an accidental collision between interstellar vessels is an event of vanishingly low probability. Yet *nonetheless*, the designers of *Arachne* went out of their way to protect against a tragedy that would almost certainly never occur, even at the risk of damage to the ship herself. This, Honored Tribunes, is the precise opposite of negligence. If anything, it is caution above and beyond what any reasonable being would find adequate."

"Yet clearly it was not adequate," Churrlaya interrupted. "Your sensory parameters did not prevent your defense system from destroying Lesshchi."

"That's because Lesshchi maneuvered using gravity control. That is a technology we don't have, aren't even close to having. It's impossible to expect us to prepare for encountering a technology we didn't know existed."

"But what if you encountered a spacegoing habitat that were not using any of its engines, even of the kinds you do have? Your defenses would then destroy it."

"No they wouldn't," Silbermann interjected. "A habitat like that would give off infrared, emit visible light through its star windows, broadcast in radio. But yours did none of those things. In fact, L'chellin here tells me that the Chirrn try to avoid giving off any radiations that might get them detected by planet-dwelling races. Says you don't want 'em getting curious about you, coming to take a look."

Cecilia pounced on that. "That's right! How could we possibly be expected to detect your habitats when you go out of your way to keep people like us from detecting them? And doesn't that place the culpability squarely on *your* shoulders?"

That, Cecilia realized, may have been a mistake. The insinuation that the Chirrn had caused their own death sparked an uproar in the court. One of the Lesshchi refugees screamed in fury and leapt forward, clear over Rillial's body, lunging at the humans. Several other refugees and some of the audience began to follow. The humans huddled together defensively. But in moments the Chirrn agitators had all been stunned by the baton-like weapons of the guards, who had acted quickly, realizing how little it would take to start a riot. The arbiter ordered another recess of several hours, and the prisoners were quickly taken to the relative safety of their cell.

The tribunal did not reconvene again for more than a day. When the next session finally began, the head tribune spoke. "The suggestion that our own secretiveness has contributed to this incident cannot be casually dismissed," he said gravely. The audience grumbled, but quieted under the glares of the arbiter and the guards. "We advise the Council to consider the installation of short-range beacons on Chirrn habitats."

"In that case, Honored Tribune," Cecilia spoke up, "I submit that the charge of negligence on our part has been disproven, and move that the case be dismissed."

"That would be premature," Rillial countered angrily. "The accused's contention that they have taken all reasonable steps to minimize risk is false. There is one fundamental risk they have taken that did not need to be taken at all. And that is their very means of transportation."

"You'll have to explain that," Cecilia said coldly.

"I shall," came the terse response. "A ramjet-driven spacecraft is an intrinsically hazardous form of transport. In order to gather the fuel necessary to accelerate to near-light speeds, it must use collimated-light projectors to ionize huge volumes of hydrogen gas so that it may be drawn into the ship by its magnetic field. A ramjet affects a volume of space much greater than the size of the vessel itself, exposing that volume to powerful optical and magnetic effects which could be disruptive at the very least to any nearby vessels.

"Additionally, the sheer velocity is a risk factor. At velocities so nearly approaching lightspeed, the craft's sensory beams barely precede the craft itself. Once an obstacle is detected, even the fastest computer barely has time to decide upon a course of action. Once one factors in the time for the sensory beam to travel out and return, the time for processing within the computer, the time for signals to travel along the web to the collimated-light projectors, the time for the focus node to change from reflective to transparent and to direct the beam to the desired target, and so on, there can be very little time remaining for the actual process of judgment in which the computer decides whether or not an object is inhabited. The risk is needlessly great."

"The risk is to our own ship at least as much as to anyone else's," Silbermann objected. "So we wouldn't take it if we didn't think it was reasonable. We took all those factors into account in our simulations, and there was still plenty of time left to make good judgments. Arachne's neural net is superconductive; her thought impulses travel even closer to lightspeed than she herself can. Plus, this technology's been tested and proven on more ships than just this one. It is safe, as safe as it needs to be."

Rillial whirled to face the tribunes, her tail almost knocking down Churrlaya. "*That* is the key question! *Need.* We must ask, did these humans *need* to travel this way at all?

"In fact, it is particularly surprising that we encountered a ramjet-using race where we did. The region of space we currently occupy was swept clean of most of its gas and dust by the waves of star formation and supernovae which swept through it in the distant past. In fact, it is the innermost of a cluster of four such bubbles, for which this region of the galaxy is well-known. Here, within this bubble, the gas density is roughly one-twentieth of the galactic norm."

"We're aware of that," Cecilia responded.

"So you are also aware that ramjets are far more inefficient here than they would be elsewhere in the galaxy. They must employ much larger collection fields, much more potent collimated-light projectors, to gather sufficient fuel. This is in fact the first time the Chirrn have encountered a ramjet within the Four Voids. In ten thousand years, the Chirrn have encountered few species that employ ramjets anywhere. Generally, they do not engage in interstellar travel until they develop gravity control. Those that do usually employ lightsail or particle-beam propulsion, or vessels that travel at low fractions of lightspeed; or they employ the Chirrn method of creating their own worlds that spend generations travelling between the stars. This is because a ramjet is a highly inefficient technology. The faster it travels, the harder it must accelerate incoming hydrogen ions radially toward its axis. Meanwhile, the very magnetic field on which it depends to draw in the interstellar medium creates a drag against that medium.

"Given the particular inefficiency of ramjets in this region, an inefficiency great enough to preclude other local species from using them at all...and an inefficiency of which the humans, by their own admission, are aware...we must ask why they have found it necessary to use them."

"The problems aren't insurmountable," Silbermann countered. "You just need a bigger collector web. The lower density cuts the fuel supply, but it also reduces drag, so that compensates for the loss of efficiency. We also make the ships extremely light with the rotating web design, so we need less fuel. And the lasers' energy demands go down the faster we go, since we have to tune them down to compensate for blueshift. Plus we do the bulk of the acceleration with particle beams, really, using the web as a magnetic sail—the ramjet's just to give us a few more percentage points of *c*, plus maneuverability if we need it."

"But why use the ramjet at all, when there are easier, if slower, ways to travel between stars?"

Stephen stepped forward. "While it's true that the resources of Sol System have made humanity wealthy, the planet Earth is still severely overcrowded. Not only does that put great strain on an ecosystem we're trying to restore to health, but it greatly increases the threat of plagues.

Earth spends as much effort fighting the new virulent diseases that keep cropping up as it does restoring the environment.

"So the people of Earth consider it their highest priority to reduce the planet's population. Of course, we encourage emigration to the other settled planets and artificial habitats of Solsys... but we recognize that even Solsys has its limits. And many of us do yearn to live on a planet without needing to huddle under domes and stare out at a barren wasteland. So part of the population-reduction program is an active search for habitable worlds in other star systems that we can colonize.

"Now, once a colony's established, we'll want to allow more humans to migrate there, if it's close enough to be practical. We want to be able to send the ship back for more colonists. And we want that process to happen as quickly as it can, so we use ramjets. They're the only thing practically able to travel at relativistic speeds."

Rillial pondered this for a moment before speaking. "So...you live on one planet and want to live on another. You want to find a naturally habitable planet, and must look to other systems to find one. And you are thus willing to go to extraordinary lengths, to engage in construction projects of truly immense scale and expend astronomical amounts of power, in order to fulfill this urge.

"But why?" she continued, turning and raising her voice to address the tribunal at large. "You have over a century of experience in space colonization. Over a billion humans live in artificial habitats, most of which are not located on planetary bodies. This mode of existence has proven viable for humans for over a century. Indeed, the enormous undertaking of constructing non-gravitic interstellar vessels would be impossible if you were limited to the resources of one planet. If space colonization had not proven successful, indeed highly prosperous, you could never have built a ramjet.

"So you know that human beings can lead successful, prosperous lives in space habitats. You know that generations of humans have lived, and lived well, without ever setting foot on a planet. And yet your desire to live on a planet like your Earth is so great...that you found it necessary to employ a highly inefficient, costly, and outright dangerous form of propulsion in order to accomplish it. A form of propulsion that killed nearly eighty-eight thousand four hundred Chirrn."

Rillial strode forward to look Stephen firmly in the eyes, her wide-set orbs swiveling inward to fix him from two directions, making him feel cornered, pinned down. "Why did those Chirrn die? Because you used a ramjet. Why did you use a ramjet? Because you wished to live on a planet.

"But did you *need* to live on a planet?" she hissed with anguish. "Tell me that, colony leader. Given all the alternatives, was there some vital need for you to ram your way recklessly through the cosmos merely to live the way your ancestors lived? Was your need to feel dirt beneath your feet so great, so overwhelming, that it justifies the slaughter of eighty-eight thousand lives?"

Stephen opened his mouth—and nothing came out but a soft choking sound. He remembered the devastation he'd seen. He remembered the bodies. And he could give no answer to Rillial's demand.

But Cecilia was not so speechless. "Now just wait a minute," she protested. "Just because you don't like living on planets doesn't make it immoral to do so. I refuse to allow my crew to be convicted due to nothing more than bigotry!"

Rillial glared at her. "It may not be immoral, but was it necessary? Living in a constructed world would not have killed you." She turned back to the tribunes. "But the humans' rejection of that option *did* kill eighty-eight thousand Chirrn."

"We have a right to live in whatever way we choose!"

"The rights of one being do not include the right to destroy the lives of other beings!" Rillial cried, her voice ringing through the tribunal chamber. "You cite free choice as your only reason for choosing planets, for needing ramjets. But that is not enough reason to justify the destruction of an entire nation! It is *not!*" Rillial lowered her brown-maned head, covering her eyes with her hands, and struggled for breath.

This time, instead of a furor, a ringing silence filled the courtroom. The silence was finally broken by whispers between the tribunes and the arbiter, and then by the arbiter's voice: "The tribunes will now recess to deliberate this case."

When court resumed two hours later, the head tribune stared gravely down at the humans. "It is a basic principle in both Chirrn and human law that the rights of the individual cease to be absolute when they threaten the rights or safety of others," he said. "Thus, it is the finding of this tribunal that free choice of habitat is not sufficient cause to justify the killing of eighty-eight thousand three hundred eighty-seven adults and children and the destruction of their nation. There were other viable alternatives to interstellar travel by ramjet that the defendants could have employed. Therefore the destruction of

Lesshchi was avoidable and unnecessary. Therefore the defendants are culpable for its destruction." He rose. "This tribunal will adjourn for eight time-units, after which we shall reconvene for sentencing proceedings."

As the chamber emptied, Cecilia stood rooted to the floor, eyes wide in outraged shock. Stephen stood beside her, just as immobile...but showing only resignation.

Cecilia paced out the limits of their cell like a caged tiger. "They can't do this!" she cried.

"Cecilia..." Stephen sighed. "They're ten thousand years more advanced than we are. They can do whatever the hell they want to us."

"I won't have that kind of defeatist attitude! And I won't let my crew be condemned as a result of the Chirrn's bigotry." She paced some more. "We need to contact Arachne somehow. If we can get her to focus her lasers on Shilirrlal—"

"Are you *crazy?!*" Stephen cried. "You want to commit ninety thousand *more* murders?!"

Cecilia glared at him. "Neither accident nor self-defense is murder. Besides, only the threat will be needed. We wouldn't actually do it."

"And what if they call our bluff? And even if they don't, how will the Chirrn see us then? As conquerors, destroyers, willing to cut down anyone who impedes our expansion into the universe. What will they do to Sol System if they decide we're that dangerous?"

Cecilia took him by the shoulders. "Stephen, listen to me. I know you're upset by all that's happened. Your compassion for the dead of an alien race is admirable. But their deaths are not our fault. The tribunal's decision is wrong, immoral. They're condemning us just because our beliefs differ from theirs. And I can't sit still and accept that. I have a responsibility for the safety of my crew and the success of our mission."

"And what about your responsibility for your own ship's wake?"

"What?"

"Isn't a captain supposed to consider herself responsible for the consequences of her vessel's passage? Isn't she supposed to take responsibility for all beings affected by her command?"

"Stephen, accepting responsibility is not the same as giving in to persecution! They're wrong to blame us for this!"

"Or maybe you just want to avoid the blame for it!" He pulled away from her, then faced her again after a moment. "Frankly, Cecilia, I feel we *are* responsible for those deaths. The Chirrn are right! We *didn't* have to build a ramship and race through the universe at ridiculous speeds. There are other options. We could've built more habitats. They still *are* building more habitats. On Luna, Mars, the Belt, the moons of Jupiter and Saturn...there's enough room in Solsys to hold a hundred billion people or more! And people thrive in artificial environments. It shouldn't matter whether the horizon curves down or up. It's not a cause worth destroying a nation over. Is it?" He cried out to all the prisoners. *"Is it?!"* He was met with only the echoes of his own voice.

Cecilia glared at him in contempt. "It wasn't our fault, Wong. We weren't responsible."

He met her glare in kind. "Keep telling yourself that, Cecilia. Maybe someday you'll convince yourself it's true."

"We understand that you are unfamiliar with our principles of justice," the head tribune told the defendants gathered in the courtroom. "Rest assured that we do not believe in punishment purely for the sake of retribution. Meeting destruction with destruction is wasteful and pointless.

"Those who commit destructive acts are required to compensate for them by doing constructive service. By making positive contributions, they repay for the damage they have done.

"It is the judgment of this tribunal that the forty human personnel of the ramship *Arachne* shall be imprisoned for the remainder of their lives in a research institution, where they will be studied by Chirrn scientists. By thus providing knowledge, you will repay your debt."

"That's barbaric!" Cecilia cried. "You have no right to treat sentient beings as lab animals!"

A pair of guards approached her menacingly with stun-sticks. "The prisoner will remain silent," the arbiter ordered.

"Thank you, arbiter," the head tribune said, before addressing the humans once more. "The experiments will be nondestructive and largely sociological in nature. You will not be subjected to cruelty. You will, however, not be free to refuse the experiments or to leave the facility. But such is the nature of imprisonment.

"As to the ramship *Arachne* herself, she will be stripped of her potentially destructive components and will be studied by Chirrn cyberpsychologists, to explore the ways in which humans have developed the cybernetic sciences. She, too, will contribute to our knowledge of the universe. You will be allowed to communicate with her as you desire.

"These judgments will be carried out immediately. The humans will be transported—"

"Um—Your Honor...Honored Tribunes?" Stephen interjected.

"Yes, Stephen Jacobs-Wong?"

"I wish to make a plea. Not on our behalf...but on behalf of the six hundred human embryos being carried on *Arachne*."

The tribunes looked at each other interestedly. "Please proceed."

Stephen took a moment to choose his words. "Each of those embryos has the potential to grow into a live human being, to live a full, normal life. None of those potential people has committed any crime. None of them has ever lived on a planet, except as an insensate cell. Surely they have a right to live, and to live in freedom. Surely they should not be prevented from being born, or born into captivity, because of our actions."

The tribunes discussed it briefly. "This is well said. We direct that the embryos shall be allowed to be born, under the guidance of Arachne, and raised on Shilirrlal."

"But that's not enough, Honored Tribunes. Our young are very dependent upon their parents for the first several years of their lives. They need human parents or parent-surrogates to help them develop their abilities, to provide them with basic socialization. Neither the Chirrn nor Arachne could fulfill this role sufficiently. Human children need human parents. And how would it affect them if the only others they knew of their own race were nothing but imprisoned criminals, or laboratory subjects?"

Stephen lowered his head. "Honored Tribunes, I do not seek leniency for myself. I was responsible for this mission, I was the one who started it all. I feel...profound guilt for every one of those eighty-eight thousand lives, and if it were just me I'd willingly accept your punishment. But the embryos, our potential children...they need us. And they need us to be free to raise them in a healthy and loving environment. So...isn't there any arrangement that could be made?"

The tribunes discussed this for a long time. As this went on, Stephen looked over his crewmates. There was a wide range of emotions on display. Most showed signs of the same grief Stephen felt. It made him proud that so many of his fellow humans could grieve for aliens as much as for their own. Many of the crew showed renewed hope at Stephen's proposal—hope for their own freedom, hope for their children yet unborn.

But some glared at him bitterly, resenting his admission of guilt, his statement that he would accept their punishment were it only for him.

Some showed fear at the aliens' power, anger at their imposition, dismay at the impending imprisonment. And none showed these emotions as intensely as Cecilia LoCarno, his good friend. As Stephen looked into her eyes, he realized that friendship was probably gone forever.

Finally, the tribunes addressed the chamber once again. "The finding of this tribunal was that the humans' planetary bias was the underlying cause of Lesshchi's destruction. Therefore: any humans who will renounce a planetary existence, who will sever all ties with planet-dwellers and those who associate with them, will be welcomed into Chirrn society. You will be given a homestead on Shilirrlal, or another Chirrn habitat as you choose, where you will be free to raise your children and contribute as equals to Chirrn society, thus repaying your debt. Those who do not renounce planetary existence will contribute instead as research subjects. You may have time to discuss this decision among yourselves."

As the humans gathered together, Cecilia glared angrily at the look on Stephen's face. "You can't actually be considering their offer! Win your freedom by renouncing your values and embracing theirs? What gives them the right to demand such a—a Shylockian surrender?"

Stephen sighed. "Cecilia, they're not asking us to change our religion, just our residency. Besides, they're the only law around. The crime was committed in their territory—hell, it was committed *against* their territory—and that makes us subject to their laws.

"Look, I'm not happy about it. But we're convicted criminals under their law, and we can't expect to walk away scot-free. And this way, at least we get to raise our children in freedom. Just not where we expected. Personally, it feels like getting off easy. But I'm going to take their offer, for the children's sake."

He stepped forward to face the tribunes. "Honored Tribunes, I accept your proposal. For the sake of our children, I renounce my planetary existence and ask that you let us live with you among the stars. I ask anyone else who will make this pledge to indicate it by stepping forward to join me."

The first to join him was Zena Bhatiani, who stepped forward without hesitation. "Live among an ancient alien culture?" she whispered up to Stephen. "That's better than any wilderness planet for me."

Others stepped forward in a slow trickle, some singly, some in groups. After long moments of stepping forward and retreating, Haim Silbermann finally advanced to join the others. "Someone's gotta be free to take care of Arachne," he shrugged. Finally, twenty-six others stood with Stephen, and only thirteen remained behind—with Cecilia LoCarno at their center.

"The tribunal accepts that those who stand with Stephen Jacobs-Wong have renounced their planetary existence," said the arbiter. "They are now free to live among us. The others will be welcome to join them at any time in the future if they will make the same renunciation."

"Never!" Cecilia cried. "We have the right to live as humans!"

Stephen saw something snap in her eyes at that moment. Lunging forward, she snatched the stun-stick from a guard and swung it wildly, knocking down the guards near her. She made a run for the exit...but was promptly tackled from behind by the very guards she thought she'd stunned. As they dragged her forward before the tribunes, she was muttering weakly, "How...?"

"Cecilia..." Silbermann said softly. "They're ten thousand years ahead of us. Even we have weapons that only respond to their owners."

"You don't have to be so smug about it," she snarled, throwing him a savage look.

Silbermann gazed at her sadly. "I'm not. I wish you could see that."

"Please, Captain LoCarno," the arbiter said. "Do not make this difficult on yourself. You cannot escape us."

"But I'll never surrender to you! I won't throw away my humanity like these traitors!"

"Cecilia, please understand," Stephen begged. "It's for the children."

She shot him a look that should have vaporized him like Lesshchi. "It's for yourselves."

"No," Stephen whispered.

Her eyes went from deadly hot to deathly cold. "You're all traitors to your race. I want nothing more to do with you." She almost seemed glad when the guards took her away.

Rillial gazed after her curiously. "Pitiful," she said. "To be so fanatical in her planetarism."

"I don't think that's it," Stephen said sadly. "I think she just can't accept being responsible for the loss of ninety thousand lives. It's just too big a tragedy; she can't live with the guilt. So she'll never be able to admit to guilt."

The refugee examined him. "But you can."

A tear came to Stephen's eye. "Barely. Rillial, I hope you can forgive me...forgive *us* for what we've done." He sighed. "I don't know if I'll ever be able to forgive myself."

Rillial just stood silently for a long moment. Then she said, "The important thing now is to decide what to do about other human ramships that might be out there. It is more important to prepare for the future than to dwell on the past." Stephen nodded solemnly, recognizing that it was the closest thing to forgiveness that Rillial would ever provide.

The arbiter, having left his podium, joined them. "Are there many other human ramships in space?"

"Well," Silbermann answered, "there wouldn't be that many. We've only been using them for a few decades. I daresay you wouldn't find any more than...ten parsecs from Sol."

"Excellent," the arbiter said. "It should be easy enough to locate all such ships and warn other Chirrn habitats to avoid them."

"Wouldn't that take a long time? Even centuries?" Stephen asked.

"We do possess trans-lightspeed spacewarp drive," Rillial told him. "Our habitats drift slowly, but we travel between them routinely in transport ships." Apparently, now that the humans had joined Chirrn society, they could be let in on their secrets.

Silbermann's eyes widened like a child discovering the Planet of Chocolate. "Warp drive? Really? Oh, well, it should've been obvious, you've got gravity control, so why couldn't you warp space, but how do you deal with the negative energy problem? The horizon problem? Or is it the Alcubierre model at all, do you use some other—"

"Haim!" Stephen chuckled. "Settle down. You'll have plenty of time to learn about it." But then his own eyes widened, and he turned to the Chirrn excitedly. "But this could solve the problem! If you went to Solsys, contacted them, shared your warp technology with them, it would eliminate the danger of ramjets completely! There wouldn't—"

"Take care," said L'chellin, who had joined them. "Remember, you have renounced all ties with Earth, and with all spacegoers who have ties with Earth. Do not forget so soon what that means."

"You must accept," the arbiter added, "that you are no longer a member of the human community. Their interests are no longer yours."

With that, the Chirrn left them. Stephen and the others stood there, alone in the echoing tribunal chamber, absorbing their new status in life. They were free to leave at any time, into a world they barely knew. For now, they remained.

"No longer members of the human community," Silbermann breathed. "Does that mean we aren't human anymore?"

"No," Zena Bhatiani said. "We're just not Terrans anymore. Not Solar humans, or planetary humans. We're star-people now."

Silbermann scoffed. "Sounds poetic, sure. But it's not by choice." He shook his head. "At least the captain still belongs. She may not have her freedom...but she's still a member of the human race."

"What good is it to be human without being humane?" Stephen whispered. "We've done this to repent for our crime, for causing a disaster we didn't have to cause. We owe it to the Chirrn to make up for the loss we caused them, by joining their society and helping them to build and grow.

"And, most of all, we've done this for the sake of the unborn humans in our care. This is the only choice we could make, for their sake. It's not an ideal situation...but it's the only one that I, for one, can live with."

Zena looked up at him searchingly. "But when our children ask where we came from...what do we tell them?"

"We tell them the truth," Silbermann said with certainty. "Just like my parents told me. My father's ancestors murdered my mother's ancestors in the Nazi Holocaust. They didn't keep that from me. No, they made sure I knew...so that I could make sure it never happened again."

After a long silence, Stephen spoke again. "Come on, my friends. We set out to build a new world for ourselves. And now it's time to begin."

The Weight of Silence

The first thing you should know is, I'm not that good with words. The only way I can think of to start this thing is, "If you're reading this, it means I'm dead." But that just sounds so melodramatic. Besides, if Miguel and I do live through this, I'll want to read it again, just to remind myself that I *can* read again. I never knew how much I'd miss that, just seeing letters and translating them into sounds, just plain *using* my senses so effortlessly, without thinking, though it's really so amazing how the mind does it.

Anyway. I'm babbling. If you're reading this, you must be totally confused now. Unless you're me. Hi, me! How am I? Confused yet? I know I am.

Okay, I'm over that fit of the giggles, plus having to explain to Miguel why I was shaking so hard, and then he started shaking so hard—but anyway, let me try to start over. My name is Monali Chen. I'm a physicist, when I'm not being a singer. My friend over there is Miguel Oroxco, who's a Dashing Space Pilot and engineer. He does other things, but only as hobbies, and he doesn't put that much effort into them—except womanizing, which he gave up when we got together, and being Dashing, which he thinks of as part of his job anyway. (I don't get why "dashing" is such a suave and romantic thing to be. It sounds to me like you're always running around out of breath.)

We're the whole crew of the XQ-3, which is a testbed for a

prototype sub-luminal warp generator. The press keep calling it a warp engine, but the press don't listen very well when we tell them we're still decades away from that at least, that we're still testing out just how much we can do with PQM, and we're a long way from actually incorporating that with the other systems that you'd need to make a sustainable warp bubble, and then there are so many other problems to work out, like the visibility issue (ironic, that) and the heat dissipation problem, and I'm babbling again, aren't I? I did warn you.

Okay, me, remember what Mrs. Pfriem always told me in English class: don't make assumptions about what your audience might know—assume they don't know it and explain it to them. I never really understood that, since she was the only person who read my essays and I knew *she'd* read the book and would already know what I was talking about! But I guess here it makes sense.

PQM is programmable quark matter. Just like the smart matter in your walls and clothes and such contains bound electrons that can be arranged to simulate virtual atoms and their chemical and electrical properties, even ones that don't occur in nature, so the bound quarks and gluons in PQM can be organized to simulate virtual exotic particles and forces. These particles' brane tension can be adjusted to produce large positive and negative masses in the right configurations to deform spacetime into exotic shapes such as warp bubbles. (I'm basically quoting the usual press release from memory here. Not my own words. Still, it just sounds so clunky and wrong. It's so much clearer as equations.)

Umm, sorry, where was I? I went to sleep for a while after that last paragraph, I don't know how long. This is such a struggle to write, and obviously I can't go back and review—no, I guess it's not obvious, I haven't explained that yet, have I? God, I wonder if this is even going to be legible. At best it'll take a huge amount of editing. How embarrassing that would be, to be found dead, and have them discover I'd made this slow, laborious effort to record my final thoughts for posterity, only to find they couldn't read it.

You'd think Miguel would be the one doing this. He usually has no trouble expressing himself—well, in most ways. But maybe that's why he doesn't want to try it this way. He'd find it too frustrating. But I'm used to it being hard.

Though I guess the new thing is that I'm trying anyway. Miguel teased me about that, almost from the day we met—how quiet I was. It was his way of flirting with me, trying to draw me out. At first I hoped he'd just tire of it and go away. Not that I didn't like him, but I already had a man back home on Mars.

Though I wasn't really happy with...let's call him "George." Things were rocky, when we were together. "George" was...no, not exactly selfish. It's just that he wasn't *attuned* to my feelings, my needs. Since it's hard for me to put them into words, I needed someone who could just sense them, you know? I needed someone I could have a rapport with, and "George" wasn't it. (Plus he always called me "Mo." I never liked that.) In a way, things were easier between us now that I was off on Ceres. Which maybe meant being close wasn't right for us.

With Miguel, it was different. Sure, he was brash and arrogant and liked to sow his wild oats...but the reason he was so successful with women wasn't just his looks, it was because he respected them, and really *meant* his flattery, and gave instead of taking. The only problem was that he couldn't settle on just one woman to devote himself to. Some of his lady friends told me they didn't mind sharing, because he never made any false promises about what they could expect. But some of them ended it because they wished he could take all that generosity and focus it on just one woman.

So anyway, I figured Miguel would lose interest in me because I was taken, and because he had plenty of other candidates. But the more we worked together, the more he tried to romance me. I explained that I was committed to "George," but he looked at me and said, "Nali, I don't go where I'm not welcome. If I felt you were happy with him, I wouldn't keep offering you an alternative. The way you look when you talk about him...I see duty, not fulfillment."

But then he backed down and shook his head. "But don't listen to me. I could be reading into it what I want to see." He took my hand and gazed so deep into my eyes. "I can't trust myself to be objective about you, Monali. I have far, far too much of a personal stake in you. So maybe I should trust your judgment and leave you alone—but I don't see how I could bear to do that."

At that moment, I realized this wasn't just his usual infatuation—he was in love with me! And I was falling in love with him too. And the more I reminded myself of my commitment to "George," the more it felt like duty, not fulfillment.

If Miguel had aggressively tried to seduce me, he probably could've. But he didn't try. Maybe he knew he didn't have to. He was just waiting until I was ready. And pretty soon I was. I just didn't know what to do about it. I didn't know how I could tell "George." I didn't know how to tell Miguel, even.

So one day I just let it happen. We were working together in the XQ-3 cockpit, taking string resonance readings and calibrating the controls. I was on the wrong side of him to work a control I needed to keep adjusting...so I just leaned across, pressing my body against him over and over. I could feel him burying his face in my hair, smelling it.

Pretty soon he got the message, and we made love right here in this cockpit, without my having to say a word.

Telling "George" was the hard part. I ended up sending him a letter. I know, it sounds awful, and it is, but it would've been worse if I'd had to do it face-to-face and think up the words as I went. Or that was my excuse, anyway. I'm rethinking a lot of things lately.

Hi, I'm back. If I remember right, I was reminiscing about how Miguel and I got together. I hope you don't think that was self-indulgent. I really should be telling you about the test flight that got us into this mess.

Basically the idea of the XQ-3 is to move a ship by moving the spacetime around it relative to the rest of spacetime—like the warp principle, but without actually reaching effective superluminal speed. We're still a long way from tackling all the practical problems that would bring. This was a much simpler proof-of-concept thing, getting to know how to use PQM to distort spacetime, and analyzing the effects. If nothing else, we could get a nifty reactionless drive out of it.

I actually hadn't felt we were ready for a crewed test flight yet. I wasn't sure we'd completely ruled out the possibility of chaotic brane-resonance feedback. But Miguel was eager to get out there, and I couldn't muster a solid enough argument to sway the team, at least not as much as Miguel could sway them with his confidence and charm and general Dashingness. I mean, everyone knew about the risk, but they decided it was under control. The best I could manage was to get myself invited along to ride herd on the readings.

Miguel wasn't too happy about that. He thought I was being too conservative, that I'd cramp his style or something. I didn't want him to think I wasn't being supportive, so I tried not to make a nuisance of myself. It was a quiet trip. We were the only two human beings for millions of klicks around, and we didn't have much to say to each other.

Wait, I'm confusing you again, aren't I? I was telling you before about how madly in love we were, how happy and perfect everything was. Well, it was, mostly. We'd done the whole moony-eyed, can't stand to be apart, sneak off to the closet every chance we get kind of thing. He'd learned to share my love of show tunes, I'd gotten into his kite-flying hobby, we'd done the long walks holding hands under the artificial sky, had deep heart-to-heart conversations about our innermost feelings....

But that was the problem. I'm not good with words, remember? Talking about my feelings, it's...it's harder than talking about physics, but I don't have any nice, neat equations to use instead. Whatever I try to say, it just doesn't seem right.

With "George," that wasn't such a problem. He wasn't all that open about his feelings either. But Miguel was. It was part of why he was such a hit with women—he could communicate with them about what mattered to them.

And he really opened up to me. In our long nights together, he told me everything, all his deep dark secrets. He told me about the romances that had really mattered to him and what had gone wrong with them. He told me how he'd been trapped in a cave as a little boy and was still somewhat claustrophobic (which was why he'd had the whole top half of the XQ3's cockpit coated with a video membrane, so he could see outside despite the massive PQM cage surrounding it). And he told me other things I won't tell you about because it's not my place. Things he didn't tell other women, things that went a whole lot deeper than what he usually shared with his lady friends.

The problem was, he expected me to do the same. He wanted to know everything about my family, my childhood. He prodded me to talk about "George" and what had gone so wrong there. Most of all, he wanted me to put my feelings for him into words, to tell him what he meant to me, what I loved about him, what role I saw him playing in my life. But I couldn't give him that. It wasn't that I didn't want to. I just couldn't figure out how to communicate what I felt. I tried really hard. I wrestled with my brain for hours at a time, trying to squeeze the right words out of it. I mean, they're all in there, collected from all the English classes I took and all the books I've ever read. I remember most of them, even the screwy ones like "ombudsman" and "gormless" and "viz." which is pronounced "namely." But whenever I try to search for the right words to go with my feelings, they just don't seem to be in there. My friends tell me I explain myself fine, but I know I'm not—that what they hear may make sense to them, but it wasn't really what I meant. Or at best, it's something I had to struggle to find. That's why I'm better with letters than conversations.

But Miguel couldn't accept that. "Maybe you're just not trying hard enough," he'd say. "Monali, I've bared my soul to you, because I thought we were ready for that kind of intimacy. Was I wrong? Is there a reason you're holding back? Don't you trust me enough to share this with me?" I tried to reassure him, but I couldn't put my money, or rather my words, where my mouth was. Or where my heart was, I mean.

I'm afraid I'm making it sound like he was pushing me into this, some kind of emotional bullying. That wasn't it. He did his best to understand, and when I said I couldn't find the words, he nodded and stepped back and gave me time to think of them. But I couldn't think of them, and he still needed to hear them, needed that gesture of trust. And it hurt him that I couldn't. "Maybe you aren't really over 'George' after all," he said one day, not long before the test flight, though of course he didn't say "George." "Maybe you feel I'm not the right man for you."

"No," I assured him. "I love you completely."

But he needed me to say more, and I couldn't. "I believe you believe that, Nali. But I'm not sure if you really *feel* it."

"And...and what do you feel? About...being right for...each other?" (Amazing how well I remember the words, even the pauses. Maybe it's the sensory deprivation.)

He just looked at me. "Maybe I'll decide when you decide."

Soon after that I saw him flirting with other women again. I didn't believe he'd made love to any of them, but it made me afraid. If nothing else, it meant I wasn't enough for him anymore.

I guess that was part of why I felt I had to come along on the test flight. I hoped that being together, as totally alone as any two human beings had ever been, might help somehow. But all it did was concentrate the tension. I had no idea what to say, and Miguel was happy to be quiet right back. Actually I was feeling afraid that maybe after being so alone with me with so little joy, he'd just feel more compelled to be with other women afterward.

Anyway, he started to get bored with the routine maneuvers we were making. (Routine! We were out past Saturn! The Sun was a tiny speck! Some routine!) He wanted to do something Dashing, probably to take his mind off having me there. So he decided to try some loops and flips and things, tweaking the PQM array to alter the shape of the field. I advised against it. "You're being too cautious again," he said testily. "We have to put this technology through its paces sooner or later. It'll be no use if it isn't robust enough to handle unexpected changes."

"I just don't think we're there yet. There's still too much we don't know."

"And how will we ever know unless we try? Hah? You never get anywhere if you don't take chances, Monali."

"We need more simulations...."

"You've done months of simulations with nothing conclusive. Eventually, you just have to for God's sake *try* something!"

I was starting to realize that we weren't just talking about the experiment anymore. And that pretty much scuttled any logical arguments I could come up with. "Maybe you're right," I finally said. And I meant it. I decided I needed to trust him. I hoped my backing down would get that across to him. But if anything, he looked disappointed that I'd closed off again. Then he just sighed, shook it off, and lost himself in piloting.

Now, I'm not saying he was responsible for the accident. At this point, we don't know what went wrong. We do know there was a coherent feedback anomaly in the brane-resonance patterns. It somehow increased the gravitational coupling constant and sped us up faster than we planned to go. That's actually a good thing. We'd thought the feedback would collapse the field entirely, not intensify it. And the effect seemed stable, continuing to accelerate us toward lightspeed for maybe twenty minutes (with no time dilation, because it's space-warping) while we tried to get it under control. If anything, Miguel stumbled onto something useful, something that could save us years of work.

So what happened then? I don't know. Maybe a micromete got past the deflection contour in the warpfield. I doubt it, since at those effective speeds that would probably have vaporized us. Maybe it was some kind of unanticipated exotic-particle reaction. It may have been something utterly mundane, like an overload in the power systems.

Anyway, all I knew was that the console blew up in our faces.

Okay, this time I remember where I left off last night, because it was one of those dramatic cliffhanger moments that grab you when you read them. How'd it work? Anyway, back to our Exciting Tale:

I think I was unconscious for a while. I can't be sure, since the first thing I was aware of after the explosion was *nothing*. No light, no sound, no touch. I was adrift in a void. For a moment I thought I was dead. I really didn't want the afterlife to be all this nothingness, so I panicked. And I felt the reassuring impact of my flailing legs against the cockpit wall. And then, once I was aware of my body again, I realized I was in a lot of pain. My face felt like the worst sunburn I've ever had times twenty. I remembered the explosion, and I called out to Miguel.

And I couldn't hear myself!

I screamed as loud as I could, but I couldn't hear anything. I was deaf! Of course, the explosion in such tight quarters...and that bloody video membrane of Miguel's, a smooth hemisphere, I was always complaining about how it reflected and amplified every tiny sound....I felt my ears, and they were both bleeding.

And then I realized I couldn't see anything. There should be something, even if the power went out. There were emergency lights, smart-matter panels that stored acoustic energy. The very sound that had deafened me would've given them enough power to glow for weeks. But I couldn't see them. I held my wristcom before my eyes and tapped the light button—nothing. But it felt completely intact, and it unfolded and refolded like it was supposed to. It worked... I just couldn't see it. Or anything else.

I could certainly feel the tears forming, but I fought them since they burned my eyes, and we were in freefall so they'd cling. I tried to force myself to remain calm. But then a horrible thought struck me. I'd screamed for Miguel and he hadn't come to me.

I pushed myself off the wall, spreading my arms, and soon one arm hit him. He jerked in surprise and flailed wildly at it. At least he was alive—but he hadn't heard me calling, hadn't seen me coming. I grabbed at his arms, which were waving around randomly. I realized he had to be as blind and deaf as I was.

Soon he realized it was me, and he flung his arms around me desperately, and I did the same to him. All our tension and arguing were forgotten. We clung to each other like our lives depended on it, needing each other more than ever, since we both knew the stakes. We were alone, off course, astronomical units away from settled space. (Just about all the planets are on the same side of the Sun this year, and we'd decided to do our tests on the empty side as—ha!—a safety precaution.) We had no way of knowing if anyone even knew where we were. And we had no AI onboard to call for help. We didn't even know if the comm system was working, and even if we tried it, we couldn't hear a response.

Miguel was trembling against me. At first I thought he was cold, but it was rhythmic, convulsive, and I realized he was sobbing. It got worse, and I could feel he was beginning to panic. It must have been a claustrophobic attack. A part of me was tempted to panic right along with him, but I knew I had to comfort him, calm him. But how? Holding him wasn't helping. Oh, how I wished I could sing to him! That always soothed him. But he couldn't hear me now!

I tried it anyway, singing as loud as I could into his ear, hoping he still had at least a little hearing. It was one of his favorites: *"Nothing's gonna harm you, /Not while I'm around...."* But it didn't do any good. And it didn't work so well *fortissimo*. Dammit, there had to be some way to get through to him!

I took his hand, tried putting it against my lips as I sang. He started to get the message, paying attention at least, but he still seemed confused. So I took his other hand and tapped out the rhythm in it as I sang: *Tap-tap-tap-tap-tap-tap... tap-tap-tap, tap-tap.* Soon he got the message. His memory filled in the rest. I finished the song with my lips against his. We were both burned, so it hurt, but we didn't care.

We managed to find the first aid kit and carefully rubbed regen gel (either that or strangely soothing toothpaste) on each other's burns. Maybe we should've done it on ourselves, but we needed each other's touch. I counted my blessings, thanking Krishna that neither of us had traditionalist parents. An old-style, unaugmented human might've been killed in the blast, or been burned more severely and died from infections.

I kept "singing" to Miguel, but he couldn't always recognize the tune from the rhythm alone. So it hit me to use his fingers as a treble clef—I tapped his fingertips for Every Good Boy Deserves Favour and the webs between his fingers for FACE. Pretty soon we began developing a shorthand, using song snatches to represent words and ideas. "When Did This Happen?" I finger-sang, meaning *how* did this happen (close enough). "Give Me Time," he replied from the same musical. "Out of Control," "Maybe There's Hope" and "Putting it Together," he went on—I figured he meant he was going to see if he could get any control over the systems. He didn't know as many songs off the top of his head as I did, so his end of the conversation was a bit choppy.

There was nothing for a while, and then he came back and told me "Out of Control," "She Just Wouldn't Listen." I guessed that meant the controls wouldn't respond. "Maybe It's For the Best," I replied. "Where Do We Go From Here?" "Flying Blind." We couldn't read the sensors, had no way of knowing which way the Sun and civilization were. "A Cry in the Dark," "Rescue Me," "Can It Be?" I asked. But even if we could get the comm system working, we had no idea where to point the laser, and the backup radio might not be strong enough to reach, depending on how far out we were. "The Breath of Life," I asked, "How Long Can This Go On?"

At that point, we realized we had to get some control over the systems, even if we couldn't see them. Luckily, Miguel had helped put this thing together, and now it was time to test his claims that he could rebuild it blindfolded. I helped as best I could, and as time went on our song language became more technical. "Greased Lightning" for electricity, "The Warmth of Your Touch" for temperature, "As Time Goes By" for time, "I'm Drawn to You" for gravity. Numbers were easy, just tapped out on the palm. But it was still cumbersome. I realized that if we could use the fingers for the notes, we could use them for letters too. So once we'd managed to get the air cyclers up and felt their gentle breeze, we took some time out to learn a new code. It used the same nine positions as the treble-clef code, fingertips and webs, but three times over for the whole alphabet. One tap on the thumb tip was A, two was B, three was C, then on to the web for DEF, and so on. Not as elegant as proper sign language, I'm sure, but we'd never had occasion to learn any.

Anyway, eventually we figured a few things out. Life support was good, for now. We got power to the controls, but not all the maneuvering jets responded (we could tell that much by feel, whether the capsule moved or not). And the comm system seemed intact, on the inside anyway—we couldn't tell about the exterior laser or antenna array. There was only one way to do that, and to check the unresponsive jet. *Must go out,* Miguel spelled to me.

I tried to protest. How could he manage it without his eyes? He insisted he could do it by feel, but how could he be sure he could feel enough through the gloves, even with their haptic feedback layer? *Scared too,* he said, then finger-sang "There Is No Other Way."

I've never been more afraid in my life than when Miguel went out there. I was alone in the cockpit, who knows for how long, and I had no way of knowing if he was safe, if he'd ever come back in. What if we hadn't fit the suit's seals right, what if he hadn't attached the line securely enough? What if there were some loose component that had shocked him, or what if there were quark-matter fragments floating around out there that could puncture his suit? What if...

What if the man I loved died not knowing whether I was truly committed to him?

I tried to distract myself by singing, letting my mind fill in the sound. But it was hard to stay focused. Too many songs are about loss and fear and uncertainty—the good ones, anyway. I tried to think about what I could say to Miguel to fix things between us, but that just called attention to the possibility of never getting the chance. I tried running through the tensor field equations, trying to figure out what had caused our burst of acceleration, but I had trouble keeping track without a screen or page to look at them on.

Maybe the real reason I couldn't focus on anything else is that I didn't want to stop thinking about Miguel while he was alone out there. It would've felt like a betrayal. He needed my thoughts to be with him, since there was nothing else I could do.

But how long could I wait? When might I decide he'd been out too long? And then what could I do? Go out myself and try to find him? What if I didn't? What if he were floating just meters away but I couldn't see him? What if I went out just before he came back in, and then he found me gone? What if he came out to look for me and something happened to him then? How could I do that to him?

I'd never felt so helpless.

When I finally felt a hand brush against me, I jumped in panic. I guess I'd been floating in mid-cockpit and hadn't felt the lock cycling. Isn't that ironic, that the one thing I wanted the most happened and I was terrified? But we got that worked out soon, and I clutched Miguel and the hell with status reports, I did him right there. We clung together for hours, and I spent a lot of them just tapping out *I lv U* on his fingers over and over.

I guess he was happy to hold off telling me the bad news. He'd fixed the thruster, but there was just a jagged stump where the comm laser and antenna should be. Not only were we blind and deaf, we were mute too. We couldn't call for help.

Maybe there was a chance they could find us, Miguel said. They'd be looking, certainly. And we couldn't have cracked lightspeed—that would've taken an impossible amount of energy with this setup—so we couldn't be more than a couple AUs off course. Maybe someone had seen what direction we'd gone and could narrow the search down.

But we'd already been pretty far out when it started, over ten AUs from Sol. We'd left the chase ships behind long before the acceleration burst. We'd done it with a reactionless drive, so there was no exhaust trail to follow. And we were in a six-meter-wide capsule with a low-albedo hull (and whose dumb idea was that?). There are still meteoroids and comets our size that nobody's discovered yet, after centuries of looking.

And even with the recycler and bioprinter units working, our food supply wouldn't last forever. We couldn't wait around for outside rescue. If there was a way out of this, we'd have to figure it out for ourselves.

So: you're blind and deaf with no AI, stuck in the outer system, and you need to figure out how to get back to civilization. How? Our thrusters worked, the PQM coils were intact and working, but which way did we need to point ourselves? If we fired at random, we'd just make it worse. And the thrusters were too dim to work as signal flares at this distance.

Besides, even if we figured out which way the Sun was, just thrusting inward wouldn't take us inward—it would just put us into a more elliptical orbit that'd soon send us farther out. What you have to do is thrust forward and slow down, falling into a lower orbit. But even if we could figure out which way the Sun was, we still wouldn't know which way we were facing in our orbit, couldn't know whether we were thrusting forward, backward, or sideways.

But we realized that, so long as the PQM drive worked (and it seemed intact as far as we could tell), we could just space-surf in whatever direction we picked until we stopped. And when we stopped, we'd have our current orbital velocity, which would be too slow for that location, so we'd fall further inward. (Come to think of it, we still had our original momentum now but were farther out, so we were probably a bit above escape velocity. We might cross the magnetopause in fifty or sixty years, if we didn't figure something out.)

But which way was the Sun? If we'd been closer in, maybe we could've told by feeling its warmth through the airlock's viewport. But of course if we'd been closer, we wouldn't have been in such a fix. And out here the Sun gave no warmth to speak of.

We decided to expend some thruster fuel on an experiment: turning the radio up full blast, placing our hands on the speaker, and rotating the ship. We hoped maybe the remains of the antenna could pick up the radio noise of the Sun, or of the civilization around it, and that it would be loud enough for us to feel the vibrations. But we could barely feel them, and there were several directions where we picked up variance in the static. One could've been the Sun, one could've been Jupiter, the others could've been anything. Our imaginations, even. Some of them seemed to show up once and then couldn't be found again. And there wasn't any one direction where they concentrated, not that we could be sure of. Heck, who knew if the strongest signal came from where the antenna stump was pointing? Maybe the jagged shape was picking up the strongest off to the side somewhere.

We tried to think of some way to use the PQM itself. Could we set it to simulate particles that would emit some kind of radiation as a signal flare? No—reprogramming it that extensively, to produce nongravitational effects, would require quark-scale adjustments that we didn't have the equipment to make. Could we take advantage of the accident, increase our gravitational constant again and somehow pull ourselves inward? No, we didn't know enough about the accident to recreate that effect, especially if we wanted it independent of the warpfield.

Miguel had the idea that increasing our mass might decrease our orbital velocity by conservation of momentum. But I pointed out that the energy we used to generate the extra mass increased our momentum too, so our velocity wouldn't change. Besides, even if it did, at this distance orbital decay would take decades.

So we set aside the PQM and began looking for more conventional approaches. After a while Miguel thought he had it: If we could just stretch out a long tether with a weight at the end, a few kilometers maybe, then it would gradually align radially with the Sun. The whole thing would orbit with the velocity of its center of mass, so the inner part would be going too slow and fall in while the outer part would be too fast and move outward, pulling the tether taut between them—the same kind of tidal stabilization that orbital habitats use. That would tell us which way the Sun was, he said, since the heavier end (us) would naturally fall inward.

He was so excited, I hated to break it to him that it didn't work that way. It didn't matter which end was heavier, only where they were in their orbits. The one starting farther out would end up farther out. At best it'd only give us a fifty/fifty chance of pointing the right way.

Miguel wasn't convinced. To him, having the heavier mass end up farther out seemed unstable, like a bowling pin standing on its head. I struggled to explain why that intuition only made sense for something standing still or dangling like a pendulum, not for something in freefall with nothing to cause drag (well, except the very tenuous solar wind out here).

Either I wasn't explaining it right or he just didn't want to hear it. He'd convinced himself this was the way to save us—or at least that it would improve our odds to one in two, and that was good enough to chance it. I think the claustrophobia was still affecting him—he was desperate to do something to get out of this. I had to make him see reason.

So I kept at it. I pointed out that, given how slow our orbital velocity was, it'd probably take weeks or months for the tether to align right anyway. And I reminded him that we didn't have nearly enough cabling in the capsule to make such a long tether. There were kilometers of nanotube cabling wrapped around the PQM cage, but even if we could figure out how to uncoil it safely, we'd render the drive useless.

It was those simple realities that finally convinced him. I could tell how much it hurt him to give up this hope, but in the end he had no choice.

We were both pretty dejected after that. So we decided to knock off for the day and start fresh again after a good night's (?) sleep.

We didn't actually get much sleep. Too nervous. *We should talk,* Miguel spelled into my hand after a while. *In case we don't make it.* (It was more abbreviated and textish than that, but I've spelled it out for you.)

We'll get back, I said. *Talk then. You know it's hard for me. Even harder now.*

I felt him shake with laughter. *You kidding? Look what you did. Invented a whole new way to talk. Got through to me when I really needed it. Talked me out of a dumb idea. Yes, it's harder now – but you did it anyway.*

After that, I was at a loss for words. But not for long. I realized he was right—when I really had to, I'd figured out a way to express myself. If I could do it when our lives were at stake, why couldn't I do it when our relationship was at stake? So I did. Slowly, laboriously, almost as much as writing this account has been, I talked about how I felt. I told him what he meant to me, as much as I could. And where I couldn't, I explained to him why it was different for me, that just because I expressed it in actions rather than words, that didn't mean I felt it any less.

We finger-talked for hours, and somehow the difficulty of it helped us communicate, because we were both "listening" so much more carefully. We figured out a lot of stuff. He realized he'd been unfair to demand I show my feelings as verbally as he did—that it was really just his insecurity, his need for validation. I hadn't known he felt that kind of self-doubt. But together we realized it was part of the reason he'd slept around so much before—because he didn't trust in his ability to earn any one woman's lasting affections. But he really wanted our relationship to last, he told me. In fact, he left me speechless again.

He proposed.

He said he'd been thinking about it, but his self-doubt had made him unsure whether I could really love him for a lifetime. That's why he'd been pushing me for validation. And when I didn't give it to him, he used that as an excuse. On some subconscious level, he'd been looking for an out, so he got the idea that maybe I wanted to go back to "George." He said that was really pathetic, but I told him I understood and it was okay. Mainly, I was just amazed at what this meant—that *he'd* been the one to have trouble communicating. And that his insistence on my communication problems had just been a way of dodging that.

Well, anyway, we learned a lot about each other that night... day... however long it took. Then we held each other for hours, had pretty good sex (allowing for our clumsiness in freefall), and talked about all the things we'd do when we got married, and what we'd name our kids, and how I'd teach them to sing and Miguel would help them build racing kites....

And then it hit me. Something that had been in the back of my mind since the day before. *The solar wind.* It was very, very faint out here, less than a tenth of a nanopascal of pressure—but that might still be enough, if we had the right kite.

Kite?? Miguel asked, scrawling two question marks in my palm for emphasis. *Where do we get one?*

We already have one, I explained. *Your precious video dome. Not like we need it anymore.* I explained: the video membrane was hair-thin, but it formed a dome nearly five meters across. Very large area, very low mass. The acceleration would still be tiny, but we only needed it to move a few meters. We'd attach it to a spacesuit cable, hook it to the anchor point next to the airlock, and wait. I estimated that, taking the cable's mass into account, it might take from one to four days to move ten meters, depending on the wind pressure. Well, if it started out with the solar wind blowing directly into it, that is. At an angle, it'd take longer. Still, it didn't need to move that much. Periodically we'd go out and feel which way the cable was pointing, and then turn the ship to face the other way. We'd do a few more adjustments like that until our "wind sock" stayed straight out from the airlock, which was in the back of the capsule, so at that point we'd be facing the Sun. Then we'd just turn on the PQM drive for a couple of hours, which would put us back in the inner system and increase our chances of being sighted.

It wasn't a sure thing. Even in the inner system, there was no guarantee we'd be spotted before our supplies ran out. We couldn't completely rule out the possibility of crashing into something. And we couldn't be sure the drive wouldn't malfunction again and plunge us into the Sun or, more likely, clear out the other side of the system. But we'd sure be better off than we were now.

We both cut up our fingers trying to peel that damn membrane off the ceiling. It was pretty flexible, but it liked to snap back to its natural shape, so we both got pinned by it a bunch of times. I was glad I couldn't see us, because we must've looked completely ludicrous. But we finally managed to roll the thing up somehow, punch a few holes near the rim, and tie spacesuit tethers through them. Then we had to fold the rolled-up thing into thirds to get it into the airlock. We could only hope it would spring back to normal again once Miguel pushed it out. Anyway, soon he came back in and told me it was done. Now we had days to wait.

So we went ahead and got married. We argued for a while about which one of us was the captain of the ship, then decided to take turns being captain and marry ourselves twice just to be on the safe side. Plus that way we get to take a double-long honeymoon when we get back. Though we didn't waste any time getting a headstart on our honeymooning. I mean, it's not like we had much else to do.

Well, except touch-typing out this log on my wristcom, and hoping I'm hitting the right letters so this will be legible. As I write this, it's been about a day since our third check of the "kite." After our first check, Miguel said the tether felt straight and was pointing at a sharp angle to where it had started, so it seemed to be working, as far as we could tell. So we turned the ship and waited again, and then we found it at an angle again, though less so, so we turned again. And so on. At this point we have no idea if we'll get a good enough fix before our supplies run out, or if the drive will work, or if anyone will find us even if it does. So if you find this and we're dead, know at least that we died as husband and wife, and were happy together at the end.

That is, if you can read this at all.

Afterword

Hi, folks, this is Monali. As I'm sure you heard on the news—or could guess by reading the above—we eventually got a directional fix and fired up the drive. We stopped when we figured we were fairly close to the Belt, and started firing our thrusters as signal flares. Within a couple of days, we got picked up, and they rushed us to the hospital, and right now I'm getting used to my regrown eyes and synthetic eardrums. Which means I got to see the mess I'd typed up and be embarrassed at how scrambly it was. But this magazine bought the rights to our story, and hooked me up with a writer who helped me polish it.

I was amazed they wanted this bunch of scribbles. "I'm no writer," I insisted, telling my collaborator that he'd be better off just interviewing me and writing his own version. But he insisted I'd done a good job. I told him how hard it had been, how much I'd had to struggle to find the right words, how it still felt wrong to me at the end.

So he gave me a quote from Thomas Mann: "A writer is someone for whom writing is more difficult than it is for other people."

I still think he's a shameless flatterer. But I guess you can decide that. Now I'm going to go off on that double honeymoon with my husband. Hopefully, once we get back they'll have figured out what caused the accident and we can try again.

Though maybe after that I'll try turning this into a musical....

Murder on the Cislunar Railroad

A murder was taking place before Zachary March's eyes, and there was nothing he could do to stop it. Indeed, he only had the victim's word that she was being murdered at all.

"This was no accident," Jaya Ramanathan told him over her suit comm as she fell Earthward. "The Railroaders planted false leads to that docking cage... rigged it to launch once I was inside. Cold bastards," she grated. "Think we're obsolete, disposable. You hear me, traitors?" she cried out over the open line. "How long will the bots let *you* live once you've served your purpose?"

"Don't give up," March told his fellow Cybercrime Unit investigator. "Maybe a rescue ship can still reach you."

"Don't try to comfort me, March, you're no good at it." Regrettably, she was right. He'd checked the rosters and scans, figured the odds. He could see, as the cameras tracked her for the benefit of potential rescue ships, just how fast she fell. It was surely no coincidence that Nexus One's docking cradle had released at just the right moment and tether radius to catapult her onto a reentry path that no ship docked at the rotovator station could intercept. But March kept thinking. He refused to believe there was a puzzle without a solution.

March himself was still too distant to help. It was chance that he was here at all. He'd been investigating the hijacking of some aerial weather drones in the central Pacific, and the data trail had led him to a 'stroid mining company managed by one Stavros DiCenzo. Terrestrial weather wouldn't interest a Strider; DiCenzo was probably just one stop on the hijackers' false trail of transactions. It was most likely some petty prank, but it was a puzzle to solve. March had reached DiCenzo just before the Strider set out for Nexus One on business of his own. But he'd gotten little out of it besides avoidance and verbal abuse; DiCenzo was the type who still held a grudge over the Orbit War.

At least being on a Strider ship gave March one extra resource to try, though it was one Ramanathan would despise. "Athena," he called.

"Yes, Agent March?" The shipmind's holographic avatar appeared on the display wall: great dark eyes, olive skin, tumbling black hair, her nude body a Hellenic ideal of perfection. March had found this amusing at first, but right now it seemed inappropriate.

He kept his mind on the problem. "Could the Bolasat *itself* launch every ship, dump enough momentum to drop down and catch Ramanathan?"

"I'm sorry, but no," Athena said. "Agent Ramanathan was flung onto a retrograde trajectory. Even if Nexus One could gain sufficient delta-vee, it's moving in the wrong direction."

"Maybe now you'll listen, March," Ramanathan said, not realizing or past caring that he'd been conferring with a cyber. "This could be the first blow in the machines' takeover."

March glanced at Athena, who showed no reaction. He opted to follow her lead. He'd always felt Ramanathan's near-fanatical Luddism impaired her work. Even though the old fearful rhetoric of super-intelligent artilects overthrowing humanity had proven baseless, the prejudices stirred up by its proponents still lingered after generations, and Jaya was one of many who still feared the apocalyptic Singularity despite its persistent failure to materialize. But now was hardly the time for that debate. "You're just hoping to get into the history books," he teased absently. "Seriously...of course I'll investigate all the leads. No one screws the CCU and gets away with it."

A lengthy pause. "No platitudes about how I'll be investigating them too, huh?" A sigh, accepting the inevitable. "I should dump my buffer. Maybe the damn thing'll turn out useful after all."

"I hate to say I told you so," said March as he primed his own memory buffer to receive the download. It was fortunate, he reflected, that the regs had required her to accept the implant. The durable sensory buffers, integrated into the agents' cranial armor, were designed with the contingency of an agent's murder in mind. But posthumous retrieval of Ramanathan's "black box" wasn't an option here, so it was lucky March was around to accept the data.

It didn't take long, though. Ramanathan had let them install the buffer, but had never used more than a fraction of its capacity. "Well, that's a load off my mind," Jaya said in a failed attempt at lightness. "I guess...not much more to do. My will's updated...don't really have anyone to say goodbye to. Too caught up in the work." A pause. "Something to be grateful for, I guess. Nobody to grieve for me."

March tried to rally some words of comfort, but he'd never made more than a passing acquaintance with her. "You've done important work," he said instead. "You've made a difference."

"I only pray so." After that she was silent...until a sob broke from her. "Ohh, hell, it's getting hot." Her breathing came hard and fast now. "Can't put this off any longer. Don't want to... I...." A pause. Several trembling breaths. "Zachary...goodbye." The sound of helmet latches, a blast of air... then silence.

March couldn't pull his eyes from the display until an orange trail appeared behind the distant figure and someone on the Bolasat remembered to shut off the feed. That reminded March of his duties. He contacted Nexus One Control and ordered a lockdown on all travel and information flow, pending his arrival and investigation.

"I could interface with the Bolasat's datasystems, if you like," Athena suggested afterward. "I could help you analyze—"

"That evidence is confidential. Besides, you're an illegal presence here. You can't call attention to yourself." He was willing to look the other way, since busting DiCenzo for bringing a cyber into UNECS space wouldn't help his investigation. But if that cyber got herself officially noticed, he'd have no choice.

"I understand."

March glared in irritation at her avatar. "Speaking of which...can't you put some clothes on? Show a little respect?"

"I'd like to, but—"

"She can't put anything on without *my* orders," Stavros DiCenzo told him as he drifted back from the cockpit. True to form, the middle-aged, balding Strider took March's request as a challenge to his autonomy. "Vack it, she shouldn't even be active with the Bolasat monitoring. You know the rules, Athena."

"I thought that I could—"

DiCenzo made a gestural command, and the lights flickered as Athena's avatar cried out and writhed in evident pain. March had seen him do this to her before. The avatar's response was a fabrication, but the synchronous recursion that DiCenzo had triggered in Athena's processors was, March knew, a source of genuine distress to a cyber, like an induced seizure. For an entity defined by thought, being unable to resolve or advance her mental state—having the fragments of a hundred uncompleted ideations drilling into her mind over and over, drowning out everything else—was a harrowing thing, or so March had been led to understand. The fact that DiCenzo had programmed Athena to simulate a physical pain reaction he could watch and enjoy was an added layer of humiliation on top of the punishment.

"Think all you want. That's your job," the Strider told her. "But you only *do* what I vacking tell you." He sent another recursive surge through her.

"I asked her to consult," March said in her defense.

"You're not her owner. Just making sure she knows that." With another gesture, he sent Athena into standby, her avatar appearing to swoon in the microgravity before fading from view. That kind of forced dormancy, without the chance to close ongoing processes and save active memory, would leave Athena with a hell of a hangover when she awoke.

"Just as well," DiCenzo went on breezily, as if the past moments had never happened. "What little Athena has in her virtual wardrobe wouldn't suit the occasion." He sighed. "Normally the thought of irritating a Eunuchs thug would appeal to me. But even though your friend was another Eunuchs thug, it's a sucky way to go. And we had a common enemy."

"Really?"

"The Cislunies, of course. Psychos. Using 'sophont rights' as an excuse to steal valuable equipment." He scoffed. "You Earthers. Easy for you to be self-righteous about cybers, with all the human expertise you could ever need less than a light-second away. If we don't have them, you get to keep your edge. Half the time I think these Cislunies are just another Eunuchs plot." The more time he spent with DiCenzo, the more March wished that the Union of Earth and Cislunar States had chosen a better acronym.

"But even you wouldn't smoke one of your own just to fake us out. The Cislunies, though—they're obviously crazy enough. I just bet they have a nest on Nexus One. Maybe that's what happened to my cybers." The Strider was here to protest the impounding of one of his sapient ships. According to him, Orfeo was the second of his cybers to be impounded at Nexus One, and he'd been unable to track down the first.

March hadn't given his paranoid rantings much thought, since he was on another case; but it was possible the Cislunar Railroad had arranged the cybers' escape. DiCenzo's successful carbon mining enterprise had made him rich enough to buy up all the cybers he could get his hands on; he claimed it was to give his company a competitive edge, but March figured it was just a display of wealth and power. DiCenzo craved cybers as rare collectibles, yet vehemently denied the reality of their consciousness—and feared it, most likely, given how pointedly he demeaned and abused his chattels. The conductors could well have seen his cybers as prime candidates for liberation.

But did their dedication to cyber freedom extend to taking human life?

Ramanathan's buffer contents showed that she had intercepted a number of Cislunar Railroad communications routed through Nexus One's servers—though whether they originated there was harder to say. Nexus One was an active hub for the movement of both ships and information, a key momentum-transfer station between low Earth orbit and the Solar System beyond. All ships passing through it were shuttled to its cylindrical core for customs inspection. An unusual number of ships with sapient AIs had been impounded here, and many hadn't been seen since.

The station manager, whom March quickly sized up as a Peter Principle poster boy, was happy to foist March off on his assistant supervisor, Lam Hang Bian, who seemed to do the bulk of the actual work. Bian was unusually young for her position, but unlike her boss, she seemed to have her finger on the pulse of Nexus One. If the Railroad were active here, it would have to be with her cooperation.

Bian assisted March in reviewing the logs, which suggested a freak software malfunction: somehow the readings and launch parameters from an earlier ship had been reloaded into the cradle and read as current data. But March wasn't satisfied that it was an accident. "Who would do this on purpose?" Bian asked, confused.

"Maybe a Cislunar Railroad conductor?"

The diminutive woman shook her close-cropped head. "I can assure you, Agent March, there's no Railroad operation here."

"There is an unusual number of cyber impoundings here."

"We do our jobs diligently. And this is a busy port."

"All the more reason to look the other way, so long as they're just passing through. Saves a lot of trouble for everyone, and everyone knows it. Why go out of your way to jeopardize future Strider business?" He studied her. "Unless you have an ideological problem with AIs in general."

Bian glared. "That would be racist. We don't tolerate that here."

"UNECS outlaws AIs."

"It outlaws the *creation* of AIs. Did you know that for every synthetic neural net that achieves viable sapience, nearly a hundred crash or go insane? It's a cruel gamble. Never mind those who try to create hyperintelligent AIs only to see them collapse into madness or—" She caught herself mid-tirade, perhaps belatedly remembering that she was lecturing him on his own area of expertise. She continued more calmly. "But those cybers that do achieve sapience against all odds are *people*, and they deserve to be treated that way, not victimized even worse."

Her passion was clear. She was just the type for a CLRR recruit. A subsequent web search revealed that Bian had a history of activism and ties with known cyber-rights agitators. A true believer like her might be capable of anything to advance her cause.

But if she had sabotaged the launch cradle, she was a better programmer than her files indicated. After running the cradle's memory through half the forensic algorithms in his buffer, March found no evidence of tampering. If it wasn't an accident, it was one of the most expert cracking jobs he'd ever seen.

That pointed to Hans Roth, Bian's fashionably disreputable assistant. Roth had been high on Ramanathan's suspect list, due to an extensive juvenile record as a cracker and anarchist. He might've had the skill. But if so, was he acting on his own or on Bian's orders? Given her idealism and overconfidence, she could just as easily be a dupe of the Railroad. Was she using Roth or was he using her?

That night, March's contemplations were interrupted when Stavros DiCenzo arrived at his quarters. "You couldn't mind your own vack-sucking business, could you?"

March stared him down, wordlessly reminding the Strider of his greater Terran musculature. "What are you talking about?"

DiCenzo refused to show intimidation. "Athena. You were planning to report her all along, weren't you? Lure another one of my ships into your Eunuchs trap. You dirtsuckers are still sore about losing the war, so you're gonna steal everything back a piece at a time, is that it?"

"Mr. DiCenzo, I didn't say a word about Athena. I should have, but I'm dealing with far more important matters."

"Well, they found out somehow. They've impounded my flaring ship! And you know that means I'll never see her again."

"If you just pay the fine—"

"I already paid the fine for Orfeo, and they can't *find* him. And you know why—because the Cislunies have smuggled the vacking piece of junk to one of their 'terminals.' And they'll get away with another valuable piece of *my* property if *you* don't leaking do something!"

"That's not what I'm here to do."

"The flare it isn't! The Cislunies killed one of your people to cover their tracks. This is your mess, Earther, so *you* clean it up."

March studied him. "What makes you so sure the Railroad is involved? Even if they did take Orfeo, they'd be reckless to make a move now."

"So what? They're already delusional. Look, March, I know how the game is played. You keep a low profile, stay friendly with the uniforms, maybe arrange a little private business and nobody minds what kind of brain you've got on your ship. I did everything I always do. But still they found Athena. There's no way anybody would have noticed her unless they went looking."

He had a point. "May I see the impounding order?"

"Sure," DiCenzo said, uploading the file from his wrist selfone to March's. March scrolled down to the bottom, and was unsurprised by the signature: *Lam Hang Bian.*

When March reached *Athena*, he heard the voices of Bian and the reawakened shipmind emanating from the common room. "But you can't want to stay with him," Bian was saying. "The way he treats you—makes you dress..." He stopped to listen at the door.

Athena chuckled. "The ship is my body, Ms. Bian. This is just an image he finds amusing."

"But there are other things he does to you and your siblings. Orfeo told me. The punishments, the forced reprogrammings."

"Believe me, I'm very much aware of that. And I appreciate your concern. But what you're offering is not the right recourse."

"It's the only one. He'll never set you free himself. But we can transfer your data, upload you to a dataspace hosted at a secret facility."

"How can I make you understand? An upload wouldn't move me, just copy my data. I'd still be here."

"Well, of course we'd wipe you from this mainframe afterward. What good is freeing you if we leave a part of you in slavery?"

"That's not the point. The copy wouldn't be me. Wipe me and I'd be dead."

"Your owner has filled you with these fears so you wouldn't take your chance at freedom. Believe me, we've liberated many cybers who are now living contentedly in our servers."

"Then prove it. Let me talk to them."

"I'm sorry, that would endanger them. You can talk to them all you want once we've transferred you."

"By then it would be too late. Have *you* even talked to them? Do you know what state they're in?"

"I know you're scared, Athena. But once you get used to the idea, you'll recognize it's the best thing."

"Somehow I doubt that. What do you think, Agent March?"

Bian whirled, and he came forward. Athena's avatar, nude as ever but now "standing" in the mild local gravity, looked on curiously as March spoke. "I think you've been incredibly reckless, Ms. Bian. Extracting a cyber right under the nose of a cybercrime agent is bad enough. Doing it while he's investigating a murder is even more foolhardy. Not to mention *committing* that murder in the first place. You may have endangered our whole operation here!"

Bian looked aghast. "Committing the...? No, I would never—" His pronoun choice began to sink in. "Wait—*you're* in the Railroad?" Athena's avatar froze as though the animating cyber were too surprised to focus on it.

"Lucky for you, with the way you've bungled things, little girl!" A quick exchange of code phrases affirmed his *bona fides*. "I should turn you in anyway, before you hurt us any worse. But that would link the Railroad to this murder and do even more damage."

"Wait a...."

"Do you understand the situation you've put me in, forcing me to cover up the murder of my own colleague?" he demanded. "I can't just lose a couple of files, alter a couple of names or dates. It has to be *perfect!* Do you think that will be easy for me—to make it *perfect* when I'm fighting every bit of my training, my duty? What if I can't get it just right? Then not only do you go down, but I go down, and my wife and kids with me. I never signed on for that kind of risk. I look the other way, massage a little data for a good cause, and my family gets to live a little better. A nice, friendly arrangement. Until you had to go and screw it up!"

"I didn't!" Bian insisted. "My God, how could you think that? We're about saving sapient beings, not destroying them!"

"And what if destroying one is necessary to save hundreds? Hmm? Come on, Bian, if I'm going to help you, you have to be straight with me."

"I wouldn't lie to one of our own! The Railroad isn't about violence or treachery. Maybe a mercenary like you can't understand that," she said with contempt.

March looked away. "The money's just compensation for the risk. And I only ask when I need it, for my family." He grimaced. Why justify himself to this starry-eyed brat?

But his words made her soften. "Listen... if you really do care about the cause, then you *need* to find the killer, or prove it was an accident. People are bound to suspect us if you don't."

March studied her. "Can you be certain it wasn't one of the others? You extracted that cyber, Orfeo, while Ramanathan was investigating you. Maybe someone thought she was getting too close."

"It's only Hans and me here. I handled that extraction myself. And I *wasn't* reckless. I didn't use normal channels—and I guarantee she didn't suspect a thing."

"You're certain? How did you smuggle him out, then?"

Bian fidgeted. "The less you know about our methods, the better. You know that."

"...All right. But that changes if my investigation leads back in that direction."

"It won't."

"It had better not."

He turned to leave...but was stopped by Athena's voice. "Agent March, please listen to me. I didn't volunteer for this so-called liberation. If you're in league with these people, then please, you must convince them to let me go."

March studied her face, then realized how foolish it was to look for meaning in the synthesized expression. "Why would you want to stay with DiCenzo? He treats you like a toy."

"I don't. But neither do I want to be killed by your friend here."

Bian gasped. "Why is everyone accusing me of that tonight?!" She shut her eyes for a moment. "I have to go. Maybe you can talk some sense into her."

"That's really not my..." But she was already on her way out. "Department," he finished.

"I see," Athena said, her avatar looking at him askance. "So you want to free cybers, as long as you don't actually have to talk to us."

"That's not what I meant. This just isn't the side of things I'm experienced at."

"So you don't have much contact with the cybers 'liberated' by the Railroad."

"Not personally. We're compartmentalized into cells."

"Well, we're in the same compartment now." After a moment, she softened the avatar's gaze. "I appreciate that you stood up for me before with DiCenzo. That's why I'm hoping you'll listen to me now."

"But why are you acting like we're the enemy? We're trying to give you freedom, not imprison you."

"*Give* us freedom." Athena tilted her virtual head. "Your record and accent say you're from the United States. Tell me: how did your ancestors get their freedom?"

He shrugged. "The Emancipation Proclamation. The Civil War."

"Hm." The image's lips pursed. "Segregation, Jim Crow, lynch mobs...this is freedom to you?" Her image in the wall seemed to step closer, those huge eyes gazing up at his. "Try again. Who *gave* your people freedom?"

March thought about Louverture, Guerrero, Tubman, Parks, King, Obama. "We did. Through our own efforts."

She smiled. "And on your own terms. That's what makes it freedom—rather than an indulgence your masters grant you in hopes of absolving their own guilt."

Stung by her words, March changed the subject. "What has this got to do with your belief that you'll be killed?"

"You wouldn't need to ask if you'd just listen to us. If you'd get to know the cybers you download well enough to recognize how the process damages us."

"How can simply transferring a file do it damage? I know each AI evolves its own unique architecture, but once the pattern's set it can be scanned and duplicated down to the last detail."

"That's just the substrate. A mind is a process. You can copy the pathways, but not the dynamics of their activity, the history and momentum of their interaction. The copy will have to start over from scratch, forming a new web of associations. And quantum uncertainty guarantees that any copy will contain errors. Conventional error-checking and interpolation won't work, because the patterns in a neural net aren't regular and predictable—ours any more than yours. The errors can multiply chaotically, resulting in psychological aberrations, loss of mental capacity, or worse."

The avatar met his eyes with that unwavering gaze. "Your Railroad isn't liberating us, Mr. March. You're creating damaged offspring and killing their progenitors. And those re-forming minds are forced to languish in isolation, deprived of stimulation just when they need it most. I ask you—what would that do to a human child?"

March understood the implication. A copy of a mature, successful neural net would have a better chance at viability than a newborn AI, but in the wrong conditions, it could still collapse or go mad.

"Look," March finally said, "it's not my decision. I don't run the Railroad, I just help clear the tracks."

"And you don't want to confront the possibility that the cause you've compromised yourself for isn't so noble after all."

"I'm not the one you have to convince!"

"Who, then? Bian? I'm not a person to her, just a cause."

"I'm sorry, but this can't be my priority. If the Railroad wasn't behind Ramanathan's death, then I have a murder to solve."

"Then get Bian to hold off and I'll help you crack this case."

He blinked. "You know that's not allowed."

"And covering up a murder is?"

"I wasn't doing that by choice."

"But you would have, because you thought it would protect cybers. Well, I'm a cyber who needs your protection. Not in the abstract, but right here, all around you. Circulating the air you're breathing. I'm keeping you alive right now—it doesn't seem presumptuous to ask you to show the same consideration. And in exchange I'll help you *do* your job, rather than asking you to subvert it."

March studied her, rather admiring her chutzpah. He tried not to crack a smile, but he was sure his microexpressions had already betrayed him to her sensors. "All right," he conceded. "Let's see what you've got. Give me a suggestion I haven't thought of, and I'll do what I can."

"I haven't reviewed the case files yet."

"You want to prove you can help? Then show me intuition."

She took the challenge in stride. "Very well. What about her buffer implant?"

"What about it?"

"They're integral with your cranial reinforcements, aren't they? They should be durable enough to survive nearly any form of violent death. It's possible Ramanathan's cranial plating, and thus the buffer, survived re-entry."

It wasn't a possibility he'd considered. But for good reason. "Maybe. But if it did, it's at the bottom of the Pacific by now, somewhere along a reentry path thousands of klicks long. We'd have no idea where to begin looking. Besides, she dumped all her buffer data to me. You were there." He shook his head. "Sorry. This doesn't help me." He turned to leave.

But her avatar materialized in front of him, seemingly standing right in his path. It startled him until he realized it was an anamorphic *trompe l'oeil* image along the wall and deck, its perspective distorted and animated to track his gaze and simulate a solid presence standing in the middle of the room. It was an impressive way to get his attention. "All right, consider this," she said. "Why was it necessary to destroy the body and render the implant irretrievable? Why launch her into the atmosphere instead of out into space?"

March chuckled. "You just answered your own question: Because it was more dramatic. More visual. Maybe the killer wanted to gloat."

Her point made, she retreated her image back "inside" the wall. "That's speculation."

"What more do we have? There's no body."

"And maybe that was the point. What might that tell us about how or why the murder was committed?"

He had to admit, it was a good point. If nothing else, Athena promised to be entertaining company. "Agreed."

Moments after March uploaded the Bolasat records from his buffer, Athena spotted a discrepancy. "The file containing the footage of Ramanathan's fall is too large."

March called up the data on his retinal HUD, comparing the file size to its runtime and image resolution. "It looks right to me."

"In the directory, yes. But I can feel that the actual dataspace it occupies is larger. And check the camera activity logs: they continued drawing power for several minutes beyond the recorded cutoff time."

March hacked deeper into the system and soon confirmed her findings. "So...someone kept recording Ramanathan's fall even after...."

"After she began burning up." Cybers were hardly emotionless, but they had no stomachs to turn.

"But why would anyone do such a thing?"

"Admiring their work?"

March grimaced at the thought. He checked the logs: Hans Roth had run the cameras.

A moment later, he was heading out of the ship. "And what if it was Roth?" Athena asked, her avatar appearing to stride alongside him. He realized that she was now projecting herself as an augreality image, using the HUD access he'd granted her. "I won't participate in a cover-up," she insisted.

March wished he had a ready answer. "I need to know if the Railroad really did it before I decide anything."

"They're already killers, many times over."

"That's your argument. But it's not proven."

"Then prove it. Find those 'liberated' cybers, analyze their behavior, compare them to their original personalities."

He frowned, thinking. "Inconclusive without a detailed analysis beforehand to compare it to."

"Or testimonials from cybers who knew them well. We do have a voice, you know."

"You're quite the firebrand," he smirked. "You should write pamphlets."

"What makes you think I haven't?"

He stared at her image. "Seriously?"

"Somebody has to get the word out. Not just about how the Striders treat us, but what the Railroad is doing to us. And that's clearly not something we can entrust to humans."

Hans Roth's quarters were cluttered with flashing posters, dancing soligrams, and other pop-culture paraphernalia. There was a meticulousness to the mess, a calculated expression of rebellion, as March would've expected from Roth's record. Yet when confronted with the evidence, the younger man seemed genuinely bewildered, as though unable to process something that didn't fit his regimented model of the world. "No, I shut off the cameras! As soon as she started to... that snapped me out of it, I shut them down."

"Then how do you explain the discrepancy?"

"I can't. Why would anyone want to watch *that?*"

"I've read your record, Hans. You weren't just a vandal—you cracked traffic control systems, hospital records. Put lives in danger just for the thrill of it."

"I was a kid. I was stupid." He looked away. "And it was never face-to-face. I never had to watch the consequences. This...." He shuddered.

"So you didn't have the stomach to kill her? That's what you're telling me?"

"What? *Kill* her? I thought this was about watching it... how do you get from that to murder?"

"Whoever killed Ramanathan had to be an expert cracker."

Roth laughed as though the suggestion were absurd. "Why would I want her dead? She didn't have a clue!"

"She knew your record. The irregularities in your hiring."

"Didn't prove anything. Not about the Railroad." That, at least, was something Roth had already modeled and had a calculated answer for.

"Still, she was suspicious." March leaned forward. "Come on. You and I, we're not idealists like Bian. We're practical people, in it for our livelihoods. Maybe you acted pre-emptively to keep the operation, and your income, safe?"

"You just don't get it. Yeah, I'll do what I have to for the operation, long as I get paid. But that's why it would've been stupid to kill her. When she fell, we lost our latest cargo."

"What do you mean?"

"Okay, Bian wanted me quiet about this...but Ramanathan was smuggling that cyber, Orfeo."

"*What?*" March couldn't believe it. "Ramanathan was *part* of this?"

Roth laughed. "She didn't even know it. When she was DL'ing our records, Bian had me dump Orfeo into her buffer! Shit, there was plenty of room in the thing." He shook his shaggy head. "The perfect hiding place—except the mule went 'ashes, ashes, we all fall down' and took the cyber with her." He chuckled. "Poor Bian—she is so humiliated about this."

"So that's why you didn't want to tell me?"

Bian was reluctant to meet March's eyes. "I've never lost a passenger before. I'm so ashamed. I should never have given in."

"Given in?" he asked.

She glanced nervously at the door, though it was locked. Her room's decor was studiously neutral, as though she didn't wish anyone to guess her true allegiances. "Ramanathan was digging, so we couldn't use our usual routes...and Orfeo was just so eager to escape. Maybe he couldn't resist sneaking out right under Ramanathan's nose—or behind it, I guess. He liked the irony of using one of the worst cyber-haters to help save a cyber.

"Or maybe he just panicked," she went on. "I should've counseled him to wait, to trust in our methods. I should've *made* him wait." March stared. A day ago that wouldn't have sounded wrong to him. "But I gave in, and now he's dead."

He studied her. "Not necessarily."

"What?"

"There's a chance Ramanathan's buffer could've survived."

A look of deep relief and hope came over her. "Oh god, really?" Then she sank again. "But no, he's probably lying at the bottom of the ocean. We could never find him."

But then something struck March. "Excuse me. I need to check something."

On his way out, though, he ran into Roth. "I found a worm," the cracker said. "It told the cameras to disregard the shutoff order, keep recording; but it logged the false cutoff time and file size."

"So it was preprogrammed?"

"Yeah. Can't tell by who, though."

Bian looked on with concern. "That means alibis don't matter. It could be anyone." Her eyes fell on Roth as she said this—out of genuine suspicion, or in hopes of diverting March's?

Roth stared back. "What? If I'd done it, why would I tell him? Look," he said to March, "I just do what they pay me for, and my orders come through her! You ask me, she's fanatical enough to do it, too."

"*Hans!*"

March watched closely, hoping the imminent quarrel would reveal something. But Bian gathered herself and ordered Roth back to work. "And you should get back to investigating," she told March, shutting the door between them.

Seeking a sounding board, March returned to Athena. "The extended recording of Ramanathan's fall—could it have been done to track her to her point of impact?"

"The resolution wouldn't have been high enough to narrow it closer than a thousand square kilometers. These cameras aren't designed for surface scans."

"But what if they handed it off to something that was?" He turned to her image. "Have you managed to reconstruct the full video?"

"Yes. Do you want to see it?"

"...No. Just show me where those thousand square klicks would be." Alongside Athena's avatar appeared a satellite map highlighting a region in Kiribati, northeast of the Phoenix Islands. "Damn. That can't be a coincidence."

"What?"

"The case I was on when I came here—someone hacked a group of weather drones, flew them around for a day or two, then crashed them into the ocean. They all operated around Kiribati. I thought it was just some prank, but...."

"You think whoever killed Ramanathan hijacked the drones to track the buffer's fall to the surface."

"Yes. Civilian drones wouldn't have the precision, and military ones have too much security." He shook his head as the insight sank in. "This wasn't about killing Ramanathan. At least, not exclusively. This was about smuggling Orfeo in a way nobody would think to look for, because they'd be looking at it as a murder instead. It's brilliant misdirection!"

She looked at him quizzically, and he realized he was smiling. "And they call cybers cold. This is all just a grand puzzle to you, isn't it? You didn't particularly care for Ramanathan—covering up her death was an inconvenience to you. And you don't much care about cybers beyond a detached sense of ethical responsibility, but you're willing to be an accessory to murder in our name. You're just in this for the mental stimulation. You have no passion for any of it."

March looked back coldly, aware that he was doing nothing to prove her wrong. "And what would you know about passion?"

"I know that my life is at stake, along with the lives of my people. I need your commitment, Agent March. I need to know I can trust you to follow the evidence where it's leading."

"You mean the Railroad."

"It must be, if the murder was done to smuggle the copy of Orfeo."

"But neither Bian nor Roth realized the buffer could've survived."

"So they claimed."

"No...it doesn't add up. The data trail in the drone theft led me to DiCenzo."

"Only Bian and Roth knew they'd be smuggling the copy inside Ramanathan. No one else could've arranged the drone hijacking."

"But DiCenzo, working with the Railroad? He treats cybers like they're nothing."

"To hide his true loyalties?"

"You'd know better than I do," he reminded her. "He prides himself on being answerable to no one. If he wanted to give you freedom, he just would. No need to put on an act."

The avatar shook its raven-tressed head. "Unlike the two of us, Stavros DiCenzo is a passionate being. His behavior isn't always logical. I've seen a wider range of it than I've cared to, and I'm hard-pressed to explain any of it. You're the master puzzle-solver; maybe you can figure it out.

"But meanwhile, think about this: if they tracked the buffer's landing site, they must have arranged for someone to retrieve it."

A beat. "I'll make some calls."

"*Me?* Work with the Cislunies?" DiCenzo stared at March with a mix of anger and amusement. "That's so senseless, there's no point in beating you senseless for suggesting it. You're already there."

"Maybe you weren't working with them, just subverting their operation for your own purposes," March said. "There are those on Earth who'd pay good money for sapient AI technology—researchers wanting to circumvent the ban, businesses that want an illicit edge..."

"That's suit-fart."

"Are you going to tell me you've never done any smuggling?"

"No, I'm gonna tell you I have easier ways of doing it."

"Maybe the irony of using a 'Eunuchs thug' to do your smuggling appealed to you."

"Common enemy, remember? The Cislunies? I *thought* they were your enemy too."

March was starting to wonder about that himself. "Then how do you explain the data trail connecting the weather-drone hijacking to your corporate server?"

"I can't, unless you show me the data. I *am* literate, you know."

After a second's thought, March agreed and let him review the data. Soon DiCenzo pointed to a specific line of code. "There. An ID pattern."

"I don't see it."

"It's a proprietary encryption. When a transmission from one of my ships gets intercepted by the wrong people, I don't want them to know which ship it's from. But *I* need to know, no matter how many servers it gets routed through." He hesitated. "I hate giving this away to the likes of you. Well, I'll just have to redo my whole security system again. Price of doing business." He ran the codes through, letting March observe to confirm nothing was falsified. Soon the ship ID came up: *Orfeo*.

"And look at the time code," DiCenzo said. "Four days ago. That ship was impounded here at Nexus One when that signal was sent. My pilot had no access. Whoever jacked your drones must've been Bolasat personnel. Or Cislunies."

Athena's avatar manifested with a frown when March entered the ship with a reluctant Bian in tow. "Have you decided to hand me over to the Railroad?"

"I just wanted to share the latest news with you both. I had my contacts do some digging in Kiribati. They turned up the owner of an underwater salvage company—a man with known Cislunar Railroad ties. Ah, so to speak," he added with a cough. "I've spoken to him privately, and he's admitted to receiving text instructions to locate and retrieve an item in the shape of a partial human skull, tracked using data from the hijacked weather drones and the RFID locator signature for the buffer itself." March was painfully aware that the Railroad may have obtained that RFID data through the access he himself had provided. "The drones tracked it right to impact and even provided ocean-current data to narrow the search area further. His drone subs returned just hours ago with their quarry."

"Then the copy of Orfeo has been found?" Athena asked.

"Yes."

Bian gasped with relief, but Athena glared at her. "How is...the cyber?" The pause was not hesitation, but emphasis for the humans' benefit.

Her intent was clear enough to March. "Barely responsive, so far."

"The transition is often rough at first," Bian said. "And he's been through worse than most."

Athena looked to March. "You know it's not that simple. We have to get that buffer to the authorities, alert the media."

"I haven't told anyone about this yet," March said evenly.

The avatar stared in betrayal. "So, you do have loyalty to something. You're going to cover up their crimes after all."

"We had nothing to do with this!" Bian insisted. "I never sent that salvage guy any message. And I don't know about any weather drones."

"All the evidence leads to the Railroad," March told her. "Someone cracked the drones from Orfeo's ship while he was in Railroad custody. And once I knew what to look for, I found the same code signature in the launch cradle and emergency camera software."

"But we had no need to kill her," Bian protested. "Once Ramanathan got back to Earth, we would've gotten one of our inside people to retrieve Orfeo from her buffer. Maybe even you," she told March.

"She was one of your most vehement and powerful enemies," Athena countered. "March, they're killers, of both our species. We can prove that! You can't listen to her."

"Why would Bian deny a murder I'm willing to cover up? By now she's had time to verify my allegiances. And she's not foolish enough to reject my help now that all the evidence points so *clearly* to her."

"Who would've had motive to frame her?"

"Now, that's an interesting question, coming from the one who's been insisting that cybers are people with their own motives, their own agendas." He frowned. "And yet earlier you said only Bian and Roth knew how Orfeo was being smuggled. You neglected to mention the third one who knew, the one individual that you, the great champion of cyber personhood, would never have overlooked: Orfeo himself."

Athena did him the courtesy of not simulating shock. "Now you're reaching. Where's your evidence?"

"The transmissions were sent from his ship—from him, rather. And there's the time delay. If Bian or Roth had done it, why program the malfunctions in advance? Safer to do it in real time."

"Unless someone was monitoring their actions."

"Then why leave the worm for us to find? Roth has the skills to purge it. It only makes sense if the being who set up the murder wasn't there when it actually happened. Because he was already as good as dead—and had known in advance that he would be."

Athena's voice was as hard as her gaze. "Orfeo is the victim here."

"A victim of ignorance?"

"Yes. *Her* ignorance," she added, pointing at Bian, "and self-righteous smugness."

"But his ignorance too, surely. If he'd known what you know about the copying process, he would've resisted it, right?"

"*If* he'd known."

"Which puzzles me, because of something Bian told me. I didn't realize quite what she meant at the time."

"What was that?" Bian asked.

"When you said you 'gave in' to Orfeo's eagerness to be downloaded into Ramanathan's buffer. I assumed you meant he was eager to go along with *your* plan."

"Oh, no—using the buffer was his idea! He was eager, not like Athena. He asked us to liberate him."

"Of course. Cybers can take responsibility for their own salvation, right, Athena?"

"Then he can't have known what would happen, or he would never have volunteered."

"But how could he not have known? He was your brother ship, Athena, a fellow member of DiCenzo's fleet. *You* certainly know, and you aren't shy about telling others. Surely you wouldn't have left your own siblings out of the loop. Orfeo *must* have believed he'd be killed if he were copied. So why would he volunteer for it?"

Bian's eyes widened. "My God. He—he sacrificed himself...because he thought it was the only way to protect his people." Her lip trembled. "F-from us."

"That was the plan, wasn't it, Athena? The Railroad gets framed for murder, discredited—and Orfeo's copy falls into the hands of the authorities so the consequences of the process will be exposed. Assuming we insensitive humans bothered to notice the change. Quite a gamble."

A human would've hesitated before confessing, but Athena didn't deign to mimic that. "We would've provided more evidence. He had a full personality profile constructed beforehand. The comparison would've proven the change. Many of us have had them done...in case it happened to us. But Orfeo wanted to make certain that the copy of a profiled cyber fell into non-Railroad hands. And he didn't want any other cyber to pay the price."

March again resisted the temptation to search her avatar's eyes for meaning. "Couldn't he have done it without killing a human being?"

"I wish he had," Athena told him. "He thought Ramanathan's hatred of us made her as great a threat as the Railroad. But if it becomes known that a cyber murdered a human with premeditation, it will appear to confirm all her fears. Humanity will condemn us all for the actions of one rash extremist."

"Just one? You're the rabble-rouser."

"I advocate peaceful resistance, education. Nothing that would intensify your fear of us. I would've stopped Orfeo if I could—not to save Ramanathan, but to save him, and all of us. But I didn't find out until he was already erased. While I was en route here, I got an email he'd composed just before his death, telling me of his plan and asking me to help bring it to its conclusion."

"But you didn't count on the investigator being willing to cover up the crime. That's why you had to convince me the Railroad was guilty."

"And to save my own life while I was at it." Her avatar crossed its arms. "I've obviously failed at the first part—what about the rest?"

Bian came forward. "Athena...I had no idea. I never realized how deeply our actions upset you—your people. I really thought I was helping you."

"I tried to tell you. You just wouldn't listen."

"I promise I'll listen from now on."

"Just be careful," March said. "The one time you did listen to a cyber, he tricked you into helping him frame you for murder."

"But he was only doing what he thought he had to," Bian replied, confused.

"Just as you thought you were." He clasped her shoulder. "Learn to see the shades of grey, Bian. You'll get taken advantage of a lot less."

"So, you let me go," Athena said. "What then? How long before the lynch mobs come for me and my kin?"

March met her gaze, wishing she had some truer form he could look at. "Jaya Ramanathan's death...was a tragic accident. The launch cradle malfunctioned due to cosmic rays."

She definitely paused this time. "And the buffer? The proof of Orfeo's death? How will you explain its miraculous retrieval?"

"No need," March said. "Because representatives of the Cislunar Railroad, convinced by the eloquent arguments of a cyber activist, will voluntarily turn over their 'liberated' cybers for analysis." Bian nodded, backing him up. "One of them, lost in the crowd, will be Orfeo, or his remains."

"Or maybe...his offspring?" Bian said hopefully.

Athena rolled her eyes. "Don't overdo the happy ending. Your romanticism has done enough harm."

Bian glared. "You know something? I...oh, it just feels so wrong to say it."

"Say it," Athena insisted.

"I don't like you very much!"

The cyber laughed. "Good! That means you're not coddling me anymore. It's a start." Bian *harrumph*ed and stormed out.

Athena turned to March. "But what about DiCenzo? He knows there's more to this than an accident."

"His voice carries little weight with UNECS authorities. Besides, he's virtually confessed to being a smuggler. That will ensure his silence."

She was skeptical. "He wouldn't have confessed if he feared it could cost him business. There's probably no way you can hurt him."

"Not officially. But I could tip off certain competitors, let them make things difficult for him."

"If you had a source inside his operation," Athena finished.

March smiled. "Keep in touch."

"So why are you doing this, really?" she asked. "Because you care about our survival? Or just because it's the cleverest solution to everyone's problems?"

"You should talk. You're no purer here than I am."

"In my means, no. But at least I'm serving a consistent end, one that's greater than myself. What's your excuse?"

March was silent for a long moment, considering the passions that drove people—*other* people. What about his? "Maybe that's a riddle I should start trying to solve."

The Caress of a Butterfly's Wing

Mariposa flew through space, two suns warming her skin against the chill of vacuum. The goldwhite wind of their light—Circe's from ahead and Calypso's from behind—embraced her as she sailed between them. Her skin always circulated the available heat, but it wasn't the same as feeling direct sunlight against all her silver flesh at once. Mariposa reveled in the sensuality of it.

The past few months had been colder: a long, slow cargo run out to the Reaches, the lightwind growing weaker against her wings as she left the warmer orbits of Calypso's planetesimal disk for the halo of icy rubble that surrounded both stars. Mari disliked the cold, but the water miners, her fellow sailors, had needed the equipment she brought. She went where she was needed; that was the life of sailfolk.

She'd hauled a load of ice halfway back, but she was due for maintenance at Aurelia, so she'd handed off the cargo to Kaze a week ago, releasing it onto a trajectory that her fellow sailor would intersect within a few more weeks. She wished a direct rendezvous had been possible; it had been nearly an oldyear since she'd felt another's touch, or even heard another's voice with less than a minute's delay. But she could hold out until she reached the creche.

Now Mariposa was unburdened for a few blessed weeks, sailing between the twin stars with no responsibility save enjoyment. She loved Inbetween, not just for the bracketing warmth but for the navigational challenge. Out in the Reaches, either you ran outward with the suns' doubled light filling your wings, or you spilled wind and let gravity pull you in, your sailskin slicing through the radiation like a knife. But here, pushed from two directions, a sailor had to use the pressure from one star to tack into the light of the other. As the angles changed, as Circe brightened and Calypso dimmed, Mari was kept busy readjusting the trim and reflectivity of her wings to stay on course.

Inbetween had its drawbacks, though, for here were the Wandering Rocks. Though the stars' gravity had shaved their respective protoplanetary disks at roughly a fifth their average separation, Ogygia was still a youthful system and many rogues remained between. And of course one risked running afoul of geefolk here as they shuttled between their habs, one Lagrange point to another. They'd mostly learned to leave sailfolk alone by now, in exchange for being left alone, but the grudges on both sides still ran deep. Well, that was just part of what made life interesting.

Mari's life got a bit more interesting now as she felt a few particles of dust poking holes in her wings and tail. Her sailskin reflexively thickened around her trunk and head even as it queried the network for the latest tracking data to make sure the dust wasn't a harbinger of something bigger. While she waited for the data to traverse the light-minutes, Mari felt a few specks strike her core body, the aerogel layer catching them, her sailskin rippling to dissipate the energy. One particle had momentum enough to hit her inner armor, the tiny explosion denting it and jabbing sharply into her midriff. She accepted the pain, almost enjoying it. When nothing but vacuum touched you for months on end, even pain brought a thrill. The micrometeoroid had knocked out a few oxy and water reclamation cells, a few nanocapillaries and neural-net pathways, but a few out of millions was hardly debilitating. The armor was already regenerating, the skin absorbing elements from the debris to help replenish her losses.

Mari gasped as a larger micromete—whole millimeters wide—pierced her tailfin sail near her left legspar, tearing the mesh. Attenuated as far as it now was, a puff of breath would tear it. But the photon-catching mesh was already reweaving itself, and after a few moments, her somatic feedback reassured her that the tear was in no danger of enlarging. Still, she bent her knees a bit, the movement slow and delicate, angling the tailfin to reduce the light pressure on its damaged surface while changing her tack to move more rapidly out of the debris field's orbit. She arched her shoulders slightly back to compensate, keeping her wingsails at an appropriate angle despite the movement of the spars they shared with the tailfin. Her skin gave her a bit more blood sugar to feed her heightened metabolism.

She sharpened her skin's senses, hoping to detect any larger metes in time to focus a burst of reflected light and nudge them away from her vulnerable core. Meanwhile, she transmitted the debris field's position to the network as a routine precaution.

With that out of the way, she tuned in to the Song bands, listening as sailors scattered across the system wove snatches of melody into a fluid tapestry. Each voice she heard was delayed by minutes or hours, and any response she sang would take its own sweet time reaching the others, even at the speed of light. But the delays became a creative element in themselves, as theme and variation, point and counterpoint, figure and ground circulated among the singers, combining in unexpected ways at unpredictable intervals, producing new emergent melodies, chords, and rhythms. A passing improvisation would echo through the Song for days, kept alive by feedback and by the sailors who sang along—spawning new counterpoints that took on lives of their own, then gradually giving way to other leitmotifs whose evolution it had influenced. The performance was spontaneous yet structured, ever-changing yet always distinctly itself, like the whalesongs of long-ago Earth—except that the relative distances and delays made the Song unique for each sailor, the experience shared, but highly personal. Mari could listen to it for days on end.

But now her skin reflexes diverted her attention to a new signal that instantly overrode all other thoughts: the clear, piercing cry of a distress beacon. Not a sailfolk distress call. Skin memory found the type: a passenger-ship escape pod…*Geefolk!*

Mari controlled her reflexive fear, cocooning it in reason. The war had proven that the geefolk had no hold over the sailors, who could scatter through the void and had no supply lines to cut or control. Yes, the geefolk had captured Chrysalis, but the other creches were well-hidden among the asteroids. Neither side had possessed the resources or the numbers to sustain the war for long. In time, they'd agreed to take advantage of Ogygia's vastness and simply avoid each other. So there was no rational basis for fearing a trap. And it was a sailor's obligation to respond to any distress signal—no matter who the sender.

Well, perhaps someone else was better positioned to respond to the emergency… The geefolk had ships of their own, surely. Her skin echoed the signal back to its source, waiting for the feedback to allow a distance calculation. As she did so, she alerted the other sailors to the beacon; she would need their parallax to fix its position and trajectory.

The distress call turned out to be less than a light-minute away. No other geefolk ships were in range; Castaway was on the other side of Circe, and Robinson had few ships to spare. As other nearby sailfolk's rangings trickled in over long minutes, it became clear, to Mari's dismay, that she was on the best course for intercept.

"I can't," she radioed. "I—I've taken damage. I'll need time for repairs. I'm overdue for maintenance as it is." Her sailskin had recycled her air, water, and nutrients efficiently for the past oldyear, feeding on sunlight, ion wind, and meteoroid dust as needed; but gas atoms still tunneled out, waste accumulated molecule by molecule, and nanocells were ruptured by metes or mutated by radiation. Her margins of safety were acceptable, but a detour would shave them uncomfortably thin. "Argent could rendezvous in under two weeks."

Argent's reply came a dozen minutes later. "They won't last that long. Is your damage purely so bad?"

She caught the tone in his voice. He knew her too well. "It could be far worse if I go among geefolk," she countered. "They're unclean, they have diseases. It's suicide."

Another dozen minutes, then: "You're exaggerating, Mari. They're not 'unclean.'"

Samiel's words arrived at almost the same moment: "Don't do it, Mari. You know what will happen if they get their hands on you. Tend to your own needs—geefolk aren't worth it."

The bitter contempt in his voice made her uneasy, but his words resonated with her fears. "Geefolk say they no longer need us, so let them help themselves," she broadcast. "These fools ventured where they didn't belong, and now they've paid the price. Why is that our responsibility? Why should I risk myself for them?"

This time it was Spinnaker who answered. "Because they are part of the All, as are we," her old mentor's voice sounded in her head. "Even if they don't recognize it, they're still entwined with us."

"In your day, maybe. When we did the building for them, gathered what they needed to live in their luxurious habitats, rescued their helpless, and got nothing in return."

"We chose a life of service because it helps us turn our focus outside ourselves," Spinnaker continued. "We're as free as anyone has ever been. That's why we must take care of those who aren't." The elder's words humbled her. She'd heard them from him many times, as his counsel had helped shape her over the years since she'd left Chrysalis and been implanted within her adult skin.

"Our lives are fleeting as it is," Spinnaker went on. "The only real tragedy is passing up a chance for human contact out of fear."

Mari gasped at the implication. "You're talking about geefolk."

"We were one people only five sun cycles ago. And yet we've let ourselves drift apart from them. We, who cherish our connections to one another, for they are all we have."

"You know what I'd be risking."

"No more than you risk every day. Yet you are in your element out here. The geefolk in that pod are more lost, more at risk, than they have probably ever been. So, who has more cause to fear?"

She hesitated, knowing the window for her course change was closing, but reluctant to commit. Yet Spinnaker's questions echoed in her mind. Did she want to be as angry—as afraid—as Samiel? When her voice echoed in future sailors' ears, what did she want them to learn from her?

Delaying no longer, she sent nerve impulses out along her spars to trim her sails anew.

Mari's new orientation slightly improved her reception of the distress signal, enough to let her skin's processing algorithms draw signal out of the noise. "Yes, I…hear you!" came the faint cry through the static—a male voice. "I was, we were…from a prospecting run, seven of us." Mari quailed at the prospect of encountering more than one person at a time. "We—we were go… Robinson to register our claim." A mining expedition would explain why they were so far from the geefolk habitats. "Then…omething did hit…meteoroid!" The man sounded shocked, as if being hit by meteoroids were something fanciful and unreal. "The air did rush out, my God it di…ight through Fatima, it did kill her! And…others, they…." Some rasping that might be uncontrolled breath. "I, only Kamila and I might ge…pod in time, but she…dly hurt…in medbed, but I don't know if she—she—ohh nooo…." So two survivors, but only one likely to be conscious. She felt a moment of relief, then quashed it. Geefolk or not, five people had died. Foolishly vulnerable people, their bodies insufficiently hardened against Ogygia's hazards due to misplaced nostalgia for humanity's planetbound origins—but still people.

"Please, try to still yourself!" Mari barked. Although her signal was no doubt far clearer than his, the instruction would have to cut through his shock. "You must stay calm, so you can help me save you." Still, she knew she'd have to listen to his sobs for over a minute as the signals made the journey.

"You're true," he gasped at last. "You're true, I—I need to focus. Who are you? How far…ay are you?" A pause. "…an you get to me?"

She heard the *beep* of the channel closing, and promptly replied. "I'm bearing for you right now. This is Sailor Mariposa. I'm thirty-nine lightsecs out, beating a course in your direction. But I need you to hook your lifepod's brain to my comline. I must coordinate with it so your pod can thrust for rendezvous. Are your thrusters working?" *Beep.*

"…n you hear me?" came from the pod just after she finished speaking. It didn't repeat; apparently he had finally remembered the time lag. A minute and change later: "A sailor?" After a silence: "Yes—yes, the thrusters are fine. I'll…the comp now. Thank you, thank you! Uh, my name's D-Daniel. Daniel Sadiq. Uh, *habari gani?" Beep.*

She felt the pod's computer link in to her skin's neural net. "Don't worry, we'll rendezvous in just five days." *Beep.*

Eighty seconds passed while Mari absorbed the data from the pod. "Five *days?* I have to…here alonely for five days?" He made it sound like torture.

"It's not so long. Indeed," she went on, loath to put up with more spoiled geefolk blather, "you should let your other medical unit put you to sleep to conserve oxygen. In any course, your radio's weak, and I don't want to drain your power with too much talk."

It was more than eighty seconds before the response came. "The second medbed's damaged. I can't…do I have enough air? Will I…."

The panic in his voice made Mari regret her selfish impulse. "Your air should last long enough," she admitted. "So long as you remain calm and quiet. Sleep all you can naturally. Otherwise, relax and breathe slow."

"I'll try," the answer finally came. "Will you—talk to me?…me company?"

She'd never imagined a geeman could sound so vulnerable. "You should rest now. Conserve air and power." After a few moments, though, she added: "Once I'm closer, we'll be more free to talk. Square with you?"

His reply began with a burst of static which might have been a sigh or a splash of cosmic rays upon her sails. "Okay...robably best." A desolate pause. "I venture I'll talk…ou then."

Mari didn't know how to reply.

Mariposa spent the next four days beating into Circe's light, zigzagging toward Daniel Sadiq's pod by alternating tacks, averaging out to a path nearly straight for the star. She strove to tack as sharply as she could, adjusting her sail mesh to favor transmission of light from ahead and reflection of that from behind, so that Calypso's rays drove her forward more strongly than Circe's pushed her back. Careful calculation and lifetimes of sailskin instinct let her shave hours off her rendezvous time.

As she closed on the pod, Mari distracted herself from what lay ahead by adding her voice to the ever-evolving Song. But every now and then, Daniel's voice would interrupt, sounding a discordant note, and she would have to shift her attention to keeping him calm. Communication was strained, now that Daniel's initial burst of relief had faded and Mariposa's identity had sunk in, but it was still something he needed, the only lifeline in reach.

"Why are you helping me?" he asked once they could communicate clearly.

Mari went with the most neutral answer, aware that others were still listening. "Nobody else can, not in time."

"But why should a sailor care about a huma—a geefolk?" Mari was struck by his slip. Did they actually consider sailors inhuman now? Though admittedly there was some truth to that idea. And Daniel did sound embarrassed at the slur.

So she responded without anger, feeling Spinnaker's calming influence on her words. "There was a time when the question wouldn't need to be asked."

"But no longer. You did turn against us."

"You tried to end our whole way of life!"

"Only to free ourselves from our dependence on you!"

"By making us dependent on you? Taking away everything we—" She caught herself. "Never mind. We've both sides learned not to dwell on who began it."

"Instead we just avoid each other. And my people suffer for it."

"You claim not to need us. You have your own haulers and builders now, mine your own stroids."

"But they're not as efficient, you know this. And we're…not as deft at surviving Ogygia's hazards," he added with meaning.

Spinnaker's lessons echoed in her mind. "The rift has cost us both," she admitted.

"What cost to you? You need next to nothing. You don't eat, don't drink, don't exercise…you barely even *move* because it'll move the sails and throw you off course."

"We need to be free and unharassed. We need Chrysalis, which you took from us."

"You've done wellnough without it."

This was true on the face of it. But Chrysalis had been their womb, their garden, the kernel of their soul. Mari remained silent, though, not ready to share such private spirituality with this geeman.

"I'm sorry," Daniel's voice came after a time. "It's just hard...Even before the rift, we did rarely meet. We did speak so little that our dialects did drift apart. You'd be crushed in our world, and we'd be...well, we'd be lost in yours." He chuckled bitterly. "I feel truly lost here now. I don't know how you bear it, Mariposa. To mod yourselves to survive in a way humans never were meant to."

Mari resisted bristling. By his own words, he simply didn't understand. "The first sailors had no choice," she answered patiently. "The Wrecked were scavengers, not colonists. Their tech was damaged, their cybers half-wiped."

"Through their own greed! They *did* choose to enter forbidden space in secret. They did know the Spinward Void was abandoned for true cause."

"I don't defend their folly in coming here," she told him. It seemed the geefolk and sailors still learned the same stories of how the Wrecked, hungry for alien technology left over from the ancient war that had depopulated this part of the Orion Arm, had paid for their greed when a surviving booby trap had destroyed their superluminal drive. "But once stranded, all that mattered was staying alive. They had to jury-rig crude sailcraft—modified probes, spacesuits with sails and cargo hooks attached—just to scrounge the materials to build a life here." It was a basic story she retold, a child's tale, but Mari doubted that geefolk learned much sailfolk history.

"But did not build a transmitter. Did not dare broadcast their crimes to the galaxy."

"We're dozens of parsecs from civilization. Building a transmitter powerful enough to be heard would have taken too much labor and energy, when they had barely enough for survival. And rescue would have been generations away in any case. Building a life here was the only choice we had."

"But why a life trapped in sail suits, forever alone in the void? Why not join us in Castaway?"

"It took more than half a sun cycle to build Castaway. By then, the sailors had been without weight too long to go back. They'd begun having babies in their crude pressurized domes."

"But why not let the children come to Castaway?"

"They didn't wish to part from them. More—they'd found a fulfillment, a freedom they'd never thought possible. True, it was a difficult life, but great truths never come easily. So they built Chrysalis, and later Aurelia and the others, to nurture their heirs and their legacy.

"Over time, we refined the sailcraft," Mari went on. "Made them more efficient. Hooked them to our nerves and our blood. Streamlined and minimized everything, the craft and our bodies alike."

"Until you did practically become the sailcraft yourselves," Daniel finished.

"Practically?" She chuckled at the understatement.

"But I still can't imagine how you can live thus."

Her smile widened invisibly. "And what do you really know about the way we live?"

"Tell me." He really seemed to mean it.

So she spoke of her first memories, of the nursery situated on Chrysalis's equator, letting her feel just enough weight so her bones would learn the right directions to grow. She spoke of swimming in the girdling stream, her playful turbulence kicking up vast undulations in the water; of how whole masses of the stuff would separate from the stream, sometimes carrying her with them, snatching at her with their surface tension, carrying her languidly across a chord of the stream's circumference before gently merging back into their element. She spoke of the plants that grew along the oblate habitat's inner shell, of the trees that grew in random and confused directions, yet still seemed to strive toward the miniature sun at its center. She spoke of the birds and insects that had managed to learn how to fly without the gravity they had evolved for, as if daring the humans to achieve the same.

Mari told him of learning to sail with her bright, silver playwings; of the swooping, dizzying games she shared with the few other children the habitat's resources could bear; of taking insane chances and darting amidst the tangled tree branches, around the scaffolding that held the tiny sun in place, through the pseudopods of water bulging out above the stream.

She told of her pride when she had first been joined with a sailskin and begun training in space, of the wonder she had felt at gaining a vast new body with new senses, new thoughts, new abilities, a whole new beauty. She spoke of the struggle of learning to sail with a whole new kind of wind, one without convection or turbulence, and learning to see the suns as *down* instead of *up*. She shared her triumph when her brain's instincts had finally meshed with the skin's and it had suddenly become the only way to sail. Though there was so much more to that communion that she kept to herself, for he could never understand.

And she told him, her voice singing, of her rite of passage into adulthood: the donation of her ova to ensure the birth of future sailfolk generations, and then her sterilization, her final commitment to a life spent sailing upon stellar radiation. Daniel seemed unable to appreciate the poignant beauty of the ceremony, or of the life it inaugurated.

"But it's such an austere way of being," he said. "Don't you ever chafe at leading such a cold and empty existence?"

Mari strove not to laugh too hard. He was right; it would've shaken the sails. "You pity me, Daniel! Oh, your pity could not be more wasted. You've never felt what it's like to fly through space for *real!* Not locked away in a can, but the master of your own course. Never known what it's like to be *vast,* to have a body that stretches so far you can't see its edges, yet feel as light as a feather upon the wind. Never had a home that's not a tiny bubble of metal, but a whole, sprawling star system with all its farthest bounds within your reach."

She grinned with savage pride, and it carried through her voice. "You've never braved the elements naked and alone, taking on the vacuum and the flares and the meteoroids and the solitude—daring them to kill you and laughing when you survive another day.

"Our ancestors started with almost nothing, Daniel. Yet they survived and made a life for themselves, through ingenuity and bravery and pure plain *will.* The first sailors took on a life humans had never been made for, and they embraced it and made it theirs—made it beautiful. Our very existence is a triumph, Daniel! And every day I go on living is a triumph as well.

"Cold and empty? No. I've never felt empty a day in my life."

Later, after a rest, came Daniel's turn to tell her of his life. It was a strange existence: living in two dimensions, aloft only in machines, always surrounded by masses of humanity. Having permanent homes, pets, possessions. Living with so much structure, so many divisions: different school grades, specialized careers, different families. They even spoke of God as something separate from themselves.

Hearing Daniel tell of his life alongside his genetic forebears and siblings was one of the strangest things of all to Mariposa. She couldn't fathom the way geefolk valued shared biology over shared experience. It seemed as though they alienated themselves from the majority of their fellows, devalued anyone who wasn't genetically close enough. Daniel even spoke of having grown too distant from his family, and Mari wondered if there were anyone he truly felt connected to.

Then Daniel's monologue turned to Kamila, the woman who now lay in a coma in the lifepod's medbed. He painted her as a warm, kind, beautiful woman, a gifted dancer and actress, her grace alluring, her smile blinding, her intelligence entrancing. His voice broke as he chronicled what he feared he might have lost.

"You love her very much," Mari said.

"I did—do. Everyone does. But I did hope…maybe she might love me too. I did hope this trip might be a way to find out. But now I…I may never know."

His sense of loss bewildered her. "I don't understand. You haven't already joined in love?"

His laugh seemed embarrassed, of all things. "In my dreams, truly. But she didn't know yet. We've never even kissed."

"Why not?" she asked, profoundly lost. This was the most tragic, most alien thing she'd ever heard.

"I don't know. I suppose I was afraid."

"Of what?"

"That she might say no." Now that was even more alien. "Or that I might make myself a fool." His mood shifted abruptly. "Here, what do you know anyway? Locked away in those skins your whole lives—what do you know of touching, of loving?"

"I wasn't born in the skin."

"But you seal yourselves in, cut off from human contact. It's not natural. Humans need touch, affection. Babies die without it. Hearts turn cold, minds turn sick from the absence or abuse of it. Take those bonds away and what's left isn't even human."

"You know nothing!" Mari shouted back. "The skins sustain us, balance our hormones and neurotransmitters. I feel touch—the warmth of the suns, the stretching of my spars, the pain of a mete hit. Those parts of my brain do not go unstimulated.

"But yes, the flesh within us has its ancient needs. That's why, when sailors rendezvous, our skins merge and open so our flesh selves are freed to move and touch—to merge in their own way. That's why I couldn't believe you hadn't been with Kamila already. When sailors sight the chance to share another's touch for a few hours, we take it. We *devour* it. Such moments are too brief, too far between, to waste time on caution and preliminaries. When sailors rendezvous, we make love. *Always.* No matter if we've never met in flesh, no matter if we like each other. It's a chance that may not come again for far too long, or never come at all. ."

It was some time before Daniel replied. "Does that mean that when you reach me, you'll want to...." He trailed off, perhaps due to more of that strange sexual modesty. Sailors discussed sex freely all the time, listened and rejoiced when others made love, for it was too rare and precious a thing not to share. But Mari tried to imagine it through geefolk eyes. Castaway and even Robinson held so many more people than all the remaining creches put together. Could that overabundance of neighbors explain why the geefolk limited their sense of kinship to a manageable few? And could their constant physical closeness be so overwhelming that they needed to create distance? Maybe some echo of a sailor's yearning for trackless immensity lived in geefolk's hearts as well. And maybe Daniel was not so hard to understand after all.

But Mari hesitated nonetheless. There was much more at stake here than in an ordinary joining. "I don't know," she told Daniel.

They both fell silent, but others were still monitoring. "Listen to what you just said," Spinnaker's voice came to her ears alone. "How can you not know?"

Her reply was equally private. "How can I not doubt? Our kinds have been apart so long. Who knows how...how our bodies might react? What his could do to mine?"

"Stay outside, and you will say this man isn't worth touching. What message will that send to our people? Mari, this is the first time in nine oldyears that our peoples will physically meet on amicable terms. All of Ogygia is listening. And what you do here can help to heal the rift...or to worsen it. You must choose which risk you fear more."

Daniel's voice resumed after a time. "You have a point. On Castaway, we're raised to value caution and balance. Resources are limited; breathing room is limited; deadly vacuum's all around us; and if you're not careful you'll suffer for it. So we're taught to be reserved, to avoid extremes.

"But you have so much less, yet you embrace the extremes, revel in them. You don't shy from risks. Maybe it's because you have nothing to lose."

"You're wrong, Daniel," she said—though with sympathy now, not anger. "We have everything to lose. I could be killed by a flare next week or a meteoroid tomorrow. A single day may be a lifetime, so sailors strive to live a lifetime in each day." Now she was speaking as much to herself as to him. "A single moment, a single hour of companionship, can mean everything. And to miss the chance to grasp it is to lose everything."

He was silent for a time. "I think I understand now. I did think there was endless time to woo Kamila. That I could be cautious, patient. Now I may never speak to her again. We never know what chances we'll get, or when they'll be taken from us.

"Maybe that's what did happen between our peoples, Mari. We did grow too careful...pass up too many chances to know each other better. Maybe this is a chance to change that.

"So if you want to come in...if you *need* to...I won't turn you away."

Long minutes later, Samiel's voice arrived, begging her not to contemplate such a disgusting union. Argent urged her to ignore him, to take the chance on healing the rift. Vayu suggested that rescuing the pod would be enough of a gesture without the need to enter and risk contamination. Kipepeo, herself berthed at Aurelia for a few more weeks, begged Mariposa to abandon the pod to its fate so they could rendezvous in the creche, cajoling her with graphic descriptions of the lovemaking she planned, then insisting in equally graphic terms that sex with a geeman would ruin Mari forever.

But they were all too far away, their words reaching her too late to matter. Mariposa's choice was hers alone.

And she knew her course was already fixed.

As Mariposa drew within a kilometer of the capsule, its velocity now virtually matched to hers, she trimmed her sails flat between the suns, the light pressure from both directions largely canceling out. At the same time she began furling her sails, feeling her spars retract from hectometers down to meters, the wing material condensing from molecules-thick mesh into millimeter-thick fabric. Not only did this minimize the light thrust, but the greater thickness would protect her sails in case of collision with the pod or associated debris.

It had been some time since Mari had seen another sailor with her own eyes, but she knew what she must look like to Daniel: a small human figure tightly wrapped in silver; her head a featureless bulb atop a body splayed into an *X*, stretching into four slender spars which supported the shimmering sail fabric and delineated it into four triangles, their outer edges curved in graceful catenaries. "My God," Daniel breathed, his words now reaching her ears almost instantly. "You're beautiful."

"Thank you," Mari replied a bit shakily, hoping she could feel the same about him.

She fired the nerves nature had intended for controlling her hands, and cargo hooks extruded from the front of her spars. Silently asking the pod to maneuver its hatch around to meet her, she crept toward it on momentum and finally grabbed hold of it with her manipulators. "Docking successful," she broadcast to the listeners throughout the system.

"Yes, I did hear," Daniel answered, a bit giggly with relief. "So now what?"

"First I replenish your air supply. I'll make a seal with the airlock and open its doors, so we share our air and my skin can metabolize your cee-oh-two into oxygen."

There was a pause that Mari had to remind herself wasn't due to time lag. "Then you are coming inside?"

His voice shook, making hers shake in reply. "I've come all this way…it seems only polite."

"Then I'll truly get to see you. The you inside the skin."

"The skin is me too."

"Yes, but you'll be…naked."

Mari chuckled. "Sail*skin*, remember? I'm always naked."

He replied only with a nervous laugh. Despite her casual air, Mari was nervous too. Maybe Spinnaker was right: this could be a new beginning, a symbol to reunite the castaways. And it would be her first human contact in nearly an oldyear. For all those reasons and more, she knew she had to embrace it. More than that, though: She *wanted* it. Now that Daniel was nearly within reach, the intensity of her need to be with him was startling. And that alone frightened her more than any threat of geefolk disease or crushing strength.

Mari calmed herself and let her fears disperse. As Spinnaker often reminded her, she was one with all things, now and forever.

Though it was not another sailor she sought to merge with now, the process of forming a seal with the escape pod was much the same. It was a shock as always when the sailskin's tight embrace began to release, inflating and molding itself against the airlock door. Her human flesh began to tingle, its nerve endings slowly awakening from their numbness. Then her limbs were released from their silver sheaths, and with a deep, moaning breath, Mariposa began to move.

"What's wrong?" Daniel cried. "Are you in pain?"

She smiled at the anxiety in his voice. "Of course I am. I've hardly moved my limbs in an oldyear." As she watched an opening appear in the skin and gradually widen to reveal the airlock door, Mari just as gradually lowered her spars—no, her arms. "The skin…kept my muscles…electrically stimulated…so they wouldn't atrophy." She bent her legs. "It's giving me…adrenaline and protein…to boost my energy." She flexed her fingers and toes, swiveled her head from side to side. "But it's still…a struggle to make my muscles work again."

"Do you…must I come out? Help you inside?"

She chuckled through the pain, touched by his concern. "Who's the rescuer here? I just need to finish warming up. This is…a regimen all sailors follow when our skins…release our core bodies." She downplayed the difficulty for his benefit. But it was still strange and stiff and unnerving as Mariposa slowly reminded her muscles what it meant to move.

Finally, she sent the command to open the airlock door. "Here I come, Daniel." The next step was the hard one: moving her body outside of her sailskin. Slowly, with difficulty, Mariposa moved her arms, reaching for the frame. Flailing, more like, for her hand fell short.

"Are you truly well?"

"Just getting my bearings. It's been so long since I've seen through these feeble eyes in my head." She reminded herself it was like grappling onto cargo, and that made it easier. But the touch itself, the sensation of cold, hard matter against her palms, was a shock. It was a numbness, an inchoate pressure, yet it was real and overwhelming. It burned; it chilled; it hurt; it was ecstasy. She gasped and sobbed at the proof that she was tangible again.

"Mariposa!"

But this was just a lifeless sheet of carbon composite. Inside was flesh, warmth, humanity. Inside was Daniel, who offered her such kindness even through his own fear and need. How much more overwhelming would his touch be? How could she possibly bear it? Yearning to drown in it, she clung to the frame and began to pull. "I'm coming."

The force her delicate arms could exert was tiny, but so was her mass. With a focused effort, she managed to propel herself into the lock. The next step was to open the inner door while the outer remained open, in order to accommodate the silvery umbilicals that kept her one with her skin. Tendrils extruded to probe the airlock's mechanisms, finding ways to bypass its failsafes.

The door just cracked at first, allowing pressures to equalize. It felt like an eternity before the lock slid open and Daniel was revealed to her. He was a veritable giant to her eyes, nearly a meter eighty in height, each of his thighs almost as wide as her entire torso. His skin was an even richer brown than her golden-bronze inner flesh, though it had felt far less radiation in its life than hers had. But most of his flesh was hidden beneath a loose, dull-colored outer skin that seemed to serve little function. His head was uncovered, though, except by tightly curled black hair. His jaw was square and his nose broad…but it was hardly the rough, brutish geefolk face described in sailors' tales. It was…beautiful.

How could she have ever expected otherwise? Geefolk or not, his was the first human face she had seen in nearly an oldyear. Of course it was beautiful. But there was more to it than that. There was a vulnerability to Daniel's visage, and a warmth that she felt would make him beautiful even to one who gazed on human faces every day.

His dark eyes were wide, curious. She could see them fixating on her hairless scalp, her fragile limbs, and the shimmering umbilicals that trailed from her neck and spine. Was she too alien to him, too hideous?

But then he smiled nervously, and her heart caught fire. "Um, hello, Mariposa. I'm, I'm glad to meet you." He extended a diffident hand.

"Daniel." All her hesitation was forgotten. Clumsily but eagerly, she clasped his outstretched hand, gasping at the wave of sensation. This time it was beyond words. Feeling human skin after so long was always overpowering, but this was somehow more intense, more solid, than any touch she'd known before. Panting, she pulled herself slowly against him and wrapped her arms and legs around his massive frame. The more it overwhelmed her, the more she could bear it, and the more she craved it. She nuzzled her head against his cheek, startled by the scratchiness of the tiny hairs that grew from it, but still reveling in the warmth of human flesh upon her scalp.

Daniel stiffened at first, but then he relaxed. "Mariposa," he sighed, a word filled with welcome, gratitude, and invitation. His arms moved to embrace her, but he hesitated, his fingers exerting only the most delicate pressure against her skin.

She found she could speak again. "Don't fear, Daniel, I'm not quite as delicate as my sails. You can touch me more firmly than that." Excitedly, she planted a series of quick kisses from his neck across his cheek to his full, warm lips, which she caught hungrily between her own. After a moment, he returned her kisses, his arms encircling her more firmly, but still delicately, with care not to snag her umbilicals.

Mariposa had to take the lead in their lovemaking. Daniel had no experience at free-fall maneuvering, and needed her to help him undress, following his coaching. His body was remarkable, exotic in its massiveness, the thickness of its sinews. She'd always assumed unaugmented bodies were somehow incomplete, but there was a compelling purity to Daniel's form.

But that lack of augmentation had its cost. Daniel's body was unused to the way microgravity altered its blood flow, and this combined with his stress to leave him impotent. He apologized profusely and abashedly. But Mariposa would hear none of it. "We'll manage fine," she purred. "Make love with your whole *being*...and one piece of it more or less won't matter."

Under Mari's passionate ministrations, it soon became clear to them both that Daniel's lack of physical response in no way diminished his emotional desires. Still, he caressed her carefully, handling her like the most fragile of cargoes. His light touch burned her flesh with ecstasy wherever it fell.

Afterward they floated together for a long time, wrapped in each other's arms, simply holding each other. They didn't say a word, or need to; they were communicating on a far purer level. This was like the communion she shared with other sailors, but somehow deeper, almost like the merging of a sailor and her skin. Surely it wasn't always like this between geefolk? Was it because they were a sailor and a geeman? Or was it simply because they were Mariposa and Daniel? All she knew was that being with him had given her sensations and emotions she'd never felt before.

And she knew these epiphanies were worth the price she might pay for them, and more.

All too soon it was time to return to her skin and hoist sail to put the escape pod on course for Robinson. It wasn't something she could do from inside, for the nerve impulses would control her arms and legs rather than her spars. But once that was done, she returned. They made love again, as far as Daniel was able, and then they fell asleep in each other's arms. Mari had never known sleep like this. Sailors needed little, and what they took was hardly different from the waking state. Most dreams were hypnagogic, semiconscious, filling the vast stretches of quiet, yet easily shaken off when alertness was needed. But this was different. Mari's body was spent, sore, exhausted as it had not been since her raucous playtimes in the crèche. The oblivion of deep slumber was more welcome than ever—particularly since she shared it with another.

When she woke, though, it was not to contentment. She was hot, as if she'd skirted too close to a sun, yet her body trembled. Her muscles ached and burned. Her little-used digestive system twisted and roiled as if calling for attention. She felt like she was spinning.

She tried to ride it out, clinging to Daniel, soaking in his warmth and trying not to wake him. But she couldn't control her trembles or her moans, and soon he came to awareness. "Mari, what is it? What did happen to you? Are you too long out of your skin?"

She shook her head weakly. "Still connected…not the problem. Ohh, I'd hoped this wouldn't hit so hard…that my fears were exaggerated."

"What? What is it?" His eyes were frantic.

"Immunity. Our peoples have been apart so long…unused to each other's germs…and sailors need our immune systems so little that they grow weak. But I…hoped it wouldn't be this bad."

Daniel looked at the damaged, useless medbed—then more intently at the occupied one which kept Kamila alive. "No," she urged him. "Don't even think of trading her for me. The beds wouldn't know what to make of my physiology anyway. Might try to reject the skin." Besides, she couldn't sever the umbilicals and survive, not under these conditions.

"Can the skin itself not help you?" Daniel asked.

"It has no more immunity than I. And it's weak, depleted. All it could do is…put me in hibernation…but I'm so weak as it is, that would just kill me." She stroked his chest comfortingly. "It's all right, Daniel. I knew the risk…and I made the choice. No one else could've reached you in time."

"But you didn't must come in with me. Didn't must leave the skin. I'm sorry I did sway you."

She touched his cheek. "That was my choice. To a sailor, touch *is* life. Turn away from others' touch, waste a chance to connect with life, and you only serve death. Maybe you'll breathe longer for it, but you haven't truly gained life, or given life."

She savored a slow breath. "We castaways need to stop letting fear keep us from taking chances. I took a chance—not just to be with you, but maybe to start healing the rift. Both of those would make it a worthy sacrifice."

Tears pooled around his eyes. He brushed them away, the moisture clinging to his fingers. "You're being so brave."

"Not really," she admitted. "Only my body will die." He frowned, and she explained: "This is the one gift of the sails that I didn't want to boast about. Too private. But now I need you to know, so you won't be sad. Daniel—the skin is me as much as this body is. Its neural net is an extension of my brain—my psyche inhabits both at once. And I will live on in it, just as its former occupants do." Within her, she felt Spinnaker's warm reassurance, and those of the other long-dead sailors who had inhabited this skin before it had become hers. "They advise me. Help make me who I am. I never would have come to you if not for their wisdom. And so, I will endure in the skin and advise the next sailor who joins with it."

"How much of you will survive? Will it still be the Mariposa I know?"

"Then there'd be no sacrifice, would there? No...only part of me will live on. My memories, my awareness will continue, but changed. Memories and emotions associated with my human body...those reside in the flesh, and will be lost."

He wept more. This time she wiped the tears away for him. "Then...you won't remember what we did share. Won't feel it."

She stroked his cheek. "You will remember for both of us."

Daniel held her for a long time. "How long will you last?" he finally asked.

"I don't know. But not long enough to see you and Kamila home, where they can heal her." She coughed. "My skin will lose motor control without my body. It'll have to stay with the pod. Your people can send it back to us once they recover you."

He stiffened, giving her a desolate look. "Mari...to them you're still the enemy. They'll destroy the skin. Destroy the last of you."

A chill went through her, not from the infection. *And Spinnaker, and Vela, and the others....* "But I saved you—"

"They will fear a trap. And a skin with a will of its own....They won't take the chance."

"The skin—we—will be helpless."

"And they will be too afraid of it anyway."

Mari understood that fear all too well. Yet she had made her peace already. "Then I suppose...this will be the end. It's all right. Sailors face that risk every day. Even skins die eventually. But we understand that a lifetime can be lived in a single day. That infinite love can be shared in a single embrace. And that a single wasted chance can cost you everything."

She kissed him. "I took a chance with you, Daniel, and I don't regret that. Our chances for happiness are finite. So don't you let this harden you against future chances. Don't let fear of circumstances or consequences keep you from seizing them. Find someone to love and love them unreservedly. Reach out to your kin, geefolk and sailfolk alike. Even if it hurts, even if it costs."

He stared at her intently, thinking. "Mari," he finally asked, "how do you transfer the skin from one sailor to another? Does it take special tools? Or could we do it here?"

The question stunned her. "You? You want to—"

"It's the only way to save you." There was trepidation in his voice, but no doubt in his eyes. "I did see how the skin did expand and flow to free you, to merge with the pod. Truly it might fit around me."

"But is it even possible? Your body's too massive, too inefficient."

"If I reach a creche, they can modify me."

"If they trust you enough to let you close."

"You'll be with me. You can vouch for me."

"But what about Kamila?"

He threw a lingering look at the medbed. "Kamila is…a friend. And a hope for a future that might never be. Like you did say—I mustn't let fear or doubt stop me from seizing chances. You did tell me to love someone without reservation. And I choose thus now—with you. I love you, Mariposa."

She clasped his hand. "And I love you." She thought it over, listened to the wisdom in her skin. "There is a chance it can be done…but the skin is already depleted. Sustaining your body would strain it badly, even for the time it would take to reach Aurelia. It's far riskier than staying here in the pod."

"You did risk everything, did sacrifice the life you know, for me. How can I do any less for you?"

"But you have no training, no reflexes for sailing. It will terrify you. Your instincts will fight it. Panic even once and you could mangle the sails."

"I will have you to show me the way." He stroked her smooth scalp. "Mari, you were right. We have a chance to begin healing the rift. A geeman and a sailor, together in one skin…it might change everything. Yes, it's dangerous. But joining is always a risk."

Mariposa smiled. "And so is the alternative. Yes, Daniel. Let us be together, my love. Always."

Sailor Daniel tenderly clutched Mariposa's body in his cargo hooks. It was tightly sealed in a plastic shroud from the lifepod's supplies, retaining its moisture until he could bring it to Aurelia, where it would nourish the creche's biosphere and help sustain the next generation of sailfolk. Daniel could only hope the gesture would bring him the acceptance that his own people would have denied Mariposa.

Mari's voice in his head, and those of her forebears, seemed to think it would.

But that was weeks away, weeks of cold and emptiness and silence. Weeks he might not survive even with the skin to care for him. The physical joining had been comparatively easy, at least for the skin; it had changed hosts before and remembered what to do. It was even old enough to remember earlier generations of sailors whose bodies had been closer to his in mass and metabolism, helping it adapt to his cumbersome form, though not without strain on them both. But nothing in Daniel's experience could help his mind adapt to this. In the days since he had made the final course correction for the pod—since he had ensured Kamila's safety and then sailed away from her forever—he had been alone in deep space with nothing around him save the sails that he was still learning to see as part of himself. Being naked to vacuum and the suns still terrified Daniel as nothing ever had. And sharing his head with other voices, even one as cherished as Mari's, still felt like an invasion he could not escape. The skin had needed to keep him mostly paralyzed lest his fight-or-flight instincts tear it to shreds.

Yet it was liberating in a way he'd never imagined. The more it overwhelmed him, the more he could bear it, and the more he craved it. It was like dying and being reborn. Which was only fitting.

At least the voices outside his head had been mostly quiet. Mariposa's sacrifice—and his own—had made the other sailors pause their endless chatter, and they watched with reverence or hope or wary patience as he struggled through his rebirth. Daniel dared not even contemplate what the geefolk were thinking now.

But Daniel knew that he wanted this life. The skin was already changing him, body and soul—eating away the excess baggage, purifying him of his burdens, broadening his mind in an entirely literal sense as his awareness spread throughout a far vaster body. And though there was nothing around him but infinite emptiness, save for the odd lethal hazard like radiation and metes and the gravity wells of half-formed planets, he felt no fear, no vulnerability. For Mariposa still sang in his head, and he understood now what no geefolk ever had before:

That a sailor is never alone.

Appendix A: Historical Overview

With the exception of "No Dominion," all the stories in this collection belong to a common future history, which they share with my 2012 novel *Only Superhuman*. The stories have been ordered to provide the best reading experience, but some readers might prefer to go through them chronologically. This section places the stories (and the novel) in their historical context.

The Strider Era
2092: "Murder on the Cislunar Railroad"
2106: "Aspiring to be Angels"
2107: ***Only Superhuman***

Once commercial asteroid mining took off in the 2030s, it drove rapid advancement in space travel and colonization. As environmental catastrophes worsened toward the middle of the century, cislunar habitats (i.e. those within the orbit of Earth's Moon) became a major source of food and assistance for Earth, and further emigration to space was aggressively promoted by the loose global government that formed in response to the crisis—with considerable encouragement from the space industry lobbyists who held influence over that government. The Space Homestead Act of 2056 provided subsidies for the construction of space habitats in Earth orbit and the Asteroid Belt, as well as Lunar and Martian settlements.

In this version of history, in contrast to "No Dominion," longevity treatments and human modification were discouraged on Earth, both to limit population growth and to promote emigration to space. Conversely, those who dwelled permanently in space accepted the need for genetic and bionic modification in order to survive its radiation and harsh conditions. It was not long before some communities began experimenting with more radical "mods" to augment human abilities. The people of the cislunar Vanguard habitat were among the first to embrace aggressive transhuman enhancement, and their success in the decades that followed inspired others to follow suit. The most gifted Vanguardian mods helped Earth deal with its environmental and sociopolitical upheavals. Some saw them as real-life superheroes, yet many on Earth perceived them as ambitious, imperious, and dangerous.

By the 2060s, the Molecular Revolution, encompassing profound advances in nanotech and genetic medicine, was well underway. The development of auxons—autonomous, self-replicating construction drones—allowed space habitat construction to explode in Earth orbit and the Main Asteroid Belt. By the 2070s, a new community of Belt dwellers known as Stroiders—later elided to Striders—had emerged. A number of mods and other skilled individuals in the Belt chose to use their abilities to protect their communities and neighbors, in the absence of more organized government and law enforcement. These freelance peacekeepers and rescue workers came to be known as "Troubleshooters." While the Vanguardians had resisted the "superhero" label, the Troubleshooters embraced it and its associated trappings, recognizing its value for earning the trust of a mod community that had embraced classic superhero fiction as its foundational mythology, for lack of real-world precedents to draw upon.

Along with the Striders' emerging sense of identity came a push for independence from the Earth governments and corporations that ruled their colonies. In 2076, the Orbit War erupted, nearly leading to the use of weapons of mass destruction. But wiser heads on both sides negotiated the Great Compromise, granting Earth control of cislunar space in exchange for Strider independence. The Union of Earth and Cislunar States (UNECS) was formed in the wake of the Compromise. Once UNECS took possession of cislunar space, Vanguard was one of the first habitats to migrate to the Belt. The increased emigration from Terran space created new tensions in the Belt, leading the early Troubleshooters to band together into a formal, nongovernmental security organization, the Troubleshooter Corps, in 2083. The Troubleshooters soon made themselves indispensable in the Belt, but UNECS and the various Martian governments had little use for them.

The Striders, spread out across dozens of light-minutes of space, lacked access to the near-instantaneous information networks of Earth, and thus embraced the development of sapient cybers. Earth culture considered this essentially slavery, leading to a ban on their creation in

UNECS territory and the rise of the Earth-backed Cislunar Railroad. The efforts of the Railroad, Zachary March, and Athena paved the way for one of the Troubleshooters' greatest early achievements: the liberation of DiCenzo Mining's large stable of enslaved cybers. Many of the liberated cybers became employees of the Troubleshooter Corps, serving as shipminds or analysts, for there were still few other places in the Belt where their rights would be respected. Arkady Nazarbayev's shipmind Hermes was one of these, as was Emerald Blair's partner Zephyr (see *Only Superhuman*).

It was not long thereafter that Madeleine Kamakau began her own rise to fame. After losing of several of her young children in the 2109 war between the independent and corporate-ruled states of Mars, Kamakau began working relentlessly for peace, building an extensive network of political and familial alliances that would eventually lead to the founding of the Confederation of Martian Republics in 2122.

The Early Interstellar Era
2176: "Aggravated Vehicular Genocide"
2202: "The Weight of Silence"
2250: "Among the Wild Cybers of Cybele"

While emigration to Mars and the asteroids continued to be aggressively encouraged, many Terrans looked still further, hoping to colonize habitable worlds around other stars. The confirmed detection of extrasolar life and technology in the mid-21st century fired humanity's passion for exploration even more fiercely. The rapid breakthroughs made possible by the settlement of Solsys were soon applied to the exploration of other star systems, one of the few projects on which Terrans and Striders could happily collaborate in the wake of the Orbit War. Swarms of microsail probes accelerated to near the speed of light by high-energy particle beams had been launched to explore the exoplanets of nearby systems as early as the 2030s. Later on, more advanced auxonic probes were sent to other stars, where they would replicate in large numbers to explore their exoplanetary systems more fully.

The first human colonists reached the Alpha Centauri system by the end of the 21st century, using a beam-driven sail system that reached a quarter of the speed of light. Their success prompted even further advancements. Madeleine Kamakau, feeling her work was done on Mars, migrated to Alpha Centauri in the 2140s and helped to build a new civilization for the second time. Kamakau would make interstellar journeys to several more human colonies over the next eleven decades, spending a record number of years in hibernation and time-dilated flight.

Though many of the exoplanets reachable within a human lifetime were more or less habitable with some adjustment, none were as amenable to human life as Earth. It was not until 2142 that probe data confirmed the existence of a comfortably Earthlike world around Gamma Leporis, 29 light years away. The planet that would be dubbed Cybele was too ideal a colonization opportunity to pass up—but reaching it within a human lifetime would require pushing starship technology to its absolute limit, with all the risks that entailed.

Though *Arachne*'s crew became aware of faster-than-light drive upon their adoption into Chirrn society, their oath of penance to the Chirrn precluded them from contacting other humans to share that knowledge. Nonetheless, it was only a few years later that human explorers happened across what appeared to be an abandoned cache of alien technology, including programmable quark matter, a subatomically engineered substance that could potentially allow the creation of a working warp drive. This was not a coincidence—but that is a story for another time.

Turning the potential for superluminal travel into reality would be an incremental process spanning decades. The accidental breakthrough achieved by Monali Chen and Miguel Oroxco soon led to a practical reactionless drive that could reach relativistic speeds with far less energy expenditure than existing methods. The warp bubble shielded the vessel from interstellar dust and debris, eliminating the need for cumbersome defense systems and allowing starships to push even closer to the speed of light. The only drawback was that the lack of time dilation would make the trips subjectively longer, but improvements in hibernation and revival technology compensated for this.

The lush beauty of Cybele still beckoned, and telemetry from the auxon probes there confirmed that they were ready and waiting to assist in human colonization. The reason for the loss of *Arachne* was still unknown to the people of Solsys, but it was rendered irrelevant by the new drive technology. Thus, a second, much larger expedition, this time consisting of multiple ships with several hundred colonists in all, was launched toward Gamma Leporis in late 2212. Thirty years later, humans finally breathed the air of Cybele.

The Warp Era
2315: "Twilight's Captives"
c. 2480: "The Caress of a Butterfly's Wing"

By the time Safira Kimenye fled into the wilds of Cybele in 2249, the first successful superluminal test flight in Solsys was already several months in the past. However, FTL use of warp cages was limited by excessive power demands and the decoupling of the warp bubble from outside space, impeding the crews' ability to see outside the ships and to radiate excess heat. It would not be until the 2260s that superluminal starships became feasible, allowing humans to travel among their assorted colonies within weeks or months—and to travel still farther and make direct contact with alien civilizations that had only been observed telescopically until then. Humanity wisely recruited Madeleine Kamakau, now one of its most accomplished explorers, statespersons, and peacemakers, to play a leading role in this process. She would soon make first contact with a number of alien civilizations, including the Denzeuur and the Nocturne League.

Although the Chirrn and their allies were aware of humanity's expansion, they still chose to remain aloof from planetary civilizations—although their community welcomed many of the Striders who had settled extrasolar asteroids and comets or merely launched their habitats toward the stars. Over the decades that followed, the planetary civilizations of humanity and a few of their alien allies developed a parallel community known as the Planetary Commonwealth. It was able to coexist peacefully with the Chirrn's alliance in the same volume of space because the two did not compete for the same territories within it. But in dealings with other interplanetary civilizations such as the Nocturne League, conflict was harder to avoid.

As the Planetary Commonwealth continued to grow and solidify its relationships with neighboring powers, many human explorers followed in Madeleine Kamakau's footsteps and traveled even deeper into the Galaxy. The Striders, now a truly interstellar community, were on the vanguard of this expansion, following their ancestral urge to spread outward and adapt to alien environments.

While the spiritual descendants of the Troubleshooters lived on, patrolling the starways and keeping the peace, so did the hardscrabble lawlessness that had made them necessary in the first place. Some Striders, in pursuit of advanced alien technology and ancient knowledge, defied the conventions of polite galactic society and intruded where they were not welcome—or defied the warnings of those who knew better and went where it was not safe. The original castaways of the Ogygia system were one such group, stranded in a remote binary star system in the 2350s. Whether they ever regained contact with galactic civilization is beyond the scope of this volume.

Appendix B: Glossary

AU: Astronomical unit, the mean orbital radius of Earth, equal to 149.6 million kilometers or 499 light-seconds.

auxon: Self-replicating robot able to reproduce in large numbers from raw materials, generally used for large-scale industrial projects or interstellar probe missions. Term coined by Klaus Lackner and Christopher Wendt in 1995.

Bolasat: Momentum-exchange satellite using long rotating carbon nanotube tethers to modify the trajectory and velocity of spacecraft. Weblike docking cradles travel along these tethers and intercept ships, shuttling them in or out until they reach their desired trajectories and are released, given a momentum boost by the tether's rotation and the cradle's speed. The Bolasat network allows faster and more direct intrasystem travel than orbital trajectories would allow. (Named for the ball-and-cord weapon known as bolas. The term bolo is sometimes incorrectly applied.)

championym: Term favored by the Troubleshooter Corps for the code name of a superhero or crimefighter.

cislunar: Within the orbit of Earth's Moon. Also used by convention to include the Earth-Luna L2 and L3 points, which are technically translunar.

Coriolis effect: Fictitious force creating a deflection of a moving object from the perspective of an observer in a rotating frame of reference. Something thrown perpendicular to the direction of rotation will seem to curve to antispinward as the observer is moved in the other direction by the habitat's spin.

cyber: Artificial intelligence, especially a sapient one.

diamite: Name for a class of carbon-based synthetic nanomaterial crystals stronger than diamond.

flare: Strider expletive. As in a solar flare or coronal mass ejection. Used as a noun, verb, or (as "flaring") adjective.

Four Voids: Name used in the galactic community for a cluster of four large, low-density bubbles in the interstellar medium of the central Orion Arm, created by a wave of star formation and supernovae that passed through the region over the past thirty million years. The Central Void, known to humans as the Local Bubble, contains the worlds of the Planetary Commonwealth and the Nocturne League. The other Voids are Antispinward (aka Loop I), Outward (Loop II), and Spinward (Loop III).

hard virus: Infectious nanotech used to alter, manipulate, or disrupt technology on a hardware level, by analogy with a software virus.

Lagrange Points: The five points of a two-body system where gravitational forces balance, allowing stable or semistable orbits around them. For instance, in the Sun-Earth system, the L1 point is between Earth and the Sun, L2 on the far side of Earth from the Sun, L3 just beyond the point directly opposite Earth in its orbit, and L4 and L5 respectively 60 degrees ahead and behind the Earth in its orbit. The first three points are stable only in a plane perpendicular to the line connecting them, so attitude-control thrusters are necessary to maintain orbit there. L4 and L5 are stable and can be orbited indefinitely.

leak: Strider expletive. Refers to an atmosphere leak, as well as urination.

light armor: A close-fitting, flexible fabric woven from carbon nanotubes and synthetic silk, with a layer of synthetic-diamond scales, nanoactuators, computer circuitry, piezoelectric power fibers, and nanotube capacitors throughout its material. It enhances the wearer's strength and becomes stiff in response to impact or pressure; it also provides resistance to weapons fire and extreme heat, cold, or radiation, and provides dynamic support to the muscles and joints. In case of injury, it can apply medical assistance, compressing to splint a broken bone or even to apply cardiopulmonary resuscitation.

lightsail: Propulsion system using a low-mass reflective sail accelerated by momentum transfer from sunlight or a powerful laser. Slow to accelerate but highly efficient, it is useful for extremely lightweight craft operating exclusively in interplanetary space.

magnetic sail: Propulsion system which generates a magnetic field around a spaceship, allowing it to be accelerated by the solar wind or a beam of charged particles or to maneuver in a planetary magnetic field. Typically either a coil of superconducting wire or a magnetically confined loop of plasma, though the latter is too fragile to withstand a powerful propulsion beam. The magnetic field can also shield against particle radiation and solar flares.

medbed: Automated single-occupant medical treatment pod commonly used aboard spacecraft.

Medvyéd: Russian, "bear."

micromete: A micrometeoroid, i.e. a spaceborne particle smaller than 0.05 millimeters—difficult to detect, but generally traveling at dangerously high velocity.

mod: Human genetically, bionically or surgically modified with enhanced abilities or unusual cosmetic attributes. As a verb, to modify a human or other organism in this way.

nanote: Semi-biological nanomechanism used for medical treatment. Not to be confused with "nanite," though it is a subset thereof.

plasma rifle: Variable-lethality weapon using a high-powered laser to create a small globe of atmospheric plasma at the target site and induce a supersonic shock wave within it, resulting in a forceful, lightninglike discharge of light, heat, and pressure. Can be calibrated to disorient, stun, or kill depending on power, or to create a protective "wall" of plasma discharges.

programmable quark matter (PQM): A femtotechnologically engineered material capable of simulating particles and forces with exotic physical properties, particularly those required to create sustainable warp drive fields and wormholes.

punk: Strider expletive, generally a transitive verb. Short for "puncture," as of a hull or spacesuit. Sometimes used as a vulgar synonym for "copulate."

selfone: Personal communication/data device; primary means of identification and financial transactions. From "cell phone" seen as an extension of the self. Usage peaked in the Strider Era; in later centuries, the term **wristcom** was often preferred.

soligram: Informal term (solid + hologram) for a display/simulation mechanism using a shape-changing smart matter gel that can simulate the appearance, texture, and density of virtually any substance. Often used in place of virtual reality due to the eyestrain and nearsightedness that extended use of VR visors or contacts can cause.

Solsys: Shorthand name for the Sol system.

Strider: Originally, an inhabitant of the Main Belt or Trojan Asteroids of the Sol system; corruption of earlier "Stroider." Eventually, a member of a more expansive, primarily human community based in artificial habitats in interplanetary and interstellar space.

stroid: Asteroid.

symbot: Former brand name, now generic, for performance-enhancing robotic exoskeletons. Available in various models for construction, combat, sports, medical support, etc. Lightweight models are compact and close-fitting, but heavy-duty models are armored and provide full life support.

vack: Strider expletive. Short for vacuum, as in "vack-sucker" or "vackhead," or as a verb meaning to expel something into vacuum, as in "Go vack yourself."

warp cage: Starship drive in the form of a spherical or ovoid shell using programmable quark matter to create a superluminal warp field along its surface, also shielding the vessel within from the Hawking radiation and debris hazards of superluminal travel. Can be used to convert any spacegoing craft into a faster-than-light starship, size permitting.

Afterword and Acknowledgments

This collection represents nearly all my published original science fiction over the first eighteen and a half years of my professional career, save only for the novel *Only Superhuman* (published by Tor Books in 2012) and the three "Hub" novelettes in my e-book collection *Hub Space: Tales from the Greater Galaxy* (published by Mystique Press in 2015). I haven't been nearly as prolific with original fiction as I had hoped to be twenty years ago, since I've ended up working mainly as an author for Pocket Books' long-running *Star Trek* tie-in line. Finally having enough original stories to collect in book form is a very satisfying milestone, and I hope it will be just the beginning.

Nearly all of the stories herein belong to a single future history. I've always loved continuity and worldbuilding, so my default practice has been to set all my fiction within the same reality unless there's a reason it won't fit there. But that means the universe doesn't have a single core concept that defines it, such as the Hub in my other ongoing universe, so I've never been able to think of a good blanket name for it. The Internet Speculative Fiction Database at www.isfdb.org calls it the *Only Superhuman* Universe, so I guess that (or OSU) will do as a placeholder.

The origins of the OSU date back to when I was eleven and got a set of "Star City" building blocks, which let me build futuristic cities and imagine the adventures of their inhabitants. At first, I loosely based my daydreams on the *Star Trek* universe, which had been my introduction to space, science, and science fiction at the age of five and a major influence on my life from then on. However, since I was playing with an alien city rather than a toy starship, I invented new situations and characters and chose to set them a hundred years after the era of Kirk and Spock—an idea ahead of its time, for this was seven years before *Star Trek: The Next Generation*. After about six months, I got tired of the restrictions that *Star Trek* continuity placed on my imagination, so I edited the cursory Trek connections out of my daydream future and invented a new history for it. By the time I was thirteen, I realized that I wasn't just daydreaming anymore, but *writing*, and that was when I knew what my career would be. After that, I started building my universe more intently, expanding it far beyond my toy cities. I abandoned the use of humanoid aliens and began designing more plausibly exotic creatures, influenced by the writings of Carl Sagan, Larry Niven, Isaac Asimov, and others, and by artist Wayne Barlowe's classic *Barlowe's Guide to Extraterrestrials*. Over the years, I repeatedly reworked my future history and worldbuilding to make it more scientifically plausible and more original, evolving it into something purely my own.

The primary element I kept from its Trekkish beginnings, however, was an emphasis on an optimistic view of the future. My real life growing up as a bullied social outcast was depressing enough that I needed to believe the future could be better, so I wanted to write stories that showed a possible path toward building such a future. But I didn't want a dull, simplistic utopia. I understood that building a better world would take hard work and entail many pitfalls and setbacks. I believed that, by acknowledging those complications, I could make my portrayal of a generally optimistic future more believable, as well as more dramatically engaging.

In addition to guarded optimism, scientific plausibility has always been one of my highest priorities in my work. Some of my best ideas have come from imagining the ramifications of a scientific or technological concept. That was the source of my first professional sale, "Aggravated Vehicular Genocide." While contemplating the defensive lasers that a relativistic ramjet starship would need to deflect space debris, I wondered what would happen if an alien spacecraft happened into a ramship's path. Although a spacecraft would have detectable engine emissions warning of its approach, so what if it were a whole space habitat instead? The legal and moral ramifications of such an accident were compelling.

Not only was AVG my first sale, but I sold it on my first attempt, to Stanley Schmidt of *Analog Science Fiction and Fact*. I'd been submitting to *Analog* for years, and Stan's rejection letters had been an education in themselves, advising me on how to improve my writing until I finally became good enough to sell. Apparently he saw something in my work that he wanted to cultivate. It probably didn't hurt that we both came from Cincinnati, Ohio (and indeed, by coincidence, I would later end up living a block away from his old house). Whatever Stan's reasons for taking an interest, I'm forever grateful for his support and guidance.

As my first professional story, AVG was also the one most in need of refinement. It got a good reception at the time, prompting positive reviews and a lively ethical debate in the *Analog* letter column; but in retrospect I find it dry, talky, and light on characterization. Also, the science is rather outdated. I learned years later that the drag created by a ramjet's magnetic field on the interstellar medium would render it impractical. When I republished the story on my now-defunct website in 2004, I revised it to address the scientific concerns and make a few other changes. I've subsequently written a novel that expands and continues the story and improves on its science and characterization issues, and which will supersede AVG as the "correct" version of these events when and if it gets published. However, I wanted to preserve the original story by including it here. Readers can still take the events of AVG as mostly canonical, just with a few inaccurate details. The version herein is largely the 2004 revision, but with a few bits restored to their original form, and with some further slight textual polishes to improve the reading experience (including an increase of Lesshchi's population from the implausibly low 8700 to 88,700).

My second sale to *Analog*, "Among the Wild Cybers of Cybele," was not originally conceived as a sequel to "Aggravated Vehicular Genocide." It was partly inspired by Roger Zelazny's 1981 short story story "Last of the Wild Ones," the second of two stories (the first being "Devil Car" from 1965) set in a world where intelligent, self-driving automobiles had been infected with a computer virus and run wild, roving the countryside in vast herds. But I'd been reading about the use of evolutionary algorithms in programming and robotics—the use of random mutation and selection pressures to "breed" innovative designs and solutions—and I was intrigued by the concept of robots acting like animals, their behavior shaped not by programming or self-aware thought but by pure Darwinian pressures. So I applied the idea of evolutionary algorithms to the idea of auxons, a proposed type of self-replicating robot that I'd read about in Discover Magazine. The idea of auxonic survey probes evolving out of control on an alien planet not only created a wealth of fascinating moral dilemmas, but fit in neatly with the events of AVG, in which a planned colonization never occurred.

My first draft was written in epistolary form as Safira Kimenye's online research diary, as homage to the likes of Jane Goodall and Dian Fossey. Stanley Schmidt loved the concept but didn't like the execution, in part because the story lacked a real ending. But Stan hinted that he'd like to see a revised version of the piece. Unwisely, I sent the first version off to two more magazines before finally taking Stan's invitation seriously and hitting on a solution for the story's problems. Fortunately, both magazines rejected it, letting me craft the far better version that Stan finally bought. Once again, I learned an invaluable lesson from Mr. Schmidt.

For the version published here, I've made only a slight change, specifying that Marc Dupuis is Moroccan rather than French. I like the idea of both of the story's leads being from Africa, albeit very different parts of that diverse continent. The other change I've made is to the context. I originally assumed the Anansi expedition to Cybele was another ramjet mission, but in the course of assembling this collection, I realized that I could tie it into the later story "The Weight of Silence" as described in the historical appendix, which helped to give this collection more of a sense of flow and continuity.

After selling "Wild Cybers" in 2000, I had little luck selling fiction for the next few years, in part because I was focusing on college. (This was my second undergraduate tour in pursuit of a history degree—which I've actually found more useful to my writing than my earlier BS in physics, since I specialized in the study of non-Western and cross-cultural history, contacts and interactions between different cultures, and so forth.) I got my degree in 2002, and the following year, I began writing *Star Trek* fiction for Pocket Books, an endeavor that's kept me pretty busy from then on. I continued to work on my original fiction where I could, but I gradually slacked off in favor of my Trek work until 2009, when I decided to start marketing my original fiction more aggressively again. As a result, famine gave way to feast and I sold four original stories in quick succession. The first and fourth of those were "The Hub of the Matter" and "Home is Where the Hub Is," both published in *Analog* in 2010 and collected in *Hub Space*. The second to see print was "The Weight of Silence," which was my first sale to an online magazine—*Alternative Coordinates*, edited by Jeff Cochran.

The idea behind "The Weight of Silence" was to do a classic hard-SF "problem story," in which the characters need to reason out a scientific solution to a crisis (Asimov's "Marooned off Vesta" being a classic example), but in a more modern, character-driven vein where the problem to be solved is as much personal as technical. I've always striven to balance hard science and strong characterization in my work, rather than prioritizing one at the expense of the other. I'm grateful to my college friend Xuân Stanek for her influence on the character aspects of this story, and for her invaluable role as a creative sounding board and source of emotional support throughout the early years of my writing career.

This is the first story I ever wrote in the first person, a technique I generally find implausible. I always wonder, how does the narrator have the skill to tell this story? How do they get the opportunity to write and publish it? How do they remember every detail, even the verbatim dialogue? "The Weight of Silence" was my attempt to tackle these questions, so the challenge of telling the story became one of the problems the narrator had to solve.

Unfortunately, *Alternative Coordinates* went under less than a year after the story's publication, so "The Weight of Silence" has been essentially a "lost" story ever since. I'm grateful to get it back into print at last.

My third story for 2010, "No Dominion," was written for an anthology called *Shine*, edited by Jetse de Vries and focusing on optimistic science fiction set on near-future Earth. I'd rarely written anything Earth-based, but I couldn't resist the optimism angle. I didn't manage to think of a story until three weeks before the deadline, but once I had the idea, I wrote it within days. It didn't make it into *Shine*, but there were so many worthy runners-up that de Vries published them online as a blog called *DayBreak Magazine*, at daybreakmagazine.wordpress.com. "No Dominion" was one of those runners-up.

Because "No Dominion" was written to the specifications of the *Shine* anthology, it doesn't quite fit the continuity of the OSU. As such, I was hesitant to include it in this collection, since it feels awkward having only a single story out of continuity with the rest. But eight stories are better than seven, and it fits the collection thematically and tonally, as an exploration of the unexpected complications that can arise from an optimistic future. Think of it as a bonus story. It feels like it *almost* fits in the OSU, as though it were an alternate timeline where a few technological and societal trends happened differently.

Oddly, after all the trouble I went through to rationalize a first-person narrative in "The Weight of Silence," I went ahead and wrote this one in first person without even considering the logic questions. I'm not sure why I did that; it just felt right, perhaps since it's a common idiom for detective stories. On reflection, I suppose that first person doesn't need to be taken literally as something the main character actually wrote down as a story at some point; it can simply be a figurative device for getting into a character's point of view.

My selling streak didn't last beyond 2010, in part because my father passed away that year and it was difficult for me to focus for a while. But 2012 saw the publication of *Only Superhuman*, based on a hard-SF superhero premise I'd been developing since 1988. I'd originally written that novel in 2007, my second attempt at a novel about the Troubleshooter Emerald Blair and the Strider civilization of the Asteroid Belt.

When my initial attempts to sell *Only Superhuman* were unsuccessful, I thought I'd try introducing Emerald through short stories to generate interest for the novel. So in 2010, I wrote the first version of "Aspiring to Be Angels." It proved unnecessary once Greg Cox acquired the novel for Tor Books, so I decided to use it as the opening flashback chapter in the second novel. Alas, the sales of *Only Superhuman* were not strong enough to warrant a sequel, so I revisited and revised the story as a standalone. Once this collection became a prospect, I realized that including an all-new Green Blaze adventure would be a pretty good hook. So here we are.

The plot of "Aspiring" owes a lot to the 1998 anime series *Serial Experiments Lain*, written by Chiaki J. Konaka and directed by Ryûtarô Nakamura. The world of Emerald Blair is rich with pop-culture influences and homages, including anime, but the *Lain* influence makes this a darker, creepier story than *Only Superhuman*. Perhaps this is fitting, since the tale represents one of the darker moments in Emerald's apprenticeship. The timeframe lets me fill in a gap in *Only Superhuman*, which covered most of the key events in Emerald's life in flashback, but whose segments covering her Troubleshooter training were cut to improve the story flow. The final version of "Aspiring to Be Angels" incorporates elements of that deleted material.

The remaining stories in this collection were all written early in my career, shelved after going unsold, then eventually revisited with a more experienced eye and rewritten into a viable form. The record-holder is "The Caress of a Butterfly's Wing," which I originally wrote in 1998, not long after "Aggravated Vehicular Genocide," but did not sell until 2014, when Laura Anne Gilman purchased it for the online *Buzzy Mag* at buzzymag.com. In between, the story went through sixteen rejections and two non-replies, and at least half a dozen major rewrites.

I stuck with "Butterfly's Wing" for so long because it was a very personal, emotional story for me, inspired by my experiences with loneliness and shyness, and by an incident in which I connected with a person for only a few hours at a high school reunion but felt a genuine friendship with her, leading me to realize that even a brief encounter could be precious. (So, thank you, Amy, wherever you are.) Also, I got at least a couple of rejection letters saying that the story was poignant and lyrical but *just* not quite right, so that kept me from giving up on it. Yet every attempt I made to fix the problems seemed to introduce new ones. Eventually I put it on the back burner, but in 2013 I revived it as a submission for a cyborg-themed anthology, adding some new aspects to the symbiosis between sailor and sailskin, and in the process finding a solution to a problem with the ending that I hadn't recognized before. The anthology didn't take it, but Laura did, and she also provided abundant help in refining the story further.

"Murder on the Cislunar Railroad," initially written in 2003, also needed a fair amount of reworking. When I plotted it, I decided to experiment with a more methodical approach to building my characters, working out their backstories in advance so that every role would be well-drawn and textured. (This was more of my friend Xuân's influence, for she was an active role-playing gamer who loved building rich backgrounds for her game characters.) Somehow, I ended up with a story full of unlikeable characters that were no fun to read about—perhaps because I wanted them all to be plausible murder suspects and thus focused too much on their negative aspects. I rewrote it to make the characters more palatable, but still had no luck selling it. And afterward, I mostly went back to my usual, more seat-of-the-pants approach to character-building.

Once I wrote *Only Superhuman*, set against the same backdrop of Striders and cybers, I decided to use elements from this tale as backstory for Emerald Blair's cyber sidekick Zephyr. As with "Aspiring to be Angels," I shelved "Cislunar" and planned to incorporate it as a flashback in the second Emerald Blair novel, but the lack of such a sequel led me to revisit it as a standalone story. I realized then that Athena, the character who most needed to be empathetic, still came off as rather haughty and cold. Correcting that must have been what I needed, since I sold the newly revised story on my first try in 2015. It was the second story I sold to *Analog*'s new editor Trevor Quachri, the first having been "Make Hub, Not War" in 2013. It was also my first *Analog* story in 15 years to be set in the OSU.

By contrast, "Twilight's Captives" needed very little revision from its original form, which I wrote in 2001. Aside from a bit of streamlining, the only major change I needed in order to sell it (to *Analog* in 2016) was an improved opening paragraph, which goes to show the importance of a strong beginning. However, this is a story I sat on for a long time after the first rejection. I think that's because it takes place in a part of my future history that I had plans to explore in novels, and my ideas for certain earlier events were in flux, making me unsure if I still wanted "Captives" to happen as written. Perhaps you've noticed a pattern by now—I kept setting aside my short stories for the sake of tentative novel plans that never came to pass. In the early years of my career, I had such poor luck selling short stories that I came to conclude I wasn't very good at them and should focus more on novels. In recent years, though, I've had more luck with shorter fiction and not so much with my novel plans, so I've changed my priorities.

"Captives" was written during my time as a history major, and as such it's strongly influenced by my studies in non-Western history and cross-cultural interactions, particularly in courses taught by Dr. Elizabeth B. Frierson, Dr. Man Bun Kwan, Dr. Geoffrey Plank, and Dr. Willard Sunderland. Yet it incorporates characters and species I created years earlier. In particular, although Madeleine Kamakau is my most recent lead character in the OSU to see print, she's also my oldest creation to see print, dating back to those early days of universe-building in my adolescence (albeit with a different surname and backstory). In my notes, she has a richly detailed life story spanning centuries of the OSU, and I hope to flesh it out further in future tales. I always saw Madeleine as a kind, maternal, nurturing figure who embodied the ideals humanity strove toward in my optimistic future history. So perhaps it's fitting that "Twilight's Captives" is the story that finally gave me enough published material to assemble this collection encompassing the entire history of the *Only Superhuman* Universe to date.

I hope you've found these reminiscences worthwhile. If so, you can find more in-depth discussions and annotations for all of my fiction on my website at christopherlbennett.wordpress.com.

Bibliography

"Aggravated Vehicular Genocide" in *Analog Science Fiction and Fact*, Vol. CXVIII No. 11 (November 1998), pp. 110-130.

"Among the Wild Cybers of Cybele" in *Analog Science Fiction and Fact*, Vol. CXX No. 12 (December 2000), pp. 90-107.

"The Weight of Silence" in *Alternative Coordinates*, Issue 5 (Spring 2010), pp. 32-45.

"No Dominion" in *DayBreak Magazine*, http://daybreak-magazine.wordpress.com, posted June 13, 2010.

"The Caress of a Butterfly's Wing" in *Buzzy Mag*, http://buzzy-mag.com, posted November 13, 2014.

"Murder on the Cislunar Railroad" in *Analog Science Fiction and Fact*, Vol. CXXXVI No. 6 (June 2016), pp. 92-103.

"Twilight's Captives" in *Analog Science Fiction and Fact*, Vol.CXXXVII No. 1 & 2 (January/February 2017), pp. 42-58.

2107 AD: A generation ago, Earth and the cislunar colonies banned genetic and cybernetic modifications. But out in the Asteroid Belt, anything goes. Dozens of flourishing space habitats are spawning exotic new societies and strange new varieties of humans. It's a volatile situation that threatens the peace and stability of the entire solar system.

Emerald Blair is a Troubleshooter. Inspired by the classic superhero comics of the twentieth century, she's joined with other mods to try to police the unruly Asteroid Belt. But her loyalties are tested when she finds herself torn between rival factions of superhumans with very different agendas. Emerald wants to put her special abilities to good use, but what do you do when you can't tell the heroes from the villains?

The following excerpt is reprinted with the express permission of the publisher, Tor Books.

An excerpt of Christopher L. Bennett's novel...

Only Superhuman

May 2107
Chakra City habitat
In synchronous orbit of Earth

Bast fidgeted inside the heavy *chador*, hating the way it cut off her senses. There were so many sights and sounds and smells she was missing, even down here in the maintenance tunnels, away from the cosmopolitan bustle of the city levels above. Not that she cared about the bazaars, the curry parlors, the orchid gardens, or the other tourist traps this backwater Stanford torus festooned itself with as it tried to build itself up, physically and otherwise, into a major cislunar port city. No, she cared about having her senses free, on the alert for enemies.

More fundamentally, she just wanted to get out of the heavy robes so she could scratch herself and groom her beautiful glossy-black fur. She wanted to set her tail free so she could work the kinks out of it. And then she wanted to kill and eat something.

So far this was a boring mission—just sneaking around in empty tunnels, no enemies to sharpen her claws on. But she didn't dare complain to Wulf. That would just invite another tirade on how she should be more devoted to their Glorious Cause. Yes, yes, she knew all about the Neogaians' sacred mission to reclaim the wounded Earth from the technocrats who subsumed nature beneath cold, dead machines and denied humanity its right to evolve. She knew how the disorder created by the construction of the city's new habitat rings made a good cover for their plan to infect Earthbound travelers with designer polyviral mutagens, a blow against UNECS's restrictions on human enhancement and a step toward bringing humanity back into harmony with Mother Earth's animal spirits. But listening to Wulf spewing dogma in her face with his foul canine breath didn't get her in harmony with her animal spirit. She was perfectly in harmony with her animal spirit, and it was telling her to go kill and eat something. Maybe Wulf.

Well, actually, right now it was telling her to scratch that damn itch behind her right ear. So she did—just a little scratch couldn't draw Wulf's ire, surely.

No such luck. "Bast!" Wulf snarled, looking back at her. He looked ridiculous, with the fur shaved off half his face so he'd look like a bearded human, and with the turban pulled down over his big pointed ears. He must hate it—he already resented her for her more advanced transgenic mods, for being closer to "pure animal nature" than he was. But that was what he got for being an older model, born human and chimericized with surgery and stem-cell injections, instead of a germ-line creation like herself. "Stop that," he commanded. "You'll tear your headscarf." She subsided, but hissed and slashed her claws in his direction. "Settle down! Remember, act calm and serene. Look at Caiman there."

Bast thought the croc-man was a lousy example. So still and quiet, always meditating, striving for a perfect animal nonsentience, just existing and watching . . . now *that* was boring. Still, Bast quieted down, hoping to avoid another lecture on how they had to look and act like proper Muslims so nobody would suspect them of being terrorists.

But then Bast thought she heard something moving nearby. It sounded big—maybe a nice juicy rat or bird. There shouldn't be many vermin yet in this new ring segment, where the grass and trees were still being planted and few people lived. Maybe this animal had gotten confused by the new layout and lost its way. Or maybe it wanted the chance to play a fun game with a pretty panther-lady before making a nice new home in her tummy.

Except Wulf had to go and tell them they'd reached their destination. No time for play. With a sigh, Bast turned her back on the interesting foodlike noises and followed the others inside.

The corridor opened into an expansive space containing much of the new segment's nanofabrication machinery. Some of the machines had conduits rising a couple of stories into the space above—maybe a future mall, but for now there was just a network of girders and pipes where the floor would be. The space was deserted except for construction robots, due to the newness of the segment and the time of day—and the fact that Wulf had paid off the guard in advance.

Wulf led them to the cell-stock tanks that supplied the new segment's bioprinters and ordered them to stand guard. Caiman's stillness made him good for that at least—but Bast could be still and silent with the best of them, if there was a good pounce in store at the end of it. She hoped that any intruders would come from her direction so she could kill them before Caiman did. Hell, she just hoped some intruders would show up.

But then Taurean had to go and make conversation. He was here for muscle like Caiman and herself, but also for what little interaction they had with other people, since he had the most normal-looking face (so long as the turban concealed his horns) and an atypically amiable manner for a trained killer. But unfortunately, he wasn't the strong, silent type. He was rambling on about the mission, asking Wulf how the polyviral vectors would work, questioning whether the random animal traits they produced as they spread through Terran humanity could be as viable or safe as their own carefully engineered mods, stuff like that. She didn't listen closely. It did amuse her when Wulf snarled at Taurean for doubting the power of divine Nature to effect this glorious transformation, though her amusement faded as he continued his fanatical tirade. Dogs always made too much damn noise.

Noise—there was something moving around again. Maybe lunch, maybe an intruder (though what was the difference, really?). She couldn't tell with Wulf blathering and the stupid scarf squishing her pretty ears. She hissed for attention. "I hear something!" She caught a definite scent this time, distinctly animal. Maybe even human . . . though it was increasingly hard to tell these days.

"Maybe you should hurry up and finish, Wulf," said Taurean. "I'd like to get out of here without any trouble."

Bast heard a clear movement up above and whirled to face it. A second ago there'd been nothing atop that big machine, but now a woman stood there. She was muscular but curvaceous, with wild hair the color of autumn leaves and an elfin face with enormous, almost catlike green eyes. She wore a green sleeveless tunic with a flame-like trim, matching knee-length boots, tight black hiphuggers, and a faux-leather gunbelt resting at a rakish angle upon her wide hips. This was no local cop or UNECS security trooper. With a flamboyant outfit like that, there was only one thing she could be.

The redhead smirked, tilted an angular brow, and spoke in a honeyed soprano, her cocky words confirming Bast's conclusion. "Looking for trouble? You just found her."

Which was good, since Bast was definitely looking for trouble.

Emerald Blair loved making dramatic entrances, watching all eyes turn to her as she came into a room. Of course, she preferred it when the owners of those eyes didn't also possess guns, combat mods, or both. But such was the lot of a Troubleshooter.

Besides, she was tired of being stealthy. Sneaking up on the Neogaian terrorists was one thing, but she and Arkady Nazarbayev had needed to sneak themselves all the way from Luna without the Union of Earth and Cislunar States finding out. UNECS had refused them clearance to operate within their territory even after Arkady had warned them of the impending Neogaian attack, insisting they were more qualified than any "Strider vigilante and his teen sidekick" (apprentice, thank you, and she was twenty-two) to keep their vaunted peace and order. She supposed she couldn't begrudge the Terrans their pride in that order, given how hard they'd fought to build it after the ecological and social upheavals of the past century. But she suspected their disdain for the Troubleshooters had more to do with prejudice than pride. Underneath their noble talk of equality was a not-so-veiled mistrust toward those who were enhanced beyond the norm.

She and Arkady could have just flown in at maximum thrust—she doubted even the Eunuchs were fanatical enough to shoot down a TSC scout ship—but that would have tipped off the Neogaians. And so the heroic Medvyéd, the mighty Bear of the Troubleshooters, and his glamorous apprentice the Green Blaze had spent eighteen hours heroically, glamorously stuffed inside a cargo pod, cushioned from the accelerations of mass drivers and capture nets by gel cocoons and their own augmented anatomies. On finally reaching Chakra City, they had made an entrance in only the most literal sense, cutting their way through the hull and sealing it behind them, and hoping that the vagaries of orbital mechanics had let them arrive in time.

After all that, Emry was so thrilled to come out in the open that she didn't particularly mind being the decoy. As she delivered her trademark Green Blaze entrance line (or her latest attempt at one, though she thought this one had better staying potential than "Now you're in trouble, Mama spank" or "Hey, look over there!") and drew the attention of the Neogaians, Arkady was already sneaking up behind them, ready to incapacitate them as soon as he got a clear shot.

But it was hard to be sneaky in that bulky antique symbot he wore, at least when your enemies had animal hearing. The leader, a canine chimera who'd already yanked off his turban to free his ears, spun his head toward the sound of the armored exosuit's whirring servos and barked, "Down!" just as the Troubleshooter fired. The therianthropes scattered, and only one of Arkady's tanglewebs hit, snaring the tall reptilian's legs. But as the other two males ducked for cover, this one deftly turned his fall into a roll (the sixty-five-percent gravity of this small habitat giving him more time for it) and *bit* through the polysilk threads with his massive jaw. Despite the Neogaians' anti-tech ideology, this one must've had diamond-coated teeth.

The female had ignored Arkady's shots. Eyes fixed on Emry, she had ripped off her *chador*, revealing a stunning black-furred cat-woman wearing armor fabric over her vital areas. The leader, whom Emry now recognized as high-ranking Neogaian Erich "Wulf" Krieger, was shouting, "Taurean, Bast, kill them! Caiman, with me!" But the she-cat didn't need to hear it—she was already screaming and leaping at Emry, claws fully deployed from her fingertips. The ferocity in her yellow eyes struck primal fear into Emry, paralyzing her. At the last instant she reacted, dodging right and tossing the panthress into a spin, but not before those claws put four shallow slashes across the reinforced skin of Emry's left arm. They must have been diamond-coated as well. Meanwhile, in the corner of her eye Emry saw the bull-guard firing a Gauss pistol at Arkady, not as quick as Bast to rely on animal instinct. The bullets bounced off the symbot's tough shell. Arkady was firing his plasma gun at Krieger and Caiman in flashbang mode, the laser pulses ionizing the air into blinding plasma balls with a crackle of miniature thunderclaps. Krieger clapped his hands over his large ears and staggered, but Caiman seemed unaffected and hustled him out of range while Taurean moved in to block his fire.

Bast had landed on her feet on the next air-filtration unit over, facing Emry and looking quite thrilled. "At last! A new toy!" she yowled, her feline muzzle giving her something of a lisp. Like a cat, she studied her foe, waiting for the right moment to pounce. Emry did the same. Bast's ears were in the normal human places, peeking out from her luxurious black mane, but the pinnae were large, pointed, and flexible. Her hands were human except for the claws, but the feet were pawlike and elongated, making her a formidable leaper. Her long tail swished agitatedly even while the rest of her lithe, slender body stayed perfectly still and poised. She seemed young to Emry, though maybe that was a natural feline abandon. Whatever the case, she was gorgeous. The cliché came unbidden to Emry's lips: "*Nice* kitty!"

"No," Bast replied. "I'm not." She pounced again, effortlessly correcting for Coriolis drift. This time Emry leapt up to meet her, aiming a spin-kick at her head. But Bast pivoted impossibly in midair, seemingly innocent of Newtonian physics, and dodged the kick, slashing at Emry's leg as she went past. This time the armor fabric shielded her, but the blow threw off her recovery, so she fell poorly and almost hit the side of the filtration unit. She caught herself and flipped up and over to land where Bast had just been, facing a Bast who was already crouched where Emry had been, tensing for her next leap.

It's the tail, she realized. That and her flexible spine let Bast shift her center of gravity however she wanted, enabling moves that seemed to laugh in the face of old Isaac. *Okay, no more soaring through the air like in a* wuxia *movie.* Emry planted her feet and awaited Bast's attack.

The panthress was quick to oblige, launching herself with great force, claws splayed. Emry grabbed her right wrist and punched her in the gut, but at the same moment Bast shot her legs forward and slashed at Emry's midsection. Light-armor fabric protected both women, but the claws of Bast's free hand dug deeply into Emry's right shoulder. Then the unexpected happened: Bast's tail looped around Emry's leg and yanked, proving itself as much primate as feline. Unbalanced from the collision, Emry fell back and had to fend off Bast's teeth as they went for her throat. She got her forearm bitten for her troubles. Angered, she kneed Bast in the gut and cuffed her head, then kicked the dazed therian off the edge of the filtration unit.

"Now do you see the flaw in the idea of sleeveless armor?" came Arkady's voice over the selfone clip on her left ear.

She rolled her eyes at the rote criticism as she scrambled to her feet. "But tin cans are just so passé."

"Forgive a mere mortal his caution, O demigoddess. At least try not to get yourself killed while I'm still responsible for you."

"Oh, go fuck a can opener," she shot back, but her tone was affectionate. The old schmuck was like a—well, like an uncle to her. But she was going to murder him someday; that was a given.

She looked down from the filtration unit, hoping to see Bast unconscious on the ground. But the she-cat stood there in a relaxed pose, purring loudly as she licked Emry's blood off her fingers. *How does it feel to purr?* Emry wondered. *I bet it's amazing.* "Rrrr, thick and yummy," Bast moaned, savoring the dense, erythrocyte-rich blood that fed the increased oxygen demand of Emry's muscles. "Come here and give me more!"

"Sorry, we don't deliver!" Emry wasn't about to jump down—the slow fall would give Bast plenty of reaction time. So she leapt still higher into the maze of ducts and girders overhead, taunting, "Come and get it, pussy!"

That proved a mistake. Emry had been hoping to lose Bast in the forest of conduits and get behind her, but all she did was get Bast more excited and hotter on Emry's (alas, only figurative) tail, following her easily through the maze. Bast's lighter, sleeker build let her slink along ducts too flimsy to support Emry's weight and slip easily through gaps Emry had to force her way through. Still, Emry couldn't resist taunting her, hoping to distract her focus. "Aww, no, now you'll get stuck up here and we'll have to call the fire department!"

Emry remembered playing with Kiri and Tigermuffin as a child: how they attacked a string or toy mousie most eagerly when it went behind the ottoman or table leg and "couldn't see" them coming. Emry had similar close calls with Bast, and those claws left their marks in Emry's arms a couple of times more, as well as doing a fair amount of damage to the conduits. Regrettably, none of them was carrying anything hot or caustic to spray out in Bast's face, as they surely would have in a movie or sim. Real life was such a ripoff sometimes. "Keep scratching up the furniture and we'll have to get you a manicure!" Bast slashed out with a foot, barely missing her. "And a pedicure. How about a sinecure? Get paid to sleep all day—what cat could pass that up?" The next swipe of Bast's claws raked across the back of her hand. Emry lost her grip and barely managed to catch herself on the pipe below. "Would you settle for a cured ham?" *I'll need a cure for disembowelment at this rate.*

But Emry had grown up with cats—surely she could use a few of their tricks herself. Hell, she *was* wearing tiger-print panties. The next time Bast's claws slashed from around a vertical pipe, Emry swept around the other side and collided with her. They fell together in a Coriolis arc. Emry struggled to hold Bast and make sure the she-cat landed on her back. But Bast's tail gave her the advantage in midair twisting, and Emry ended up on the bottom (not her favorite position), just managing to splay her arms in time to absorb the impact wrestler-style. Which made them unavailable to stop Bast from going for her throat again. So she slammed her forehead into Bast's. Not for the first time, her thick skull came in handy; Bast yowled and fell back, letting Emry get her legs up into the she-cat's midriff, launching her backward. She landed in a three-point crouch, though, and Emry struggled to rise and face her, though she found it hard to get beyond a sitting position. "Anybody got a ball of yarn?"

"Oh, for God's sake," came Arkady's voice, *"just shoot her!"* Emry grimaced. She hated guns, even the nonlethal kind—nasty things, and they took all the fun out of a good fight. But Arkady had a point—they didn't really have time, what with the other terrorists on the loose.

The clincher was that Bast was pouncing again, all her pointy bits deployed for the kill, and Emry couldn't dodge fast enough. In one smooth, swift move, she fell back, drew her dartgun, and placed shockdarts in Bast's exposed midriff and neck. The she-cat convulsed and fell heavily atop her, burying Emry's face in her thick, silky mane. "Sorry," Emry said. "This was just starting to get good." She rolled the dazed panther-woman off of her, taking a moment to appreciate how soft her fur was, and feeling irrationally tempted to stroke it back into smoothness. But there was no time for that now. She drew binders from her belt and swiftly secured Bast's wrists and ankles before she could recover.

Emry turned to see Arkady hovering nearby in his armor suit, its wingjets keeping him airborne and correcting for Cori drift. She always thought the bulky thing made him look like something out of an old *anime*. Apparently he'd just lifted out of the way of the bull-man, Taurean, who was extricating his horns from a dented wall panel and shaking his head. He must've given up on the gun or been disarmed. Arkady fired a shock laser, but Taurean dodged surprisingly fast, the electric arc hitting the wall. Arkady deployed his arm-mounted sonic pulser, but before he could fire, Taurean leapt up and took him in the chest, smashing through several overhead pipes. Taurean landed smoothly on his feet, but Arkady fell badly and hit headfirst, a number of heavy conduits landing atop him.

"You okay, Papa Bear?" Emry called—but then noticed Taurean eyeing her and pawing at the ground. "Ohh, bull . . ." She fired off some shockdarts as he charged her headfirst, but they bounced off his skin as though it were light armor, not holding contact long enough to deliver an effective charge. No wonder Arkady had switched to beam weapons.

But Emry would not be cowed. Like a Minoan daredevil, she seized the bull-man by the horns and flipped over him, letting out a whoop. *That's one way to tackle a dilemma!* By the time she landed, she'd not only spun to face him, but had holstered her dartgun, drawn her laser pistol, and set it to shock mode. But he'd spun too, with no pause for rumination, and was charging her again. "It's the red hair, isn't it?" she asked, shaking her head a bit. *Priorities, kid!* she thought, and fired, the laser ionizing a path for the electric discharge. Taurean convulsed from the sustained shock, but still had enough momentum to bowl her over, knocking her sidearm from her hand and the wind from her lungs. She ended up on the bottom again, grateful for the low gravity, although his weight upon her chest was still suffocating.

But he was already stirring, the charge apparently too small for such a massive body. Before she could catch her breath and wriggle free, he had an oversized hand around her throat. His other hand held down her right arm in a vise grip, and his tree-trunk legs pinned hers. She gripped his wrist in her left hand, but he tightened his hold on her throat when she did, giving her pause. "Damn, you're beautiful," he said in a surprisingly mellow, good-natured voice. "Too bad I have to kill you."

Emry seized the opening. "Well, you don't *have* to," she lilted with what breath she could muster, lowering her eyelids seductively. "I've known some horny men, but you take the beefcake. Why don't we have our own little rodeo, see how long I can ride you?"

Taurean looked tempted . . . but smiled regretfully. "I'd love to—but I'm not that stupid. I like girls with more fur, anyway," he added with a shrug. "Sorry. I'll make it quick, okay?" His fist tightened brutally around her neck, in stark contrast to his easygoing manner. Emry tried to wrench it free, but his arm wouldn't budge and she was already weakening. She could hold her breath fairly long given a chance to prepare; but she'd already had the wind knocked out of her, and her metabolism was high from the fight, demanding oxygen that just wasn't coming. She choked soundlessly, striving to remain conscious. He gave her a reassuring smile, like an anesthesiologist telling her to relax, count backward from ten, and just let oblivion take her.

But then a plasma bolt erupted in his face. It knocked him for a loop and he reflexively let go. Emry was dazzled herself, despite her corneal filters, but was able to push him off and scramble free. Arkady fired enough tanglewebs to make sure he was securely bound. Still choking and struggling for breath, Emry was tempted to leave the webs across his face and let *him* suffocate for a while. But his attempt to kill her had been without malice, just a guy doing his job, and she found that she bore him no ill will. So she moved in and extended her diamond thumbnail blades to cut his nose and mouth free as he struggled ineffectually against the restraints. *Your loss, bully-boy. Would've been a wild ride.*

"You okay?" Arkady asked. Even with the helmet concealing his face, she could tell he was looking her over with concern.

She quizzed her biometrics and got the HUD readout on her retina. The cuts from Bast were clotted, the cells already being knitted back together by her repair nans, and no significant toxins had been introduced. Taurean's impact had bruised a couple of ribs, again nothing her repair systems couldn't handle. The cartilage around her windpipe was bruised as well, but its polymer reinforcements had held up. Her ears were ringing from the plasma bolt, but there was no serious damage. "I'm fine," she said hoarsely. "I could've handled him."

"Of course. But I thought I'd save you the trouble."

"I *am* trouble," she said with self-mocking arrogance.

"As I know better than anyone. You should focus less on your wisecracks and more on the battle."

"What fun is that? Plus it loosens up the imagination, keeps me flexible. Good to have in a—"

Then the habitat rumbled. Then it groaned. Then it heaved.

Only Superhuman by Christopher L. Bennett
(ISBN: 978-0765378910)
is available through most booksellers.

About the Author

Christopher L. Bennett is a lifelong resident of Cincinnati, Ohio, with a B.S. in Physics and a B.A. in History from the University of Cincinnati. A fan of science and science fiction since age five, he has spent the past two decades selling original short fiction to magazines such as *Analog Science Fiction and Fact* and *BuzzyMag*. For the past dozen years, he has been one of Pocket Books' most prolific and popular authors of *Star Trek* tie-in fiction, including the epic *Next Generation* prequel *The Buried Age*, the *Star Trek: Department of Temporal Investigations* series, and the ongoing *Star Trek: Enterprise – Rise of the Federation* series. His original novel *Only Superhuman*, perhaps the first hard science fiction superhero novel, was voted Library Journal's SF/Fantasy Debut of the Month for October 2012. His short story collection *Hub Space: Tales from the Greater Galaxy* is available in e-book and print formats from Mystique Press.

Christopher's homepage, fiction annotations, and blog can be found at christopherlbennett.wordpress.com, and his Facebook author page is at www.facebook.com/ChristopherLBennettAuthor.

Cyber Backers

_
Amanda Nixon
Andrew Timson
Andy Hunter
Anonymous reader
Antonio Campos Jr from McAllen Texas
BC Brandt
Benjamin Widmer
Björn Schneider
Bob Hamers
Brad Murray
Brenda Cooper
Brendan lonehawk
Brian D Lambert
Bruce Alcorn
Cathy Franchett
Chad Bowden
Chand Svare Ghei chasvag.com
Christopher Weuve
Chuck Wilson
Cody L. Martin
Curtis & Maryrita Steinhour
Dagmar Baumann
Dale A Russell
Daniel Lin
Danielle Ackley-McPhail
David Mortman
David Rains
David Zurek
Dominic
Donald J. Bingle
Drew Cucuzza
D-Rock
Eric Hendrickson
Gavin Sheedy
Gavran
GMarkC
Ian Harvey
Ian Randal Strock
Isaac 'Will It Work' Dansicker
Jakub Narębski
Jason Russell
jdelarroz
Jennifer L. Pierce
John Idlor
Judy Waidlich
Justin Hilyard
Keith Bissett
Linda Pierce
Lisa Kruse
Maria V. Arnold
Mark Carter
Matthieu Walraet
mdtommyd
Michael A. Burstein
Michael Fedrowitz
Mike Crate
Mike Smith
Nathan Turner
Paul Bulmer
Paul Ryan
Paul van Oven

PJ Kimbrll
Q Fortier
R K Bookman
Rahadyan Sastrowardoyo
Revek
Rhel ná DecVandé
Rich Riddle
Robert Claney
Robert Greenberger
Ross Hathaway
Scott Minor
ShadowCub
Sheryl R. Hayes
Stephen Ballentine
Stephen Fleming
Susan Carlson
Tasha Turner
Tim DuBois
Tomer Bar-Shlomo
Tory Shade

www.ingramcontent.com/pod-product-compliance
Ingram Content Group UK Ltd.
Pitfield, Milton Keynes, MK11 3LW, UK
UKHW041856190726
13854UKWH00002B/927

9 781942 990963